JUDAS COUNTRY

Kapotas gave him a key. 'I have put you in 206, near to Mr Case.'

Ken took it and picked up his bag. 'Thanks. Drop in and take a glass with the Professor, Roy. You'll like him. I haven't met the daughter.' He ignored the lift and bounced lightly up the stairs.

Kapotas said in his most blank voice: 'I would welcome your opinion of the champagne.'

I looked at him, but he turned away. So I followed through the service door and down the corridor to the wine cellar. He unlocked it, and we went in. It was a small square rough-plastered room with no window and just a single unshaded bulb glaring down on the near-empty wine racks, the heavy scarred old table in the middle, and in the middle of that the opened box of Kroeger Royale '66. Behind me, Kapotas carefully locked the door again. What the hell . . .?

When he turned around, his face and voice weren't neutral any more.

'Will you tell me,' he hissed, 'exactly how you take the cork out of a sub-machine gun?'

**Also by the same author,
and available from Coronet:**

Blame the Dead
The Conduct of Major Maxim
The Crocus List
Midnight Plus One
The Most Dangerous Game
The Secret Servant
Shooting Script
Uncle Target
Venus With Pistol
The Wrong Side of the Sky

About the author

P G Wodehouse greeted Gavin Lyall's first novel, *The Wrong Side of the Sky*, in 1961 by exclaiming 'Terrific! When better novels of suspense than this are written, lead me to them.' *The Most Dangerous Game*, *Midnight Plus One* (Winner of the Crime Writers' Association Silver Dagger), *Shooting Script*, *Venus With Pistol*, *Blame the Dead* and *Judas Country* followed. Then he created his Whitehall troubleshooter, Major Harry Maxim, hero of first *The Secret Servant* (televised with Charles Dance as Maxim), followed by *The Conduct of Major Maxim*, *The Crocus List* and, most recently, *Uncle Target*. He is married to the distinguished journalist, Katharine Whitehorn, and lives in London.

Judas Country

Gavin Lyall

CORONET BOOKS
Hodder and Stoughton

British Library C.I.P.

Lyall, Gavin *1932–*
 Judas country.
 I. Title
 823'.914[F]

ISBN 0 340 51581 3

Printed and bound in Great Britain for Hodder and Stoughton Paperbacks, a division of Hodder and Stoughton Ltd, Mill Road, Dunton Green, Sevenoaks, Kent TN13 2YA (Editorial Office: 47 Bedford Square, London WC1B 3DP) by Clays Ltd, St Ives plc.

1

A few minutes ago the sky had been a place. Of clouds, winds, pressures, turbulence. Now, it was just the décor of a flashy Cyprus sunset. The propellers wound down and stopped with a brief, violent shudder, but I went on sitting there, running my hands over the still-unfamiliar avionics switches and trying to wriggle some of the stiffness out of my neck and shoulders. A small Ford van dashed up and stopped just in front.

By the time I'd worked my way back past the champagne boxes and stacked passenger seats and swung down the door, he was waiting below with a small piece of paper and a large anxious expression.

'Landing fee,' he said. 'You have cash money?'

'Yes, sure.' But I must have looked puzzled. I've known airports that were hungry to get paid, but this was a new record. Still, service with style – it says so on the tail of the aeroplane, just under the Castle Hotels International symbol. I found the wallet of Castle's money, sorted through to the Cypriot pounds and paid him. 'What's the rush? – are you behind with the rent?'

He tucked the cash away, receipted the bill, and looked happier.

I said: 'When you get back, will you ask the refuelling boys to step over?'

'You pay them cash?'

'Of course not. I've got a Shell carnet.'

He smiled, a little maliciously. 'No. Is finished. No good.'

'What the hell are you talking about?'

'Your company – Castle – is bust. Finished. Broke.'

*

Loukis Kapotas was aged about thirty, with neat black hair, a long Grecian nose and the standard Cypriot business uniform of white shirt, tie and dark trousers, only his shirt was real advertisement white.

What he wanted from me was my money, my traveller's cheques, credit card and fuel carnet.

'If you've got a pair of clean scissors, you can have my balls, too,' I said. 'What's going *on*?'

'I am a chartered accountant. My firm acts as the Cyprus associates of Harborne, Gough and Co. of London, who are – unfortunately – acting as receivers to Castle Hotels International.' His English was good and his voice was calm, but his fingers crept nervously on the counter of the airport café. And he hadn't touched his coffee yet.

'Receivers?' I said. 'Somebody finally blew the whistle on Kingsley, did they? When?'

'We were informed just this afternoon.' So I was lucky to have got this far; the refuelling lads in Crete, and Naples before that, hadn't got the bad word. They'd accepted my carnet; I hoped they eventually got their penny in the pound or whatever.

Kapotas added carefully: 'Have you known Mr Kingsley long?'

'We met when he was in the RAF, twenty years ago.'

'And you have worked for him – for Castle International – all that time?'

'I don't work for them. This is just a one-off job; their regular pilot quit the other day.' Because he'd foreseen stormy weather? Well . . . I sipped my beer. 'I was looking for a free trip down to this end of the world, and happen to be type-rated on a Queen Air, so Kingsley took me on for a week. What does all this do to my chance of getting paid as well?'

He remembered his coffee and took a careful gulp. 'In theory, you understand, a certain amount of wages and salaries have a certain priority. But first we must find if we have the money. Now, Captain . . . er . . .'

'Case. Roy Case. And just Mister.'

'Thank you. Now – you understand that a receiver is responsible only for goods delivered or debts incurred *after* he has taken over? The credit you pledged yesterday, or this morning, is not my concern. But what you do now with the company's credit and carnet and cash – that is very much my concern. Please?'

He held out his empty hand.

It all sounded real. And it was typical enough of Kingsley to go in for high finance without visible means of support, but . . .

'I suppose you have some proof of all this?'

He'd been expecting that. He did a fast draw, and dealt me a business card, his driving licence, and a slip of telex paper. It read:

Have been appointed receivers to Castle Hotels International stop please take over Nicosia Castle soonest and intercept company aircraft Beech Queen Air en route Beirut stop bank informing local branch separately ends Harborne Gough.

'And since then,' he said, 'of course I have spoken on the phone to them in London for instructions.'

'So you're running the hotel as well?'

'Yes,' he said grimly. 'The manager left before I arrived – I think not with empty hands. I have told the police. Now . . .'

'All right.' I took out the carnet and credit card and traveller's cheques that Kingsley had given me less than two days before and . . . and carefully tore them all in half. Cyprus still *is* the Middle East.

He grinned quickly and picked up the pieces. 'And the cash also, please.'

'There's only about thirty quid left, and I'm not walking around town stark financial naked. Call it drinking money.'

He frowned. 'Your room at the Castle is free, of course, and I can give you a lift in my car . . .'

'Drinking money,' I said firmly. 'So I'll pay for your coffee.'

*

He had a new Escort station wagon and he drove as carefully as a profit-and-loss account – though that sort of driving isn't so rare in Cyprus as in some parts of the Eastern Med.

When we were out on the main road into Nicosia, I asked: 'What happens to my flight, then?'

'That's not for me to decide.' He hesitated, then said carefully: 'Harborne, Gough did not seem too clear what the flight was actually for.'

'I'm taking a dozen of champagne into Beirut for the grand opening of the Cedars Castle.'

He frowned. 'Do you normally send champagne by air?'

'Probably not. I think somebody forgot to order it in advance

7

– but the aeroplane was going anyway, so why not use it? I'm supposed to stay on in the Lebanon and give some of the travel writers and VIP guests free flights around, seeing the sights. All part of the Castle International tradition of service with style.'

'But champagne, by aeroplane . . .' he muttered.

'I flew low so the corks wouldn't pop. That's why I came down through Nice and Naples instead of over the Alps.'

'Perhaps, but it means the aeroplane is full of champagne.'

'Half full. Just a dozen cases, 144 bottles. But all good stuff: Kroeger Royale '66.'

'How much is it worth?'

'It's insured for five hundred quid, but you could sell it through the hotel for at least twice that.'

'Not an inconsiderable asset.'

'The aeroplane itself must be worth thirty thousand.'

He glanced at me. 'But does Castle International own it outright?'

'I don't know.' But now I thought about it, I doubted Kingsley had nailed down his own money for that Queen Air. It would be on some sort of lease or never-never.

'Well, London will know by tomorrow. Is the aeroplane safe where it is?'

I shrugged. 'It's in a Customs Area. Sort of in bond. When d'you think we'll know what I do next?'

'Tomorrow, perhaps.'

I filled my favourite pipe, the only Dunhill of the lot, then decided it would be too tricky to light in a car with the windows open so just parked it in my face and waited. The road widened and straightened as we reached the outskirts of the town, and the first street lamps were going on, just faint sparks against the lingering brightness in the sky. The air was gentle and smelt of coffee.

'I like Cyprus,' I said. 'Particularly I like Nicosia.' The new town outside the walls is a rambling, shambling place, but both people and traffic move at a stroll. I said: 'It's a calm sort of place.'

'Calm?' He snatched a glance at me. 'My God.' We passed a bunch of United Nations soldiers – Swedes, I think – deliberately conspicuous in their blue berets; they have to wear uniform at all times, even when they're planning on disgracing it.

'Well, at the moment anyway. But better than most of the Middle East, and at least your driving's much better here.' He instinctively slowed, though he'd been crawling already. 'And usually your guns aren't loaded.' You see them at all the road-blocks that cut the old city clear across the middle; a Greek carrying some modern sub-machine gun, then twenty yards on a Turk with one of those old Thompsons with the brass receiver. But neither have magazines in, and both guards grin cheerfully as you pass.

'They *can* be loaded,' Kapotas said dryly. 'One of our National Guards put in the magazine the other day. A friend had stopped for a chat and they got into an argument and the guard put in the magazine to impress him.'

'What happened?'

'He shot his own foot off, of course. And all the Turks dived for cover and the United Nations rushed in five hundred men and after a few hours they just about calmed things down. The friend, I think, is still running.'

Over the river and down Byron Avenue past the government buildings, the traffic thickened – but stayed polite. Kapotas asked, 'Do you know the Castle Hotel?'

'I've passed it.' And kept on going, though I didn't say that. I remembered it as being on Regina Street, just inside the walls : a gloomy, tall-windowed old place that had been modernised with a new name and a paintbrush when Castle bought it. I'd never stayed there, and with one of the best hotel bars just a few hundred yards away in the Ledra Palace, I hadn't done any drinking there, either. Well, I'd have to do some now; it would hardly be the sporting spirit, in these hard times, to sneak off and spend Castle's cash in the Ledra.

We went through the Paphos Gate in the vast sixteenth-century Venetian wall that runs a three-mile ring around the old city, weaved around a few of the narrow car-jammed streets and came out just alongside the hotel and opposite as obvious a knocking-shop as even Regina Street could produce. I'd for-gotten what that road did best.

Kapotas did some nippy parking and I took my flight brief-case and grip out of the back seat.

'You travel light,' he commented.

'Aircrew mostly do.' Some of them live pretty light, too.

The lobby was narrow and dimly lit, with the original worn marble tiles on the floor and rather garish green and gold paint on the plaster mouldings of the ceiling. A man built like a Regimental Sergeant-Major, with a scruffy red uniform and a big moustache, came out from behind the desk. He seemed sadly pleased to see us.

Kapotas waved a hand at him. 'This is Spyridon Papadimitriou, our hall porter.'

'*Sergeant* Papadimitriou.' He clicked his heels and bowed half an inch, which was all his shape allowed. So I'd been almost right about his rank, and now I could see two rows of faded medal ribbons across his heart.

I said: 'Roy Case.'

Kapotas was looking around nervously. 'Where is everyone?'

Come to think of it, it did seem a bit quiet – for April, when the tourists begin.

'They have all gone. *Vamoso.*' The Sergeant rocked on his heels and looked quietly happy.

'You mean the staff? Gone where?'

'They have not been paid for two weeks. And this afternoon you come and tell them perhaps it will be never, so . . .' He looked even more happy.

I said: 'Why not you?'

'I have not been paid for *six* weeks,' he said proudly.

'Oh God,' Kapotas said quietly, almost like a real prayer. And maybe it was. His fingers rattled on the desk top.

I said: 'I have to carry my own bags, then?'

'Your own bags?' He looked at me with sick pity. 'You have to help me cook dinner for the guests.'

2

In fact it wasn't that bad, except for the parts that were worse. There were only twenty guests, and only the dozen that were paying *en pension* rates and would lose by going out decided to stay and face our menu. And the menu itself was easy since the late staff hadn't been in such a hurry that they'd forgotten to pinch every bit of food that wasn't too heavy, like half a deep-frozen sheep, or too bulky, like the fresh vegetables, or too wet like several red mullet, a flayed octopus and three kilos of minced meat, family tree unknown. 'They must have hired *taxis* to take it all,' Kapotas said, looking into a larder that was empty of everything except a few sauce bottles and a dead mouse.

'They shared together and got a van,' the Sergeant said helpfully. Kapotas just looked at him.

It also turned out that Sergeant Papa wasn't the only one left. There was a small, dark, ugly chambermaid who was supposed to be his niece, and – surprisingly – the barman, Apostolos. I'd assumed he'd've been the first to go, plus the tools of his trade. But Sergeant Papa leant his big backside against the kitchen sink, lit an expensive cigar, and explained why not.

'He has brought in too many bottles so, naturally, he does not want to take them all out again.'

'Brought them *in*?'

'All barmen bring in bottles. They buy whisky for perhaps two pounds, then sell it in drinks for six pounds. Naturally they do not want to use hotel stocks and give the hotel the profit.'

'Naturally. But that being the case, hop out to the bar and bring back a bottle of Scotch for cooking purposes.'

'I am the *hall porter*.' I'd given him a corporal's job.

'If the pilots are doing the cooking, at least the sergeants can fetch them a drink.'

He looked me in the eyes, didn't quite smile, and went out at his own pace. Kapotas wiped his forehead with a shaky hand and said : 'You did say for cooking purposes?'

'For purposes of the cook; it comes to the same thing.'

'Can you really cook?'

'Can't you get your wife to come in?'

'With three children?'

'Oh well. Most unmarried men over forty can tell one end of an egg from the other. Have we got any eggs, by the way?'

'Yes. They must have been too difficult to carry.'

'Fine. Hard-boil a dozen and some of the beans and we'll start with an egg salad. Then we make the mince into meatballs – what d'you call them? – *keftedes*? – and we'll do something to the fish. I'm buggered if I'm touching *him*.' I glared at the octopus and the octopus stared blankly back.

He sighed and got started. I looked around. 'You know, if I worked here for any time, I'd scarper whether I was paid or not.'

The repainting job had stopped at the service door; the kitchen looked like a Crimean War hospital before Florence Nightingale got into the game. The stone walls were decorated with fifty years of spilled sauces, the ceiling was black with oily grime, and there was fungus growing from the food scraps in the cracks in the floor. The only ventilation came from a couple of small barred windows, above head height over the blackened old cooking range.

Kapotas nodded gloomily. 'But we are lucky that Papadimitriou stayed loyal.'

'Don't kid yourself. All the others'll get their usual jobs as waiters and cooks and things, particularly with the tourist season just starting. But he wouldn't get to be hall porter anywhere else. And I never heard of a hall porter living off his salary yet. I wonder how much he charges for that "niece" of his?'

'Oh God. Am I running a brothel as well?'

'You and every other hotel manager. Is this fennel or last week's spinach?'

*

Kapotas and the niece did the serving, the Sergeant found that his dignity allowed him to double as wine waiter, and I remembered that the real gourmets say red mullet should be grilled complete, not even with the scales scraped off. Our *en pension* guests would live like kings and ruddy well like it.

12

Afterwards we settled in the 'bar', which was just the other end of the dining-room; a few tables, a short counter and a dark brown décor that might have driven you to drink but couldn't make you enjoy it. Kapotas and I got stuck into a bottle of Scotch while the Sergeant passed round a bunch of old photos. Each one showed him, younger and thinner but still neither young nor thin, wearing a wartime uniform and standing proudly next to some general. Each a different general, but each a general; no brigadiers or colonels or suchlike.

We made impressed noises, then I asked Kapotas: 'How long d'you think we can keep it going like this?'

He shrugged. 'If London – or the bank here – would tell me I can spend some money, then I can look for new staff tomorrow. But myself, I am just a nightwatchman. And daywatchman. I check the inventories, the stocks, the books, make sure all the assets are insured – often they let the policies lapse as a last economy – and . . . Oh God!' He looked at me, wide-eyed.

I said nothing. Just took out the Queen Air's insurance certificate and passed it over. He skimmed it, then relaxed. 'Thank you.'

I began to pack a pipe. 'So the big decisions are taken in London?'

'Yes. A receiver acts as the agent of the debenture holder, whoever it was that lent the company money in the first place and now wants to move in and try to rescue some. Most of the time, like this, it's a bank.'

'Which d'you think they'll do?'

'Compromise – as usual. Get rid of the worst hotels individually, sell the rest as a unit. But to have time to decide, we have to keep everything running anyway. Or try.'

'Welcome to the hotel business.'

He smiled weakly and took a gulp of Scotch. 'I can always remind myself of other accountants doing the same thing in the Rhodes Castle, the Malta Castle, the Corsican one, Elba, Lebanon I suppose, if they ever *do* open . . .'

'Only they don't have me and the aeroplane to worry about as well?'

'Yes, exactly.' We drank on.

Around ten, the Sergeant said he fancied a couple of hours'

kip before coming back on duty at midnight – since there wasn't a night clerk.

Kapotas flapped the idea aside. 'Tonight we'll lock up as soon as the last guest is in. Not stay open. Have another drink.' The Scotch was turning him auld-lang-syne.

But Papa was horrified. 'We do our best business after midnight. When the bars and nightclubs begin to shut.'

'*What?*'

The Sergeant spread his hands. 'Of course. Here in Regina Street . . .'

'I get it,' I said. 'When the other places shut, their guests need some place to take the girls they've picked up there. And we're almost next door.'

Kapotas poured himself another drink, quickly but shakily. 'My God, I *am* running a . . . But what about our proper guests?'

'They are usually in before midnight. And we put our short-night guests only on the first floor. Never above our residents.'

'What goes into the register?' Kapotas asked.

The Sergeant's big shoulders lifted a fraction. Nothing, obviously.

I asked: 'More to the point, what goes into the till?'

'The night clerk takes one-third; it is a tradition. Because, of course, he is to blame if the police raid us and find people whose names are not in the register.'

'And I imagine the manager's been taking the rest of it? Well, tonight do us a favour and give it to Castle International. And make the split after you've deducted for overheads, like clean sheets.'

'Not many of them care about clean sheets.'

'As from now, they'll get 'em and pay for 'em regardless. Service with style, remember.'

'Yes, sir.' He stiffened into a mocking but still professional salute, about-turned, and marched out.

Kapotas said soulfully: 'You are much better at managing a hotel than I am.' In a couple of drinks he'd discover I was his only real friend.

'That's the nastiest thing anybody's said to me this week. But don't believe it; it's just that I've seen a lot more crummy hotels around the world than you have.'

'But this should be a de luxe hotel, the highest category – and he talks of police raids!'

I shrugged. 'If there'd been an *honest* crook in charge here, it would've been like printing money. This place has got everything going for it.'

Kapotas shuddered. A while later, he asked: 'Didn't you say you only took on the flight to get to Cyprus – was it?'

'I wanted to meet a friend who's been in Israel.'

'Is he coming over here?'

'I hope so. I booked him a room here before I started the flight.' And I'd checked this evening and, surprise surprise, somebody had actually written it into the book.

'But you are not sure?' Kapotas persisted.

'I'll ring tomorrow. He can't get away until then anyhow.'

He opened his mouth to ask another question, then shovelled some Scotch in instead. I was glad the Sergeant had gone; his suspicious little mind wouldn't have stopped there.

Then the lobby phone rang. I remembered the Sergeant was in bed, decided Kapotas was too near a state of liquidation, and went out myself. Behind the desk was a small switchboard old enough to be steam-driven, and I almost lost the call finding the right plughole, but at last—

'This is the Castle Hotel, good evening.'

'I began to think you were closed,' Female voice with a faint German? – East European? accent.

'We almost are, but can I help?'

'Do you have a room booked for Mr Kenneth Cavitt?'

I paused. I didn't need to look at the book about that one. But could I ask why she wanted to know? I decided not.

'Ah yes – there seems to be a Mr Cavitt on the list.'

'Thank God. I have asked at five other hotels. Now, please can you book me also two rooms, beginning tomorrow.'

'Well . . . we're in a bit of a mess here.'

'Full up?' She sounded incredulous.

'Anything but. The trouble is, most of our staff's scarpered and we can't really cope with the guests we've got already . . .'

'Never mind that.' She brushed the problem aside impatiently. 'So, two rooms please, and I want it also very secret, *verstanden*? If somebody rings up about *us*, then you say we are not staying there.'

'Ummm . . . I suppose we might put you on the hourly rate and count you as five Swedish soldiers and friends.'

'*Bitte?*'

'Sorry. Just thinking aloud. Hold on.' Sergeant Papa had just arrived in his best imitation of a hurry, looking puzzled and buttoning his uniform trousers.

I put my hand over the receiver. 'A girl – German or something – wants two rooms from tomorrow and no names on the register. Any views?'

He blinked, frowned, scratched his gut and finally grunted: 'It might be possible – at a special rate. We can say it was just a mistake in all this confusion if the police find out. But *we* must know the names.'

'Sure. And see the passports.'

'Naturally.' He nodded approvingly.

The phone was squawking: 'Where are you? Hello? Hello? Ah, *Scheisse*!'

I said smoothly: 'Sorry, I've just been consulting the assistant manager. Yes, that will be quite all right; we can agree on the rate when you've chosen the rooms. But may I have the name, please? – just for us, not for the register.'

Pause. Then: 'Spohr.' She spelt it out. 'My father's name.'

Well, I'd believe what the passports said. I said: 'Thank you, ma'am. Now, if you don't want to appear conspicuous, would you be wanting all your meals in the rooms?' Frightening how easily you become a bill-building little reservations clerk.

'Perhaps. But I want you to have waiting for us some good champagne – good – and caviar. We shall arrive before Mr Cavitt, soon after lunch. *Wiedersehn*.'

I wrote it all down as a note for Kapotas – or reminder for me – come the morning, then rang the operator and asked where the last call had come from. He footled around a bit, then told me Limassol, the main port down south.

Then I went home to the bottle, leaving the Sergeant still standing there, trying to worry out what particular secret depravity needed two rooms and took longer than one day. It hurt him that he couldn't spot it immediately.

*

Back in the bar, Kapotas had reached the stage of having trouble sitting on a chair, let alone standing up. Apostolos the barman was watching him calmly.

I jerked my head. 'Get him a taxi, then you can shove off home. Leave the keys: I'll lock up the liquor.'

He didn't much like that, of course, but we both knew it was what Kapotas would have wanted. Apostolos went out and I helped the accountant to, give or take, his feet. 'Come on, the wife and three kiddies are wondering where you've got to.'

'I doubt it,' he said thickly. 'I doubt it. You're the only friend I've got, Case. You're a damned good chap as you British say. *Damned* good. Damned good.'

'There's a taxi waiting for you.' I helped him towards the door.

'I gotta car,' he remembered.

'Leave it till tomorrow. Taxi's easier. Don't worry about a thing.'

A taxi actually *was* waiting, but Regina Street would be their best hunting ground at this time, of course. Apostolos and I poured him in, got the address to the driver, and watched the tail-lights out of sight. I wondered if Mrs Kapotas understood the pressures of being a receiver.

Apostolos said: 'You need not worry, Captain, about the bar. I will—'

'The keys, chum. The keys.'

He handed them over.

I spent twenty minutes and an extra drink roughly clearing up the dead glasses, counting the money in the till and finding the way to lock the grille down across the shelves. When I got out to the lobby again, the Sergeant was already on night duty.

'It's only half past eleven,' I pointed out.

'I could not sleep more. And you have had a long day, I think.'

'Well, thanks.' I looked through the glass doors at the shiny street. 'I think I'll take a stroll around the block. About twenty minutes.'

Papa cleared his throat. 'If you want a girl, I—'

'Actually, I want a stroll.'

He just nodded and I went.

The night air was gentle, although the sky was clear and sparkling with a thousand stars you never see through Europe's smoke-screen. I went out of the walled city and drifted along the wide bright street beside the dry moat and its little kebab stalls. It was pretty empty; just a taxi-driver leaning on his cab, a bunch of UN soldiers – Canadian, this time – staggering home leaning on each other, a cop loafing on a corner. A nice, un-hurried Cyprus pace.

It would still be there tomorrow. So I turned back into the city from Metaxas Square and along Regina Street from the Regina Palace. Narrower, jammed with parked cars, and darker: just a ribbon of starry sky above and the neon lights of bars and strip joints down below.

I was almost at the Castle when a voice said: 'Mr Case,' and I turned towards the car parked beside me. Then a hand pulled my shoulder from behind and I turned my head back – just like sticking up a target. It's easy to say that now.

My vision smashed into a thousand coloured pieces, my jaw jumped sideways towards the car, dragging the rest of my head with it, and my knees just gave up and I started towards the gutter.

I didn't quite make it. Somebody caught me, hefted me, my face bounced on warm rough plastic, a door slammed and we were moving. This wasn't quite unconsciousness, just instant Sunday morning; zig-zagging between sleep and wakefulness, time tearing past or unmoving. I felt hands rumple me, but wasn't sure where my own hands were so I didn't try to do anything. Voices muttered, the car droned. Then a something was wrapped around my head and eyes, we stopped, I was picked up and put down and the car whined distantly . . .

I was alone in the dark. Carefully I levered myself up on one elbow, grinding it into the gravelly pavement. The world beyond my bandages was swinging in soggy orbits and my stomach swung in tune with it, so I stayed very still and thought of cool calm things . . . and slowly the feelings passed and I could sit up.

I unwound the bandages slowly – the bastards had used wide sticky insulating tape and it ripped out half my scalp as it came free – and looked around. I was in a narrow street of derelict houses, sitting a few yards from a complete roadblock of con-crete blocks, oil drums and sandbags. A little bit of no-man's-land between Greek and Turkish areas.

Forty yards the other way there were lights, the sound of cars passing. I staggered out on to Paphos Street, a few yards from the Paphos Gate and a quarter of a mile from the Castle. Using two feet and a wall, it took me just under ten minutes, and I used the rest of my strength shoving open the front doors.

Sergeant Papa stared.

I croaked: 'Don't just stand there: open the damn bar.'

*

Five minutes later I was sitting at a table with the second Scotch in my hand and the Sergeant chewing his moustache and watch-ing me – curiously more than anxiously. 'Shall I call the police?'

'Not for a minute.' I was running my fingertips gently over my face. There were sticky bits that I knew must be black streaks, and a small hard lump half-way along the right side of my jaw. 'I can't think what to tell them, yet.'

It's funny how you can feel that way: not wanting to do the simplest things until you're in charge of yourself again.

'What did they steal?' he asked.

I hadn't even thought to ask myself that. 'Money, I suppose,' and I started turning out my pockets.

My wallet was still there – and the notes still inside it. And a handful of coins, and my keys – to the Queen Air, my boarding-house room, flight briefcase. And papers: passport, aeroplane insurance, the champagne cargo papers (a whole bunch of them) cheque book, vaccination certificate . . .

'You know,' I said slowly, 'I don't think they've taken a damn thing.' Or had I been carrying something I'd forgotten about?

The Sergeant frowned. 'Perhaps they mistook you for some-body.'

'One of them knew my name.'

He shrugged helplessly. 'Then you did not have what they hoped for. Shall I telephone the police now?'

'What do I tell them? I can't identify anybody, not even the

19

car. Nothing stolen – so it's just a simple assault, even if they believed me. The hell with it.'

He nodded doubtfully. Then: 'Somebody telephoned for you, after you went out.'

'What did you say?'

'That you were out, but just for a walk and you would be back soon.'

'They didn't leave a name? Or ring back?'

'No.' After a while he added: 'Do you think it was . . .?'

'It sounds like it.' I finished the Scotch and stood up. And swayed and grabbed for the table. 'No, I'm all right.'

But he stayed close, just in case. 'I'm sorry, Captain.'

I was about to say 'Just Mister' but then realised he'd meant it as a compliment. 'Give me a ring about seven-thirty and I'll start cooking eggs. Good night, Sergeant.'

3

Next morning, Kapotas arrived at about half past ten looking in roughly the same state as the octopus in the kitchen only weaker. He was about the one man in Cyprus I wouldn't have swapped heads with; my own was merely sore, with occasional shooting pains. I still had the lump on the jaw, but for some reason it hadn't coloured up so I only looked a bit lopsided.

To Kapotas I probably looked triplicated. 'Oh God, I am so sorry,' he croaked, clinging to the reception desk. 'I will never drink whisky after dinner again. Never.'

I diagnosed him. 'Better have one now to seal off the nerve ends. Or a Bloody Mary—' I lifted my own glass from under the desk top; '— the hair of the dog with food value.'

'No, no, no.' He shuddered. 'What happened at breakfast? – I should have been here.'

'They got a choice of boiled or fried egg and black or white coffee.' The Castle only served Turkish or instant coffee anyway. 'No mutinies yet. Next time, sleep here.'

'My wife said the same thing only she took half an hour. What happened in the night?'

'We sold six short-stay rooms and the hotel cut came to ten pounds, 300 mils. Four of them were still around by morning so I served 'em a compulsory breakfast at 500 mils each. Two families have checked out early, we've got three new guests coming in this afternoon. And an order for champagne and caviar. I'm damn sure there isn't any caviar, what about champagne?'

He shook his head very very carefully. 'They took it all.'

'Ah. I'd been wondering why they hadn't nicked all the ordinary wine. Well, you're the man with money: you'd better go shopping.'

'Oh no,' he said limply. 'Please – it would be better if you ... I must think about our problems ...'

That did it. I swallowed my drink and stood up. 'Listen, Jack—'

'Loukis.'

'Listen, *Jack*: yesterday I got up at six and flew nearly eight hours and two refuelling stops, solo, before I even got here. Then I find I probably won't be paid for that, so I sit down and cook dinner for twelve when I could have told you to stuff the whole kitchen sideways. As far as I recall, what *you* did was boil some eggs, pass some plates and get smashed on company whisky. Today . . . today go shopping, Jack.'

By now he was standing up straight and looking a good quarter bottle less hungover. I sat again. I don't know why I'd stood up, really, except these things don't sound the same sitting down.

He muttered: 'Yes, of course . . . I . . . just a cup of coffee . . . will you stay here?'

'Sure. I'm waiting for a call to Israel.'

He tried a quick smile and tottered off towards the kitchen.

*

Actually I was waiting for my third call to Israel. The first two hadn't got me anywhere, though I'd been pretty thick to expect an Israeli airport to tell me if a certain person would be on a certain aeroplane. The way they feel about airport security, they wouldn't tell me if there were wings on that aeroplane. So now I was trying the British consulate in Tel Aviv.

Somebody came through on a rough line. I yelled: 'Does anybody there know anything about Kenneth Cavitt?'

'What about him?'

'He's supposed to be coming out of Beit Oren today. Have you heard anything?'

'The prison?'

The Sergeant came downstairs, looking pink, clean and dignified. He nodded graciously to me, then planted himself out on the doorstep and studied the sky.

I lowered my voice. 'Yes, that's right.'

'Are you a newspaper?'

'No, no. I was his partner. Name's Roy Case. I'm waiting for him in Nicosia.'

'I see. Hold on.'

The line went quiet except for the atmospherics. The Sergeant clasped his hands behind him and rocked gently on his heels, sniffing the warm coffee-flavoured air.

A new voice came on. 'You were asking about Mr Cavitt? We've been told he'll be aboard the afternoon flight to Nicosia. That's EL AL 363.'

'Thanks very much.' Then something about that phrase 'we've been told . . .' made me wonder. 'Who told you about him?'

'The Ministry of the Interior. It's standard procedure. They always try to get us to pay the fare and we never do.'

'Every time a British citizen gets out of jail?'

'No, just whenever one is being deported.'

'He's being *deported*?'

Now we were both surprised. 'What did you expect? That's also pretty standard for a foreigner found guilty of espionage.'

*

Kapotas got back from his shopping trip just before noon, having bought a small pot of caviar, two cooks and a waiter. No champagne.

'Do you know the *prices*?' He stared disbelievingly at the caviar. 'So I remembered: we have an aeroplane full of champagne.'

'And a grand opening in Lebanon.'

'No. That is postponed indefinitely. I got the message from London when I called at our office just now.'

Well, it didn't surprise me. Opening a new pad would be a pretty pricey commitment.

Kapotas added: 'They say, can we try and sell the champagne out here?'

'Not without an import licence. And paying duty and all.'

'I think the hotel has a licence to import some wines . . . I saw something in the file . . .' He went through into the little cubbyhole of an office behind the desk and started rummaging.

I called after him: 'And who do we sell it to? It would take years to get rid of 144 bottles of that stuff over the counter here, so unless the Ledra Palace or the Hilton want some . . .'

He came up with a piece of paper and studied it, frowning. Finally: 'I don't understand it. I will ring the Customs and ask.'

He started dialling, and I drifted back to the desk and to brooding about deportation. Ken wasn't going to like it. A pilot's life is travelling and he can't afford having places he

23

can't travel to. The big airlines even put it in your contract: getting yourself barred from a country can be a valid reason for dismissal.

The trouble is, deportation isn't a 'legal' thing, if you see what I mean. It isn't a court decision, but a minister's one. In some places you can appeal it through the courts, if you can invent some grounds, but it likely won't help. And just because it isn't a court sentence, it can last forever – or a day. All you can do is wait and hope for a change of government, policy, wind or the minister's liver and – bingo – you're back in favour again.

If, of course, you're important enough for it to be worth somebody changing his mind about you.

Kapotas came out of the office looking almost cheerful for once. 'They understand our problem: it is okay to bring in just one box, on this licence, as long as the others stay "airside", if you understand that.'

I nodded. 'On yonder side of the barrier, in the aeroplane or a Customs store. There's no point in unloading it and renting store space until we know we'll get an import licence for the lot – *and* we've got a buyer waiting. So leave it on board.'

He was ready to agree to any scheme that saved money. 'Good, then. If you go to the airport now you will be back by half past one. You may use my car,' he added magnanimously.

'Hold on, now. I'm meeting a flight at two-ten so I shan't be back before three anyhow.'

'But we must have the champagne before then!'

'Then come with me and bring the box back while I hang on there. We can use your car,' I added magnanimously.

*

Stand 8, the visiting light-aircraft park, was just about next door to the Customs supervised store, so they let us take the box out through that. They even offered to rent us a porter, but Kapotas had just found out about the duty on imported wine and gone mean again.

'£3.70 a gallon! That means more than seven pounds for a box! Of course, it would be better if it was Commonwealth champagne.'

'A fine old Nova Scotia blanc de blanc '53, for instance.'

'Ummm. Well . . .' and after that he saved his breath for humping the box – it weighed just on fifty pounds – while I locked up the aeroplane and sorted out the paperwork. Standing out in the sun, the inside of the Queen Air was like an overheated greenhouse; it wouldn't hurt the aircraft, but I didn't think champagne was normally served lightly boiled. Maybe we really ought to move it into store . . . the hell with it; I'd probably end up paying the rental myself, on Kapotas's past form.

The Customs sorted through my wad of papers, down to and including a Certificat d'origine from Comité Interprofessionnel du Vin de Champagne swearing that no unprofessional grape had been allowed to get its pips into the tub. I'd never seen a certificate like that before, though I'd never carried champagne before, either.

So finally Kapotas paid his duty and staggered away with the box still unopened, while I drifted over to the terminal for a beer and a look at the menu. The latter was a pure formality; whatever they offered, it was sure to be better than what the Castle's new cooks did to that sheep and/or octopus.

*

EL AL flight 363 was an old Viscount 800 they must have borrowed from Arkia, and late, just as you'd expect with the way they search passengers at Tel Aviv nowadays. It was pretty full, mostly with a returning old folks' pilgrimage, each carrying a bottle of duty-free brandy and a bundle of Jerusalem walking-sticks. Then a couple of American families – and finally Ken.

I was watching from the terminal restaurant, looking down to the tarmac. He and another man came out of the door, paused at the head of the steps, then Ken walked quickly down, carrying what looked like his old flight briefcase. The other man stayed up there, watching. Ken came across until he was almost at the immigration entrance below me, then turned and jerked a stiff two fingers at the man back on the steps. The man didn't react. Ken vanished inside.

Twenty minutes later he came out of the Customs hall with the briefcase and a battered brown leather grip I remembered him buying in Florence eight years before. He was wearing an old pair of khaki trousers, faded to near white, and a new white shirt. For a few moments he stood there, letting the crowd flow around him, not really looking for anything and maybe only smelling the air. To me, the scent was sweat and floor polish, but it could have meant something different to him.

He was a couple of inches shorter than me and now thinner as well. The long lines down the side of his bony nose were cut deeper, his eyes barricaded with sun-crinkles, and for the first time there was grey in his lank black hair. But he'd been moving easily, though maybe a little warily, and he was still Ken Cavitt. And I was very glad to see him.

He sensed, rather than saw me moving towards him and jerked around. His face was blank for a couple of seconds, and then he began to smile. That hadn't changed.

We shook hands, sort of politely, and I said: 'Hello, Ken.'

'Hello, matey. Nice of you to remember.'

'Oh, I hadn't got anything better to do today, so . . .'

'Sure, sure.' He looked me carefully up and down; I was still wearing yesterday's smudged khaki drill trousers and shirt. 'Millionaire dress, huh?' He tapped my stomach. 'And a deposit account.'

'I'll slim tomorrow.'

'What happened to your face?'

I touched my jaw carefully. 'Got slugged last night. I'd say mugged if they'd taken anything.'

'Weird.' He looked along the terminal lobby. 'Can we get a drink or ten in here?'

'It comes wholesale back in town, but we can run some taxiing trials here first.' I headed us towards the stairs up to the restaurant – the bar downstairs doesn't serve spirits – then took out a packet of menthol-tipped cigarettes and offered them. 'You still on these?'

'I gave it up. You can't afford to have vices, inside. Somebody gets a hold and screws you.'

I nodded and tossed the unopened packet into a wastebin alongside an airport cop, who did a double-take and then carefully ignored the bin until we were out of sight.

I ordered two Scotches and two Keo beers – an old pattern, but only with Ken. I hadn't drunk like that in two years.

He took a bite of the Scotch and shuddered violently. 'Christ! Is that what whisky tastes like?'

I sipped cautiously. 'It seems normal . . .'

'Hell, to think I've spent two years dreaming of that.' He gulped at the beer, then took another cautious sip of Scotch. 'I guess I'll get used to it again. Where are we staying? – the Ledra?'

'Nicosia Castle.'

He frowned. 'Why that dump?'

'It's a bit complicated. But about your licences: I talked to the Civil Aviation people before I left London, and—'

'Ah, that can wait. Just tell me how rich we are.'

It was a moment I'd known would come, but that didn't make it any easier. 'Ken – we aren't rich.'

'Not quite millionaires, then. Have we still got the same aeroplane?'

It's funny how few British pilots say 'plane'; I don't myself. Somehow, it would be like calling a woman you loved 'a good lay'.

I said carefully: 'We don't have any aeroplane.'

His face was suddenly very calm. 'Why not?'

'We only owned half of it – and d'you have any idea what a hot lawyer costs in Israel? By the time I'd got through paying for your defence . . .'

After a time, he said slowly: 'I knew it must be adding up, but . . . you should have let me go down without a fuss. Came to the same thing, anyway.'

'It wasn't sentiment. The business wasn't the aeroplane: it was you and me, and damn-all use in jail. You can get an aeroplane any time at any money.'

'If you can show the bank a cargo contract . . . Why didn't you tell me? You were writing.'

'Didn't think it would make two years go any faster.'

'You could be right, there.' The loudspeaker gurgled an announcement for a CSA flight to Prague, passengers please go to . . . Ken cocked his head to listen, then shook it, annoyed. 'You get too used to listening for orders. So, we're broke?'

'Within a few hundred.'

'D'you mind if I say "knickers"?'

'Make it "cami-knickers" if you like; I don't shock easily.'

'It can't be that bad.' He gulped the rest of his Scotch. 'Or should I have given it back and taken a refund?'

'We'll live.' I waved for refills.

He stared into his empty glass, then grinned suddenly. 'Busted. Well, we've been there before. More comfortable, somehow.'

'And all we have to do is start again. I may have ballsed things up, but you can't fly a business one-handed.'

'I know . . . It's just that you sit there on top of that mountain and bugger-all to do – not even needlework or carpentry classes – and damn few to talk to, and you think "Well, at least Roy's making our fortune".'

'I know. Sorry.'

'Ah, the hell with it. What've you been doing?'

'A while with an air-taxi outfit, Aztecs and Comanches. Then a North Sea oil company – that's where I got rated on the Queen Air—'

'What's so marvellous about that?'

'Sorry, I hadn't told you.' Our drinks arrived, then I told him about Castle's aeroplane and the firm going broke. 'So we spend a few days here getting you back on the primrose path, then they'll tell me to fly the aeroplane home. You come along, you can fly every inch of the way and that's ten hours' free practice. After that, all you have to do is take a medical and instrument rating, get a type-rating and once they've looked at your logbook you've got your licence back.'

He nodded approvingly. 'And you'd got all this worked out?'

'I didn't know Castle was going broke, but I knew I'd have to fly back empty anyway.'

'Neat. What mark of Queen Air?'

'The 65-80. Lycoming 380's, no long-range tanks, usual ADF, VOR, ILS, weather radar that's trying to pick up dirty pictures.'

'Radar's improved since my time. What's the weather up to, here?'

I told him as much as I remembered about the met situation – I hadn't picked up a report today – as we walked out towards the taxi rank.

He listened carefully. 'It's funny – it's almost the thing you miss most, not knowing the weather, not getting a report. You can work out a bit for yourself, when you can see the sky, but not knowing what's really happening up there . . . then you feel cut off. Shut in.'

'Uh-huh.' We were almost at the rank, but then the Czech Tu-104 started its takeoff and we stopped to watch, as pilots always do. It did it the old-fashioned way, getting the nosewheel off early and running nose-high for a while before sagging up into the sky.

'Takes you back,' Ken said. And it did: that was the way we'd learned to handle the early jets in the RAF, Meteors and NF 14's.

'It's an old design. When did it first come out? – '53? – '54?'

'As a bomber, earlier than that . . .' he watched it howl ponderously away to the north-west, and his eyes were screwed tight against the bright sky.

I offered my sunglasses and he took them; he hadn't seen too much sun in the last two years. His face had a thin, superficial tan of the exercise yard over the deeper pallor of the cell block.

'I'll buy some in town – if you can afford it.'

I nodded and we walked on to the taxi rank. The car park was pretty much uninhabited; it was a quiet time between flights. Just one man who'd paused to watch the takeoff and was now climbing into a white Morris 1100.

We were heading for town in the back of an old Austin A60 when Ken suddenly said: 'Whatever happened to Linda?'

'Linda? Oh yes, her. She was shacked up with some air traffic controller in Scotland, the last I heard.'

'Damn it.' He went depressed. 'I was probably going to marry that girl.'

'Oh yes? And what about Angela and Judy and—'

'What? I didn't know any Angela or Judy.'

'You would have done, mate; you would have done.'

He thought this over and it seemed to cheer him up a bit. 'Maybe you're right. Which reminds me: I hope you weren't thinking of an early night tonight?'

I'd been thinking of it but certainly not expecting it. 'I'll start organising things when we get to the hotel. Incidentally, you've probably got company waiting there: a certain Spohr, plus daughter.'

'Professor Spohr?' He seemed impressed. 'That's quick.'

'Professor? Where did you meet him? – not in Beit Oren?'

'Yep. He did a year. Came out about six weeks ago.'

'You're getting a better class of jailbird these days. He's ordered champagne and caviar to be waiting for you; what did you do? – save him from drowning in the cell bucket?'

'No, just that most of the time we were the only English-speaking Christians in the place.'

'And you spent a year talking about Christianity? You don't know anything except the churches have pointed tops.'

'Very interesting bloke. He's a medieval archaeologist.'

'So what did he go down for?'

'Well, he was excavating a site without permission—'

'They don't give you a year for that.'

'They do if you pull a gun on the cops who've come to arrest you.' He was twisting uneasily to look over his shoulder.

'Ah. So this is just an old boys' reunion.'

'Could be.' He was still glancing back.

I said: 'What's the trouble?'

'There's a car . . .' he said softly.

'The white 1100? It was in the park with us, but this is still the normal route into town.'

'Yes . . .' He studied the road ahead, trying to remember. We were coming up to a big roundabout. 'If you go right here, you come in over the river on George Grivas Street, is that right?'

'I think so.' He looked at me and I shrugged and then nodded and leant forward to tell the driver to make the turn. 'I know it isn't the quickest way, but my friend wants to see something of the Engomi area.'

So we turned right. So did the 1100.

Ken said: 'Would they have told Cyprus I was coming in?'

'Sure to have done.' After all, you don't pay the airline fare to deport somebody unless you've made sure you won't have to double it by bringing him back when the other place won't take him either. 'But the authorities here wouldn't bother to tail you. All they have to do is check the hotel registers.'

'Ye-es ... I'm not going back to jail, you know.' He said it quietly, as much to himself as to me.

I looked across, a bit surprised. 'No reason why you should. Specially if you don't go back to Israel.'

He just nodded, and looked back. The white 1100 was staying about fifty yards back on a fairly empty road. If he *was* tailing us, it was quite an efficient job. But just his hard luck that he was behind two pathologically suspicious characters.

We came over the river Pedieos – a steep green gorge but with only a flabby brown trickle at the bottom – and the town began to thicken up. The 1100 closed in, casually.

Our driver slowed to make a left turn that would have brought us along Evagoras Avenue to Metaxas Square, Nicosia's busiest junction and the closest entrance to the walled city. I tapped him on the shoulder hastily. 'Keep going, keep going. Go down Makarios instead.'

'But it's stupid—'

'It's our money on the clock.'

The big shoulders shrugged but we kept going. And it *was* stupid, an unnecessary loop, doubling back. And if the 1100 was just as stupid ...

He was. Makarios Avenue also brings you down to the Metaxas Square traffic-lights, and from a hundred yards away we could see we'd be caught by a red.

Ken looked at me. 'Shall we dance?'

'If you like. But don't hit him before I do; my record can stand it better.'

We stopped and the 1100 stopped immediately behind and we were out. I heard the taxi-driver's surprised shout dwindle away and then we had both doors of the 1100 open.

I said: 'It's a nice day for a drive, but what makes you think we know the only good route on the island?'

He was maybe my age but more solidly built, with a soft-edged square face, brown hair that was thinning back from a high forehead, fluffy side-whiskers and very calm blue eyes behind rimless glasses. He just rested his forearms on the wheel and looked coolly from Ken to me, and finally asked: 'What are you doing?' A slightly clipped accent.

'Louder,' Ken suggested, 'and more worried. You're an innocent citizen out for an afternoon drive and we could be the Hole-in-the-Wall gang for all you know.'

'I do not think you will rob me here.' We had quite a nice little traffic jam building up around us, with innocent bystanders watching curiously. Our own driver was climbing out.

I said: 'It's a hire car. He's not resident.'

'Sure,' Ken said, leaning in and punching the preset buttons on the car radio and watching the wavelength needle jump along the scale. 'But ... that's 292 metres, isn't it?' He turned the on-off switch and the car flooded with a fast-talking gabble in ... Hebrew.

Ken said reprovingly: 'That's not clever, is it? Staying pre-tuned to the Voice of Israel. Ha Mosad wouldn't like it.'

'Ha Mosad?' I queried.

'The Establishment. Latest name for the Sherut Bitachon.' The Israeli secret service. 'Ask him what he does for a cover job here.'

'What do you do for a cover job?'

'Not that he'll tell you.' Ken added.

'Then why ask him? We know what he looks like, we can find out his name by reporting his car number.'

By now a couple of cars in the rear rank were hooting impatiently, and our own driver was shaking my arm and making imploring noises.

Ken said: 'What do you think, friend?'

The new friend looked at me and his voice was as calm as ever. 'I think you are Roy Case.'

I stepped back and said politely: 'You have the advantage of me.'

'Not yet.' He pulled the doors shut. 'My name is Mihail Ben Iver. I deal in non-ferrous castings.' He swerved out past our taxi and on across the square.

'You see?' Ken said. 'All done by kindness.'

4

I overtipped the taxi driver without changing the suspicious
stare he was giving us, and Sergeant Papa saluted and swung
open the glass doors for us. And gave Ken a rather careful look.

Inside, everything was calm, except Kapotas, of course. I
introduced Ken, gave him the register to sign, and asked: 'Did
the Spohrs arrive yet?'

'Yes. Father and daughter.'

I raised an eyebrow and he said: 'Austrian. They are upstairs, in 323 and 321, the best rooms.'

That niggled me a bit. So why wasn't *I* in a best room, instead
of tripping over holes in the carpet of 208? 'Did you send up
the champagne?'

There was a peculiar neutral look on his neat accountant's
face. 'Not yet. They said they would wait for Mr Cavitt.'

Ken said: 'Well, they can wait a bit longer; I'm having a bath
first.' He rubbed his palms together as if he could still feel the
prison grime – and maybe he could; he probably hadn't come
out more than a couple of hours before they stuck him on to
the airliner.

I said: 'I'll tell them you're here.'

Kapotas gave him a key. 'I have put you in 206, near to Mr
Case.'

Ken took it and picked up his bag. 'Thanks. Drop in and take
a glass with the Professor, Roy. You'll like him. I haven't met
the daughter.' He ignored the lift and bounced lightly up the
stairs.

Kapotas said in his most blank voice: 'I would welcome your
opinion of the champagne.'

I looked at him, but he turned away. So I followed through
the service door and down the corridor to the wine cellar. He
unlocked it, and we went in. It was a small square rough-
plastered room with no window and just a single unshaded bulb
glaring down on the near-empty wine racks, the heavy scarred
old table in the middle, and in the middle of that the opened

box of Kroeger Royale '66. Behind me, Kapotas carefully locked the door again. What the hell . . . ?

When he turned around, his face and voice weren't neutral any more.

'Will you tell me,' he hissed, 'exactly how you take the cork out of a sub-machine gun?'

*

Five of them, actually. Partly dismantled to fit into the box, and wrapped in newspaper to stop them rattling, with other twists of newspaper holding a few cartridges each.

Kapotas unwrapped a long straight magazine that looked fully loaded. 'Five to one box, so if the other eleven boxes are the same *vintage*, that makes sixty guns. And over a thousand bullets.'

'Christ.' Stupidly, my first thought was the risk I'd been taking by flying with an unmeasured weight on board. But the Queen Air had been nowhere near her maximum load anyway – and of course, somebody had made sure the boxes weighed just what a dozen of champagne would, making it up exactly with those extra cartridges.

I fingered the box with its neat lines of staples and paper taping. 'This was done properly. On a machine.' Probably at the Kroeger bottling plant one quiet weekend? Then I remembered: 'But one box got opened at Rheims. It had got ripped. And that was champagne, all right.'

'Did you collect this in France?'

'Sure, that was the whole point. It was a last-minute order and they didn't know how the hell to get it here in time and then remembered I was flying down anyway, so told me to stop off and pick it up direct from the growers.'

'This was no last-minute order.' And by now I was wondering for myself about how much of the story I'd just told him was true, plus exactly why Castle's regular pilot had left in a hurry. Then Kapotas added: 'But did you bring the torn box?'

'No, they'd brought down a couple of extra boxes by mistake – so they said. So I left the torn one and another – of course.'

'Very clever,' he said grimly. 'They bring some real champagne and tear it open as a decoy – and if you had taken it also, what does it matter? Very neat.'

I'd smoothed out a bit of the newspaper wrapping: it was a *Le Monde* of nearly a month ago. What did that tell us except an earliest possible date for the packing? Kapotas had picked up the major part of one of the guns.

'What are they?' I asked.

'Not even French. American. The M3; they called them 'grease guns' because they look a bit like them.'

'Ah. You know quite a bit about it.'

'We all know about sub-machine guns in Cyprus,' he said, just a little sadly. 'Some of our National Guards have these.'

'Ah. But at least you don't believe I knew what I was carrying?'

He thought about this. And took rather too long, in my view. But finally: 'No. You would not have let me open this box if ... but what matters is what the police believe.'

'Now, hold on, hold on, don't let's rush things—'

'Don't *rush*?' he hissed. 'Do you know how they feel about gun-running out here?'

'Much the same as they do in the Lebanon, I'd guess, except here I'd probably get a fairer trial.'

He shut up, thinking – for the first time – about what might have happened to me if the flight had gone ahead as planned. 'Well ...'

'Look: this is nothing to do with Cyprus. If I'd been flying on today, nobody here would know anything about the guns. So let's start again from that premise.'

'Do you mean *not* to report them?'

'What do we gain? – except the chance of being disbelieved. And whatever happens in the end, we'll have a bad time getting there. The newspapers'll be full of it ...'

I let him write his own headlines, and from his expression they were good ones. Meantime I counted the rounds in one of the magazines: thirty. Oddly, the cartridges themselves had been made in Spain. Or maybe not so odd. Somewhere down the line, somebody had kept his hands clean by selling empty guns, somebody else had stayed a virgin by selling only cartridges without guns. Some minds think that way.

Kapotas asked: 'What do you want to do, then?'

'Get 'em off the island.'

'Where to?'

I shrugged. 'It doesn't have to be further than the sea. I can take out the escape hatch and just feed them into the drink.'

'Are they all right where they are now, though?'

'As long as they stay airside they're no concern of Customs. And they know our problem – or think they do – so they treat it as entrepôt cargo; as if it was just changing aeroplanes. Happens all the time.'

He considered this and decided that it really must happen all the time.

I said: 'Now, on the more pressing problem: what about the real champagne? – you've got guests waiting.'

'I rang up and had some sent round from the shop. For cash.' He made it sound like he'd paid in his own blood. 'It's cooling now, but it could not be the Kroeger Royale. The best they had was Dom Perignon 1966. Is it good?'

'Some say it's the best, but I only drink for effect. What are you going to do with this *cuvée*?' I waggled a hand at the bits of weaponry. 'Stick it in the boot of your car?'

He shuddered at the idea, but had to admit it was a good one. Anywhere in the hotel was too risky. 'All right – but what do I do with them then?'

I shrugged. 'Bury them, if you like. We can't try taking them back through Customs.'

'I suppose so. But—' he showed a new flash of annoyance; '—you should have been suspicious. Bringing champagne by air!'

'People charter aeroplanes to send boxes of cut flowers. *I* wouldn't hire a bike to send a bunch of them.'

'Now I understand how you have avoided being married,' he said bitterly.

*

In the end, I took the champagne and caviar upstairs myself. Pure snoopiness; I'd never met a professor who'd done time before, let alone one who pulled guns on coppers.

The hotel was an L-shaped affair with the low-numbered rooms – like mine – on the street front, and the better ones in the quiet wing that stuck back from it. The view from 323 was the blank wall of the apartment building next door, but blank walls don't throw bottles, rev up jeep engines and sing Swedish drinking songs at one a.m. Apart from that, it was a bigger room than mine, and with a bathroom, but the furniture was the usual heavy Victorian mahogany and chintz, just more of it.

When I went in, the Professor was the only one there. I put the tray down on the round table by the window, took the first bottle from the ice bucket and started a careful job of opening it.

'I'm sorry the hotel's in a bit of a muddle at the moment, but I expect you heard about our troubles.' That was just to try and get him talking; he didn't look like the type who normally chatted with servants.

In fact he looked like the last of the hairy English kings: neat sharp imperial beard, black flecked with grey, on a square face with cold grey eyes above a solid square body. But all a bit shrunken, which could have been a year of Beit Oren food. With a deep tan – the jail pallor had gone – and an elegant Chinese silk dressing gown over a bare chest, and Moroccan slippers, he looked as fit a sixty-year-old as I'd seen in my life.

He screwed a small cigar into an ivory holder and said: 'You are not the floor waiter, then?' A slight German accent and a touch of dry humour.

'No, I'm sort of the company pilot.'

'Ah so?' He was interested. 'Perhaps you are Mr Cavitt's friend, Mr ...' I suppose Ken must have mentioned my name at some time, but he'd forgotten.

'Case, Roy Case.' I'd got the wire off the cork, and now—

'Please do not work it with the thumbs. Twist it out gently with a napkin. We waste less that way.'

Of course, I hadn't brought a napkin. He sighed, took a folded maroon silk handkerchief from his breast pocket and passed it across. I got the cork out without any bang, poured a glass and took it over to him.

'Please to give yourself one.'

'Thank you, Professor.' And so I did. 'Can I give you some caviar now?'

We'd done what we could, like finding a poncey-looking dish and filling it with cracked ice and the caviar pot in the middle and a plate of bread and butter ... But he wasn't offering to share all *that*.

'I will wait for Mr Cavitt. He seemed well?'

'I think so. He tells me you're a medievalist?'

He moved a chunky, strong hand in a deprecating motion. 'Only a humble artisan. I dig things up; it needs a real scholar to decide what I have found.' And he sipped his Dom Perignon like any humble artisan.

'D'you find much from that period out this end of the world?' I was thinking of medieval times as being knights in armour and most of the ruins out here being Greek or Roman or Hebrew or Islamic ...

He looked mildly surprised. 'The Crusades, Mr Case, the Crusades. Four centuries of holy warfare leaves its mark.'

'Silly of me. And where you find a mark, you dig?'

'When there is permission.' He smiled gently.

'Found any new Lost Cities recently?'

'God grant nobody finds any; the Middle East is full of old cities that nobody has the money to excavate yet already. But no – my business is artifacts, not so much buildings. Coins, pottery, a fragment of a helmet, a lance tip.'

'Where were you working when ... er ... ?' I didn't know quite how to put it to a professor. But he just smiled again.

'At Acre, then Caesarea. Both, as you know, were important Crusader ports and fortresses.'

Actually, I did remember something like that. 'Wasn't Richard the Lion Heart involved around there?'

'Certainly. He recaptured Acre in 1191 – his first battle with the great Salah ed-din.'

'Huh?'

'Saladin, you would say.'

'Oh, him.' I sipped my champagne – although I don't like fizzy drinks much. Then asked: 'Are you going back to Israel to carry on the good work?'

'Probably. Permits may be a little more difficult to come by, but ...' He flapped the problem aside.

So *he* hadn't been deported. Or was good at hiding the fact. And just then there was a knock on the door.

The Professor bounced on to his feet – he'd locked the door

behind me – and moved pretty nippily across, opened it, and let in a girl. I'd expected Ken.

His daughter – it had to be, since they let go a quick rattle of German as she stepped inside – was a short, properly shaped girl in her late twenties. Almost everything about her was mousey: the colour of her hair, the neat quick movements, the sharpness of her face, the polite hesitant smile as her dark eyes followed the direction of his nod and she saw me.

'Mr Case – my daughter, Mitzi Braunhof.' He shut the door behind her.

I held out a hand. 'Frau Braunhof . . .'

'No.' She took a few quick steps and shook my hand quickly. 'My marriage is finished. Just Fraulein again.' She was wearing a simple black skirt, thin black high-necked sweater and a light suede jacket. I bowed in what I thought was a formal German way, turned back and poured her a glass.

The Prof said: 'Mr Case is a friend of Mr Cavitt, *Liebchen*. Also a pilot.'

'Ah?' she looked politely interested and took the drink. 'Thank you. You must have arranged for him to stay here.'

'Mr Case,' the Prof said gravely, 'flies for the Castle Hotel company.'

Mitzi cocked her head and said, a little curiously: 'You are not going back to work with Mr Cavitt?'

'Oh yes. Soon as we can arrange it.'

'There is a problem?'

I shrugged. 'It takes time to get back to where we left off.'

'Ah yes . . .' and she gave a quick mousey nod, just as if my remark had meant something.

There was another knock on the door and this time it really was Ken. Looking a little pinker and cleaner from the bath and in a pair of fawn twill trousers with a lot of horizontal creases from lying on a shelf for – maybe two years. But the same new white shirt.

I put down my glass. 'I'll leave you to it. I want to get to some shops before they close, anyway. Anything you want besides a pair of sunglasses, Ken?'

Ken shrugged. 'Just about everything. But it can wait.'

The Prof said: 'Ledra Street is not quite Bond Street, Kenneth.'

I went past them to the door. 'See you downstairs, Ken?'

'Sure. About seven.' He gave me a quick, and perhaps slightly nervous smile. I went out.

*

Sergeant Papa was sipping coffee at the lobby desk. No sign of Kapotas. I asked, 'Any messages?'

He turned his head ponderously and took a slip from my pigeon-hole: a Mr Uthman Jehangir had called from the Ledra Palace. He was news to me. 'Did you take the call?'

'Yes. I would guess he is Lebanese. He said he would call again. And somebody asked for Professor Spohr. I said we do not know him.'

'Good. You checked the passports?'

'Ye-es.' He frowned. 'The woman's name is Braunhof.'

'She's still his daughter. Busted marriage, I gather.'

He frowned on. 'They changed the Austrian passport in 1970. Now it does not show the maiden name or even if women are married.'

I didn't know women's lib had taken over in Vienna. 'Well, don't charge them the immoral rate – though I suppose we are already, for secrecy. Anyway, I'm out until about seven. Then Ken Cavitt and I are going on the town.'

'He has just come out of ... ummm ... ?'

'Biet Oren.'

'Yes.' He nodded slowly. 'They all have the paleness under the sunburn.'

'We'll be looking for some bright lights and dark corners. You must advise us where we won't get screwed.'

'Where you *won't* get screwed?' he frowned.

'Not expensively.'

5

In the afternoons they close Ledra Street to all traffic except
taxis and delivery vans, so I could just drift down the middle
of the road with the easygoing crowd, mostly local and mostly
in bright cheap clothes. Just a few uniforms and blue berets, a
few old ladies wrapped in the traditional black. The sunlight
was warm and soft, not the trip through the toaster that it
would be in a month or so, but there were thunderheads stack-
ing up on the mountains to the south-west, and an occasional
distant grumble of thunder.

I drifted, stopped for a cup of gritty sweet Turkish coffee,
bought a pair of sunglasses, bought myself a pair of nylon
socks – and then, because that seemed mean, bought Ken a pair
as well. It's funny how you never get time to buy ordinary
things at home; I'm always getting my handkerchiefs in Frank-
furt and my paperclips in Brussels.

So by then I was almost up to the permanent roadblock to the
Turkish quarter. I could have gone through – they don't mind
foreigners – but there didn't seem much point right then. So I
turned left and drifted towards the Paphos Gate, and once I
was there it wasn't more than five minutes to the Ledra Palace
and goodbye to my resolution about spending Castle money
only in Castle Hotels.

The little old barman was just setting up for the evening,
filling bowls of nuts and crisps. He did a quick double-take and
said gravely: 'It's been a long time, Captain.'

'Nearly two years.'

'Whisky and . . . soda, is it, sir?'

'And not too much ice.'

He put a bowl of overcooked peanuts in front of me and
trotted off to organise the drink. It's a tall, dim room and the
stone-tiled floor gives a slight echo that makes it seem even
cooler than it is. Almost empty, now, but full enough at other
times for them to have started punching out the arched french
windows to make an extension into the garden. And then the
old hands from all over the world will sit in there and complain

that it just isn't the same any more, and they'll be right but they'll still be there.

He came back with the Scotch. 'And Captain Cavitt – is he with you, sir?' He'd remembered Ken's name; not mine.

'He'll be around. Mind if I ring somebody in the hotel?'

He put the phone in front of me and went back to the nuts and crisps and ice. I asked for Mr Jehangir's room and got a polite voice that said it was jolly good of me to call and he'd be down as soon as he could get some togs on. Sergeant Papa must have quite an ear to spot the faint trace of accent; I wouldn't have got it if I hadn't been listening for it.

I sipped my Scotch and ate a peanut and waited and ... and now what? Back to Britain in a few days – but what after that? Well, for the summer we might find some charter outfit that wanted a couple of extra bods; that would build up a bit of fat against the cold. But it wouldn't be heading us towards our own aeroplane again. For that, we needed capital – or a personal introduction to Father Christmas. And he'd have to be in a pretty good mood even for Father Christmas: Ken and I weren't bright young things with decades of earning power ahead. At forty, we'd only got about fifteen years before a medical downcheck put all the future behind us. By then, we had to be in a position to hire others to do the flying, or ...

The woods are full of old pilots who just assumed they'd have it made before the doctor pulled the sky from under them. Or assumed they'd be dead, of course; plenty escape that way.

On that happy note, somebody leant over me and asked: 'Captain Case?'

'I'm Roy Case. And just Mister.'

'Oh splendid. Uthman Jehangir,' and he held out a long brown hand.

The rest of him was a lean, tanned fifty-year-old with crinkled grey hair, a square white smile with gold trimmings, a very formal blue suit and white shirt. Beirut, for sure; they all dress like bank managers over there. Of course, half of them *are* bank managers.

I asked: 'What are you drinking?'

'No, please, allow me.'

Any time. So I took another Scotch and he asked for a red

Cinzano and soda. Then, as he moved and sat down on the next stool, I realised he was lame in his left leg. Or no: something about the businesslike way he arranged the knee with his hand, the shiny uncreased stiffness of the shoe ... an artificial leg, from above the knee.

He lifted his glass: 'Cheers.' And we sipped. 'I rang your hotel ...'

'I got the message. What can I do for you?'

'You fly the Castle International plane, don't you?'

It isn't a plane. 'I did last, I will next, but at the moment it's—'

'Oh yes, I know about Castle going into receivership.' He had the silly habit of flashing his white grin as a full stop at the end of each sentence, but his eyes were bright and watchful. 'I heard that you got stuck with a cargo of champagne?'

All the fire-warning lights in my head flashed on at once. 'Uh-huh.'

'D'you think the receivers could be persuaded to sell it?'

'Better ask them.' Oh no, don't for God's sake call London! 'I mean – ask their man here. Loukis Kapotas. He's at the Castle most of the day.'

He whipped out a little leather notebook with gold corners and wrote it down. Then looked up and grinned once more. 'What marque is it?'

'It says Kroeger Royale '66.'

'Splendid. Jolly good stuff. How many boxes?'

'Only a dozen.' I was beginning to feel a bit uneasy. I mean, the man might be honest or something. 'But why do you want it?'

'For resale, of course. I supply wines and spirits to ... er ... *private* houses in Beirut. And next week we have a rather sudden visit from some friends down in the Gulf. I expect you know these ... er ... gentlemen with their oil revenues? In their own countries they have to set a good example by being strictly Muslim, so when the weather starts boiling up and they escape to Beirut ...' he spread his hands and grinned; '... naturally they want a rest from their devotions.'

I knew – no, I'd only *heard* about these private parties of oil sheikhs in the big houses of Beirut's hillside suburbs. A lot of everything and everything of the best – at a price, of course. But when you've got oil derricks sprouting like weeds, what's a bottle of Kroeger Royale to help launch the latest Swedish virgin?

'But can't you pick it up around Beirut?'

'Oh, I just got caught short with the rush, and the St George and the Phoenicia won't sell me any ...'

'And bankrupt stock comes cheap at any time.'

The grin flashed on-off. 'And that, of course. If you could persuade your Mr ... er, Kapotas to sell at a reasonable figure, I'm sure you'd find your time hadn't been wasted.' So I could take a cut as the middleman – and he'd assume I was taking a commission from Kapotas for finding a buyer. Jehangir would normally do business that way ... And why not, come to think of it?

'And,' he added, 'the matter of getting it on to Beirut: how much would it cost for you to fly it there?'

About 140 nautical miles, say fifty gallons there and back plus landing fees ... and *my* fees, this time ... 'Call it a realistic sixty quid sterling.'

He twitched his elegant shoulders. 'Splendid. If you have a word with Mr Kapotas first, I can call him tomorrow.' And if he could get it at four quid a bottle and resell at a minimum of ten, then he'd clear an easy £750 after all overheads ... Hell, maybe the man *was* honest, if you see what I mean.

'Fine,' I said slowly. 'I'll do that right now. I wanted to be back before dinner anyway.'

'Is the food any good, there?' he asked, genuinely interested.

'Last night it was terrible, but they've got rid of that chef already.'

*

It was just on dusk when I got back to the Castle, the eastern sky turning a dark velvet blue and the first stars coming on with that odd abruptness that must be something to do with the eye of the beholder. Sergeant Papa came to attention in a slow-motion parody of his army days. 'Good evening, Captain.'

'Sergeant.' I stayed out there on the step with him, filling a pipe and watching Regina Street switch on around us. 'Any more news?'

'Mr Kapotas talked to London again but he told us nothing. And somebody called again for the Professor. Again, I said we did not know.'

'Popular, isn't he? Seen anything of my friend Ken?'

'He has not been out.'

I nodded and lit my pipe. The first smoke puffs just hung there, dissolving before they could drift away. It was the moment of stillness between the day wind and the night wind. Then two young ladies who wouldn't have known a day wind if it had jumped into bed with them click-clacked past on their high heels, on their way to work. Sergeant Papa bowed solemnly.

'I have been thinking about your problem,' he said when they'd passed. 'I think you should go to the Atlantis Bar—' he nodded down the street, and about fifty yards off I could see the red neon sign; '—and I will send somebody to meet you there. It would be ... safer. And I will make sure you are not treated as tourists.'

'Thanks. That sounds fine.' It didn't; I wasn't looking forward to this evening much, but I didn't want to let Ken out on his own, either ...

I said: 'Fine,' again and went inside to look for Ken or Kapotas.

I found Kapotas first, sitting in the little office behind the front desk eating a plate of something and sorting through a small black cashbox. He didn't seem to be finding tidings of great joy in either.

'Have you been taking stamps out of here and not paying?' he demanded. The box had only a handful of coins, a couple of scruffy 250-mil. notes and about half a dozen stamps in it.

I sat on the edge of the desk. 'No, I've done all my Christmas thank you letters. Is that the dinner?'

'Yes.' He stared at the end of his fork. 'I can think of no bit of a sheep shaped like that.'

'I can. Any news from London yet?'

He pushed the plate away and shut up the box. 'They say there *is* a finance house with a first charge on the plane. Now Harborne, Gough have to decide whether to default on the

45

payments, whether to pay up and sell the plane themselves, or to keep on operating it.'

'Any and either way, it's got to get back to Britain; any news on that?'

'No.'

'Well, any news on my pay?'

He didn't look at me. 'You should have got payment in advance.'

'Now, I agree with you. But is that all the bloody help you're going to be?' He didn't say anything. So I said: 'Oh – by the way, I've found you a buyer for the champagne.'

'Oh God.' He leant his head on his hand and shuddered. 'What can I do?'

'I've heard suicide highly recommended, though never by anybody with practical—'

'This is serious!'

'So's my pay.'

He stood up shakily. 'I need a drink.'

So we went through to the bar and sat at a table out of earshot of Apostolos and two other couples who were anaesthetising themselves to face the dinner.

Kapotas asked: 'Who is this man?'

'A Beiruti, Uthman Jehangir. Says he wants to sell it to visiting oil sheikhs.'

'Is he . . . genuine?'

'He's got a poncey English accent and a nice blue pinstripe, but underneath I'd say he was just a simple old tiger-shark.'

He suddenly remembered something. 'Did you tell him we'd opened one box?'

'Of course not. If he *is* after guns, that'd tell him we knew.'

'Yes, of course. I'm sorry.' He stared into his whisky. 'But . . . which is he mostly likely to be after?'

'Champagne or sub-machine guns? In Beirut it's a fifty-fifty chance, isn't it?'

'I suppose so,' he said miserably.

'But if you know anybody in Beirut you could ring up and try to get the word on him. It's a small town in that sense.'

He cheered up a bit. 'Yes, I can do that tomorrow.'

'And sooner or later you're going to have to tell London we

can't sell this cargo. Only don't put the real reason in a cable or telex.'

'I'm not stupid.'

'No, but you're drinking whisky after dinner again.'

'Oh God, so I am.' He shook his head sadly and then drank some more anyway. 'But why should anybody send you on a flight like this?'

'There's an obvious profit in it – probably paid for in advance and certainly not going through the company's books. If Kingsley saw the crunch coming he might want to squeeze the last drop of blood out of the firm while he still had it.'

'A man like Mr Kingsley?'

'A man exactly like Mr Kingsley.' A charming, handsome, well-dressed polite man with the morality of dry rot. Who'd come as near parking me up the creek as I'd been for ten years. So why wasn't I more resentful? Probably because I was too busy being annoyed at myself to be surprised at him I'd been concentrating on getting a paid ride down here instead of looking for snags. And the bastard hadn't even made the mistake of overpaying me for an apparently simple job. In fact, he hadn't made the mistake of paying me at all.

Oh well. With Ken back, things might be different.

I asked: 'I don't suppose there's any news of Kingsley himself, yet?'

'Nothing.'

'I see why, now. For all he knows, there's a gun-running warrant out for him.'

6

Appropriately enough, the Atlantis was below normal ground level, although probably it hadn't been down there for three or four thousand years; it just smelt that way. We were the first into the place except for a bunch of Canadian soldiers at the bar. We squeezed past them and parked around a small round table in a corner.

A waiter came over, lit the small night-light candle on the table and took our order for two large Scotches and two Keos.

Ken peered around. 'Difficult to be colour prejudiced in a place like this.' The room had a lighting level a bit better than a coal hole in a power strike.

'Cheapest décor you can get: don't pay your electricity bill. But it must be an improvement on Beit Oren.'

'Yes, you could *see* some of that.'

'Was it bad?'

'Oh . . .' Just then the waiter put our beers, two small glasses and a bottle of soda on the table; '. . . not really tough or anything, just bloody depressing. Grey stone and brown paint and bugger-all to do. No art classes and all the books in Hebrew . . . You name it, they haven't got it.' He picked up his glass. 'Do I make the old joke about Hey this glass is dirty! No, sir, that's your double Scotch.'

I'd been expecting something like that. 'Put in some soda.' While he did, I sneaked out the tonic bottle that I'd filled with Scotch from the hotel bar. If the manager here didn't like it, he could turn up the lights and catch me at it.

Ken watched as I poured. 'Nice to see your brain hasn't gone to fat. Cheers. What are these girls like?'

I shrugged and drank two-handed. 'All the usual mod cons, I expect. I haven't met them; I just passed the word through Sergeant Papa.'

Ken chuckled. 'That man . . . Did he show you his army snapshot album?'

'Sure. How d'you think he got to know all those generals? — those are all real.'

'He procured for them. Hell, couldn't you guess?'

'I should have done, I should have done . . . So let's hope he gives us five-star service.'

'It isn't the service *he* gives that interests me . . .' Ken smiled hungrily in the candlelight. 'How much money have we got?'

'Here and now? – something over twenty-five quid, that's all.'

'They didn't pay you for the flight down here, yet?'

'Not yet – if ever. Just a nice line about receivers not being responsible for earlier debts.'

'Bastards,' he said unemotionally. 'What was the whole idea of sending you down here, anyway?'

I took out my sole Dunhill pipe and began to fill it carefully. 'They were opening a new hotel in the Lebanon – but that's off, now. I was coming down to fly the VIP guests around a bit, and bringing a spot of cargo.'

'Like what?'

'Like boxes marked champagne.'

He caught my tone. 'Boxes *marked* . . .?'

I looked casually around, but as far as my non-radar eyes could tell, there wasn't anybody within hearing. 'They sort of turned out to be M3's. New M3A1's to be precise.'

He frowned and stared. 'You mean you didn't know what you were carrying?'

I nodded and put my pipe in my mouth.

'Je-sus. Delete what I said about your brain not going soft.' He thought for a moment. 'Where are they now?'

'Still airside. Except for one box we brought through – we were going to serve it to the Professor. That's how we know what it is.'

'We?'

'Kapotas, the manager-accountant chap. He's the only one.' I hoped.

'Where did it all come from?'

So I told him about Kingsley and he vaguely remembered the man from our RAF days. Then he asked: 'Who was supposed to take it off you in Beirut?'

'I was just told to contact the hotel and they'd send round a cargo handling agent with the paperwork. There's nothing suspicious in that.'

He nodded agreement and finished his drinks. I banged on the table for the waiter – there was no question of 'catching his eye' in that blackout, short of throwing a chair at him.

He brought over two more beers, more 'doubles', another soda and two menu cards: the place was supposed to be a grill as well as a bar. But I waved them away. 'We'll eat when the girls get here.'

Ken got the hungry look again. 'Where the hell have they got to?'

'Spill some soda in your lap and cool down. It's early yet.'

'I suppose so . . .'

I did my party trick with the extra Scotch and we drank. Ken wasn't rushing the drink, but it's surprising how you can lose your capacity for alcohol if you're off it for a time. And we'd had a couple at the airport, then he'd had a glass or two with the Professor, and maybe he'd treated himself at the hotel bar as well . . . Anyway, I'd keep an eye on it. He'd certainly hate himself in the morning if he slept through the evening.

I asked: 'What did the Prof want?'

'Oh . . .' he frowned into his glass. 'It was mostly just a celebration. He did mention something he dug up in Israel, before he got picked up. He thinks it would be easier for somebody else to export it.'

'Oh brother!' I made it a long outward breath. 'We really need a job smuggling something out of Israel, don't we? Not while there's still vacancies for night shite shovellers in Calcutta.'

Ken nodded without meaning much. 'It may not still be in Israel – he didn't so much say it was—'

'He wasn't very chatty, was he?'

'In his business would you be? Anyway, we can't do much about it, not without an aeroplane.'

And with Ken being barred from Israel, if that's where the thing was. But I wasn't going to mention his deportation until he did himself; bad form and all that.

But then he remembered the guns again. 'The M3A1, you said? In the normal .45 calibre?'

'Right. There were five in the box we opened, plus about two loads for each. That weighs exactly the same as a dozen bottles of Kroeger Royale, if you want to know.'

He shook his head slowly. 'That's ridiculous ... who wants a .45 calibre gun out here? It's almost all 9-mil. or the Russian stuff. And only two loads? – you'd fire that just learning the gun, and then there's no more ammo this side of the American Army in Germany. They just become scrap metal. Ridiculous.'

I relit my pipe and added to the quaint, truly Cypriot atmosphere of the place. 'That's what I thought. But, mind, we don't *know* what's in the other eleven boxes. They might be all ammunition. They could be anything – even champagne.'

'Yes, there's that. What happened to Kingsley, by the way?'

'Nobody knows, but I get the general idea that he was last seen with a Montevideo brochure in one hand and the office safe in the other.'

'That sounds likely. But he wasn't so stupid, was he? If you'd got picked up by the Lebanese or Cyprus cops—'

'You mean if I do yet.'

'Yes, but – with your reputation, who'd think of blaming Kingsley? He picked the right pilot for the job. You've got to admire the bugger.'

'Have I? Show me the law.'

A woman's voice asked over my shoulder: 'Mr Cavitt and Mr Case?'

✳

There were two of them, as ordered, and we scrambled awkwardly on to our feet and pulled and pushed chairs until we were all seated again, with the waiter almost perched on my shoulder like a parrot.

The smaller, darker, girl said: 'We seem to like champagne, these days.'

It's funny how long 'these days' have been going on. Ken gave her a quick sharp look and I knew she was mine. Well, it was his evening. So I just nodded over my shoulder and the waiter faded away.

The girl said: 'I'm Nina, this is my friend Suzie.'

The names fitted, but they'd probably been chosen for the fit. Nina was smallish but certainly not thin under her tight primrose sweater. Neat sharp features, big dark eyes, and hair that might have been jet black even in a good light, in a loose, silky pageboy bob. Her voice was just English English without any accent that I could spot.

I said: 'I'm Roy Case, the gentleman with the X-ray eyes is Ken Cavitt.'

Suzie said: 'Charmed, I'm sure,' and smiled absently back at Ken's hot stare. She was another English girl – I suppose the Sergeant had chosen them deliberately – and while she might not have been a genuine blonde, she was certainly one at heart. She had a cheery open face, a pert nose, slightly chubby arms and hands and a powerful overdose of figure more or less inside a thin silk blouse. And she positively radiated sex of the simplest kind: just bouncing about in a bed with no hangover to come.

Ken was obviously getting the same perfume; his eyes were practically licking her.

I said: 'I must apologise for Ken: he just spent the last two years in a monastery.'

Suzie said: 'Ooooh, how interesting,' and went on smiling out of her big blue To Let eyes. Ken finally got his mind off her chest and back to his glass.

Then the waiter came back with the champagne and menus.

'What d'you recommend?' I asked Nina.

'Kebabs. Four shish kebabs.' Quite firmly. Ken looked disappointed – he'd obviously been dreaming of steak – but he had the sense to guess what it would taste like in a joint like this. A kebab is about the one thing no Cypriot could louse up.

I said: 'Right, four kebabs,' and it was the waiter's turn to look disappointed; he'd been thinking of steaks, too.

Nina lifted her glass. 'Well, here's to us.'

We all drank, and Suzie said: 'Ooooh, lovely,' in a practised way. Myself, I'm no connoisseur of champagne, but my guess is that if they'd aged this another twenty-four hours it would have made a big difference. I stirred my glass with a fork.

Nina asked: 'Don't you like champagne?'

'I prefer the taste to the bubbles. Somebody once gave me a glass of a 1911, I think it was, and that was exactly what the angels have for teabreaks. And it was practically flat.'

'I remember,' Ken said. 'It was that Portuguese mining man

in Monte. *I* thought the stuff tasted like mushroom soup.'

I shrugged and sipped; without the bubbles I'm not sure there was any taste at all.

Nina asked: 'Have you just arrived in Cyprus?'

I nodded.

'Have you been here before?'

Ken said: 'A few dozen times.'

She lifted her thin dark eyebrows. 'What business are you in?'

I said: 'We're pilots.'

Suzie said automatically: 'Oooh, how interesting.'

'In the RAF?' asked Nina.

I shook my head. 'Just civil.'

'Which airline?'

'Our own,' Ken said. 'From time to time.'

'Oooh,' said Suzie, almost waking up. 'Do you really have your own airline?'

'Sure. It's just that we can't remember where we put it.'

Nina was frowning slightly. Even if Sergeant Papa hadn't briefed her, she'd priced us pretty accurately. Ken had simply added a black uniform tie to his white shirt and twill trousers rig. I had on a white shirt, for once, and the trousers of my blue uniform. Not the jacket with its three stripes that mean nothing except impressing customers without quite annoying four-stripe airline captains. In fact the only expensive thing about us was our wristwatches: Ken's Rolex and my Breitling. You daren't skimp on the tools of your trade.

'What does – or did – your airline do?' she asked.

I said: 'Freight.'

'But no monkeys, no strawberries,' Ken added.

Suzie was looking more puzzled than asleep by now. 'What *do* you mean?'

'Three cargoes most freight airlines don't like,' Ken said. 'Monkeys because they just plain stink.'

'Why would anybody want a load of monkeys?'

I said: 'Medical experiments.'

'Oooh.' She shuddered – or quivered. 'I don't think it's nice to think of things like that.'

'What's wrong with strawberries?' Nina asked.

Ken explained. 'They stink, too, only differently. Haul a couple of tons of them and the aircraft's left smelling like . . .' The usual phrase aircrew use is 'like a cheap whorehouse' but luckily Ken remembered who he was with. 'Well . . . you just can't describe it,' he finished feebly.

'And the third cargo?' Nina asked briskly.

By now Ken was wishing he hadn't mentioned three cargoes, and so was I. I sloshed some more carbonated wine into the girls' glasses and said: 'Anything you might describe as political.'

Nina cocked her eyebrows again. 'And you never carried strawberries or monkeys.' She had a pretty good idea of what a 'political' cargo might be; anybody who'd spent more than a couple of weeks out here would be able to guess.

'That's right,' I said.

'But then, I don't suppose the pilots who carry strawberries and monkeys feel they have to spend two years in a monastery.'

I said: 'They're less devout.'

'I mean, it must be so difficult to keep in flying practice in a monastery. You'd keep on bumping into those stone walls.'

Ken lowered his head slightly and stared very hard at her, and for a moment I thought he was going to launch her with the champagne bottle. So did she, but her reaction was to sit upright, chin and breasts sticking out defiantly.

Just then the waiter dumped our kebabs on the table. Either his timing was lucky or he had an instinct for interrupting trouble, and a place like the Atlantis would need such instincts. Anyway, Ken relaxed and for a few minutes we just listened to each other chewing.

Suzie fed as if she was going to hibernate the rest of the year; Ken worked slower, savouring each piece as if it was the best food he'd tasted in two years – which it likely was; Nina just filed it away as so much protein. In fact it wasn't too bad; just a bit burned.

Halfway through, Suzie remembered that a real lady drinks red wine with meat, so I spent a few moments trying to catch a waiter and then went over to the bar and asked for a bottle of Othello. The place had filled up in the last quarter of an hour, with a dozen little nightlights twinkling through the smoky gloom, waiters weaving about on instrument landings and sweating into the food. I couldn't see who the customers were, but their feet sounded mainly military.

I had to wait while the barman first tried to sell me a bottle of the classy Domaine d'Ahuera, then went to fetch what I'd asked for. The man alongside me at the bar seemed to be drinking alone: a broadish bloke in a well-fitting lightweight suit with those raised seams. His face was turned away from me; all I could see was the darkish hair thinning on top, the glint of spectacle earpieces.

I took the bottle back to the table. Nina glanced at the label and confirmed her private opinion of us, airline tycoonwise. But she sipped a glass politely enough and asked: 'Are you staying at the Castle here?'

'That's right,' Ken said. 'My associate seems to have gone into the hotel business as well.'

I grinned at Suzie's blank look. 'It figures: all the big airlines are getting into the hotel racket – Pan Am, BEA and all. Just keeping in fashion.'

Nina said coolly: 'Didn't I hear that the Castle was closing down?'

Ken said: 'Just going broke, dearie. It isn't always the same thing.'

Suzie sighed. 'Well, I just hope Sergeant Papa doesn't lose his job; he's such a *nice* man.'

All three of us stared at her; whatever we each thought of the Sergeant, the word 'nice' certainly didn't come into it. At last Nina said: 'Never mind, darling – the Sergeant is sure to manage somehow.'

'He could always go back into the army,' Ken suggested. 'Armies have still got generals, and generals have still got—'

'Ken!' I snapped. He grinned at me, a little loosely, and with a faint glitter of sweat on his forehead. The steady drinking had suddenly begun to grip. Just as suddenly, he realised it. He turned to Suzie.

'Tell you what: let's you and me go for a little stroll in the moonlight.'

'Moonlight?' Nina snorted. 'It's probably raining like a drain out there. It was thundering when we came in.'

Down in the Atlantis we wouldn't have heard World War Three get started.

'Hell,' said Ken; neither of us had brought coats. 'Well, it's only a few yards to the Castle.'

Suzie said plaintively: 'But I was going to have some ice-cream.'

Ken stood up. 'The nice Sergeant Papa will find us some ice-cream,' he said in a controlled voice. She sighed and stood up, and then sort of rubbed herself against Ken the way a big cat might except not exactly the same way. Ken twanged like a guitar.

Suzie said: 'Ooooh,' in an interested tone for once. 'Come on, dear,' and grabbed his hand and hauled him away between the tables.

Nina gave a dramatic sigh. 'Your friend—' but then I was on my feet and taking several fast steps towards the bar and colliding with the man in the spectacles and natty suit.

'Why, if it isn't Mr Ben Iver. Shalom.'

'Shalom,' he answered automatically, and then tried to ease past me. I leant against him like neither cat nor Suzie. His glasses gleamed as he cocked his head, and his hand dipped towards his pocket. I slapped downwards and his hand and jacket swung aside; the pocket clunked as it hit the bar stool.

By then my own hand was in my own pocket and pointing. 'It's raining up there, they tell me, and I expect you've forgotten your umbrella. Sit down and have another milk-and-honey. It'll clear soon.'

He looked down at my pocket. 'Shoot through your pocket and it jams,' he said softly. 'If it's a revolver you won't even get off one shot.'

'Not if you use a Smith Bodyguard, the one with the enclosed hammer. Get off all five, most likely.'

'Only five?' he said, slightly mocking.

'I don't suppose I've got more than five enemies left in the world.'

A silly conversation, but it had already achieved all I wanted. He shrugged and lifted himself back on to the bar stool. 'You're right, I did forget my umbrella.' By now, Ken and Suzie would be well out of sight.

'I'm sure you're doing the right thing.' As I turned away I took my second pipe out of my pocket and shoved it in my mouth. Maybe I heard a sharp little hiss behind me.

I sat down again. Nina asked: 'And what was all that?'

'Call it a delaying action.'

'Who is that man?'

'An Israeli, Mihail Ben Iver.'

'What does *he* do between drinks?'

'Ken thinks he's in their secret service. Could be: they don't give up easy, over there. Though I don't know what they're not giving up easy on right now.' I picked up the Othello bottle and shook it: still about a third full. 'Shall we finish this?'

She held out her glass. 'Did your friend . . . was it in Israel?'

I nodded, filled our glasses, started to pack a pipe. 'Well, what shall we talk about now?'

She stared. 'Good God, where did you spend the last two years – in a nunnery?'

I grinned and struck the first match.

'Or,' she added acidly, 'are you afraid of losing your amateur status before the next Olympics?'

'It was more Ken's party than mine. Now make with the light chatter.'

'Trust me to get the one who had an accident with a bicycle saddle,' she growled. 'Well, the usual question you start with is How did I come to be on the game?'

'Okay – how did you come to be on the game when you're so ready to pick fights with the clientele?'

For some reason she didn't throw a bottle at me. She just nodded, and her voice was suddenly gentler. 'Yes, I don't really know why I do it. That's what's so sweet about Suzie: the way she sticks with me. Would you believe she's had two offers at good houses in Beirut in the last six months but she wouldn't go without me? And I can just see anybody offering me a good place in Beirut.'

'You mean you *want* to go on the game in Beirut?' My second match died of surprise.

'Haven't you seen the money they throw around over there? A girl can do pretty well for herself if she knows the business. Oh, I don't mean getting yourself sold off to some old goat in

Saudi Arabia; that happens to some poor kids. But if you've got a work permit and the proper protection . . . Well, if I was a tennis player I'd want to play at Wimbledon, wouldn't I?'

'I suppose so. I'd just never thought of Beirut as the Wimbledon of . . . Well.' I finally got the pipe drawing. 'How did you get to Cyprus?'

'I was born here; my father was in the British Army. So I can speak Greek pretty well and when I left home it seemed better to come a long way . . . And that's all I'm telling you about my family.' She took a defiant swig of the wine.

'Fair enough.' I sipped quietly for a while.

Then she asked: 'Have you known your friend Ken for a long time?'

'About twenty years. We met in the RAF, on my first squadron. Night fighters. Then we did a tour on Transport Command together, some work on tactical transport development . . . then we got the idea of coming out and setting up our own show.'

'Just like that.'

'It took a couple of years before we were really on our own: getting civilian licences, working for charter airlines to get marketing experience. Nobody would lend us money for our own aircraft until we knew the civilian ropes."

'What are they going to lend you after this little trouble?'

I shrugged. 'I suppose we may have to change our style a bit. I haven't had time to talk to Ken about it, yet.'

'Who takes the decisions?'

'On the operations side – the flying – I'd take Ken's word; he's the best pilot. But mostly it's a straight partnership.'

She finished her glass and about a second later a waiter appeared, looking expectant.

I said: 'D'you want any more?'

'I don't think so, thank you,' she said steadily.

So I asked for the bill and he simply said: 'Fifteen pound, please.'

When I'd got my breath back, I said: 'Look, chum, I expected to get bitten but not swallowed whole.'

'Fifteen pound,' he said impassively.

Then Nina said something fast and low in Greek and without

changing his expression by a millimetre, he said: 'Ten pound.'

I paid him, said to her: 'I know some governments who could use your touch with price control.'

She smiled briefly and stood up.

As we reached the bar I peered around, but it was solid Canadian soldiery. Ben Iver had vanished without me noticing.

She found her coat, a thin white mac, and I helped her into it. 'Well, where would you like to go now? Ledra Palace for a last jar?'

'Good God.' She swung around and glared at me. 'Are you going to screw me or not?'

I made shushing noises, but far too late. About half a dozen soldiers turned on their bar stools and looked at us – mostly at her.

Then one said: 'Say, pal, if you've paid for your ticket and don't feel up to the ride, I'd be happy to oblige your lady friend.'

'Save your strength for the mooses!'

He got his feet on to the floor and swung his right at the same time.

In that light, he wasn't likely to be too accurate, but I had to duck anyway. And if I hit back, I'd make another five enemies ...

Something small and shiny-black swished over my shoulder like a scythe and clunked solidly on the Canadian's cheekbone. He slammed back against the bar and his knees melted. Two of his mates reached him before he hit the floor, Nina grabbed me and we ran for the stairs while they were still regrouping.

As we galloped upwards, I identified the secret weapon as a small handbag covered in black sequins; I just hadn't noticed it before.

'What the hell d'you keep in that bag?'

'Just a load of pennies,' she panted. 'It doesn't look as suspicious as a piece of lead.'

'When you've reformed the Treasury, try for the Ministry of Defence.'

We reached the front door and she said: 'I *told* you.'

7

It was raining like something out of Noah's memoirs. The street, pavements and parked cars were covered with a grass of spray two feet high and the only sound was a steady roar like a waterfall. Until the street was lit by a neon-coloured flash and almost immediately a gigantic explosion of thunder right overhead.

Mediterranean thunderstorms always have an over-melodramatic quality that makes them seem unreal. Unless you're up in among them. I said: 'Pity poor airmen on a night like this.'

'What?' she shouted. 'We'll have to go back inside and wait.'

'With all those mad Canucks? They'd rape both of us, and personally I'm not used to that sort of thing.'

'Coward!'

I nodded. 'Come on – run!'

So we ran. The moment we hit the rain, visibility went down to nil. But nobody else was fool enough to be on the street, even in a car, so we blinded up the middle and reached the Castle in about fifteen seconds – soaked through.

I was, anyway. Nina was a bit better off: her hair looked fairly lank, her legs were wet to the knees and her face was dripping, but the mac had saved the rest. It didn't seem to cheer her much.

She shook herself angrily and said: 'My shoes were new last week and I had my hair done only this afternoon. Blast you.'

I was taking papers from my jacket pockets and laying them on the lobby desk. They were only slightly damp and buckled. 'Never mind, you can have a free bath while you're here.'

'That solves everything, of course.' She sounded rather bitter. 'Oh, hello Papa.'

The Sergeant didn't even notice her. His face looked lemon yellow in the thin light and his red jacket was undone at the neck. 'Captain – thank God you've come. Thank God. The man – the Professor – I think he's dead.'

*

I thought so, too.

He was in the bathroom, sprawled over an upright kitchen chair, head hanging over the back so that . . . so that . . . well, so that what had been in his head had dripped into the bath.

It's the suddenness, not the sight itself. You walk up to a wrecked aeroplane and you have time to think what you'll see, to pull the lace curtains behind your eyes. I stepped back into the bedroom and wanted to sit down with my head on my knees, but also didn't want to, with the Sergeant watching from the corridor. And there'd been a spatter of blood and something on the wall behind the bath . . . Gradually the hot-cold feeling passed and I stopped swallowing.

I said: 'You were right first time. Get on to the police.'

'Perhaps a doctor, too? It's normal when something like this . . .'

I shrugged. 'It's a waste of money, but . . . You'd better ring Kapotas as well, so let him decide.'

He nodded and moved off, for once briskly.

Then I just stood and looked around the room. It looked tidy enough: even the glasses, champagne bottles and caviar pot – empty – were all back on the tray on the window table, beside a square rigid black briefcase. Two black suitcases stacked neatly in a corner. The silk dressing-gown folded neatly on the bed – he'd been wearing just trousers, shirt and slippers.

A tidy, economical man, the late Herr Professor. Gunshot suicide's a messy business at best, but he'd done what he could to minimise the damage. Always assuming that it *was* suicide, of course.

Had there been a gun?

I could go back in and look, of course . . . I shut my eyes and tried to visualise the scene in there, and then tried to forget the parts I recalled best. But after a minute or so, I was sure I hadn't seen a gun. And after another minute, I accepted there was only one way to be sure.

*

Downstairs, the Sergeant, Nina and the chambermaid were huddled up by the desk. They looked at me with various expressions of pale apprehension.

'Did you get the police? And Kapotas?'

Sergeant Papa nodded. 'He says he will come.'

Nina said: 'I think perhaps it would be best if I went—'

'You'd better hang on, love. The cops might get snarky if they find you'd been here and gone before they arrived.'

'Oddly enough, I was thinking of your reputation.'

I grinned. 'Thanks, but let my reputation look after itself. It's big and ugly enough by now.'

She smiled lopsidedly.

I turned back to the Sergeant. 'Where's Ken?'

He nodded at the ceiling. 'He came in an hour ago. Not alone.'

Any point in waking – I mean disturbing – him yet? I couldn't think of one. Then I suddenly remembered. 'Where in hell's the daughter? – Mitzi.'

'Out.' Papa looked at the wall clock, which showed five past midnight so it was only ten minutes fast. 'Before Mr Cavitt got back. Perhaps about nine o'clock.'

I looked round to check that her key was hanging on the proper peg by the pigeonhole: it was. And in the pigeonhole for 323 there was a bright green envelope. 'What did they do about dinner?'

The Sergeant shrugged and looked at the chambermaid and they swapped a few words in Greek. Then: 'They did not eat downstairs. I think the Professor did not eat at all, except the caviar. So perhaps she went out for food.'

'I don't blame her, but she's taking her time with it.' Still, she could be just waiting for the storm to ease. I turned to the chambermaid. 'Can you start making coffee? Buckets of it. It's going to be a long night.'

Nina sighed.

*

First to get there were a uniformed sergeant and constable – just a reconnaissance party. They shook themselves dry in the lobby and asked if I'd sent for a doctor.

'No.'

'Not?' The sergeant seemed shocked. 'But why not?'

'Because I didn't know one that does head transplants.' But he didn't get it. I said impatiently: 'Just go up to 323 and have a look, then tell me I was wrong. Go on.'

He frowned and led the constable upstairs. They were still there when Mitzi came in. She wore a long lightweight black coat that was hardly damp, and I saw the lights of a taxi pull away behind her. And so now somebody had to tell her . . . Somebody like Sergeant Papa or the chambermaid? I took a deep breath and stepped forward.

She looked puzzled at our little group. 'Is something wrong?'

'I'm afraid your father – he's dead.'

Her face just froze, expressionless. Her mouth moved in an odd independent way, like a puppet's. 'No. But how?'

'I think he shot himself.'

She looked at the stairs. 'Is he up there?' She moved and I stepped in the way.

'The police are there. Better wait until . . . until they've cleared up a bit.'

Then her face slowly crumpled and she leant over the desk, head in hands, sobbing: *'Ach, mein Vater . . .'*

I just stood, feeling like a bundle of hands and feet without a purpose. Then Nina came forward and put her arm round Mitzi's shoulders, and Mitzi clung to her.

The police sergeant came downstairs looking a lot paler. I pushed the phone across to him. 'Thank you. Yes, I see what . . .' he started a fast patter in Greek.

After that, things moved quite quickly. A carload of mixed uniforms and plainclothes arrived, led by a CID inspector with the hot eyes and grubby shirt-collar of a man who's already been on duty for more than his shift. After that, some sort of doctor or forensic man who swapped half-hearted banter with the police sergeant, sighed heavily and went upstairs. And soon after, Kapotas got in.

He was fully dressed except for a tie, but unshaven and more worried even than usual. But by then we'd opened up the bar and were sitting in groups at the tables, chain-drinking coffee and local brandy. Kapotas looked around, asked a quick question of the nearest cop, got a shrug for an answer, then came over to me. 'My God, this is all we needed.'

'Keep your voice down.'

He noticed Mitzi, so sat down beside me.

'Is he really dead?'

'He's really short of half a head.'

'Oh God.' He rubbed his palms into his eyes. 'When did it happen?'

'Don't know. Some time after nine, probably before eleven.' Some of the blood had almost dried.

'Who found him?'

'I gather the chambermaid; she'd been ringing the room to see if she could collect the champagne tray, finally she went up and stuck her head in. She called the Sergeant. I got in just after that.'

'He hadn't locked the door, then?'

'Apparently not.' Was that another example of the Professor's thoughtfulness?

He shook his head sadly. 'What will this do to the hotel?'

'We hadn't quite got the Hilton worried before.'

Then his eyes widened in horror. 'The register! The police are sure to want to see the register!'

'Oh Christ.' I thought about it. There was just one uniformed cop lounging around the lobby. With luck . . . I got up and went over to Mitzi.

'Miss . . . Braunhof – I'm sorry about this, but if we can do it without the police noticing, can you sign the register for us? It's a small point, but . .'

She looked back, red-eyed but calm. 'Yes, of course.' So I led a little deputation out to the desk.

Sergeant Papa started chatting up the cop while Kapotas and I pretended to be looking for something under the desk; Mitzi leant across and watched and – well, it worked. We could only hope that her signature would do for both, but at least it looked as if we'd been more careless than crooked.

I shuffled the register back into place and took a look around before heading back. That green envelope in the Prof's pigeon-hole – maybe Mitzi should open it. No, wait a moment—

'Who in hell put that envelope up there?'

Everybody looked round, startled. Sergeant Papa cleared his throat and said: 'I think I did – yes . . .'

'You mean somebody came and gave you that—'

'No, no. It was just lying on the desk, so I put it in the box.'

I took it down. It just had *Professor Spohr, Nicosia Castle* typed on it, no stamp. It felt thin and looked cheap, like some advertising handout.

'Neat.' I nodded grimly. 'And not a little bit gaudy. Somebody walks in, waits till nobody's looking, leaves that there. Then maybe he has a drink at the bar or walks round the block, comes back and takes just a glance and he can see the Prof's staying here – even which room he's in. And nobody knows he's even been asking. Neat.'

The cop was looking at me, puzzled. I hoped it was because he didn't understand English too well.

Kapotas said: 'But he would have had to do it for all other hotels, too.'

'Not too many. He'd start at the Ledra and Hilton and work down until he struck oil. The others would just chuck it in the dead-letter box. It wouldn't take him long.' I held the letter out to Mitzi. 'Here, you'd better open it.'

Slowly, timidly, she took it, and her hands shook a little as she ripped open the flap. Then relaxed as she handed me a folded one-page timetable for coach tours of local archaeological sites.

I nodded. 'It's even appropriate enough not to seem too suspicious, unless you knew how secret you and your father were trying to be.'

Sergeant Papa said mournfully: 'I am sorry. It was stupid.'

'It does not matter,' Mitzi said, and turned back to the bar.

'She's right,' I reassured him. 'And anybody would have done the same.' We followed her back to the bar-room.

Five minutes later, the cop came and said the Inspector wanted to talk to the hotel management. After a bit of hithering and dithering Kapotas decided that that included me, so I went up with him and Papa.

8

They'd taken over room 105 on the first floor, dragging in half a dozen chairs from other empty rooms and a pretty squalid collection they made, seen together and none of them matching. A young plainclothes man sat at the dressing-table ready to take notes, a uniformed sergeant guarded the door from the inside – and the inspector himself.

All experienced detectives can't look the same and I know they don't, but when I'm in front of one . . . well, there's always that something. A sense of completeness without depth, a man without personal problems or involvement, a pathologist of events dissecting from behind a professional mask. This one had it.

That apart, he looked about fifty, which any forty-year-old has a right to do at that time of night. A pale grainy skin starting to sag off the long face into pouches under the eyes, slight jowls, the beginning of a turkey neck. Thin-rimmed glasses and bloodshot blue eyes. But sharply dressed, except for that wilted shirt, in a browny-gold suit with a slight sheen, flowered tie, fake crocodile shoes.

He sat on the bed with an open notebook, scattering cigarette ash near a crammed ashtray and waved us to sit down. Then said something in Greek, noticed my expression, and added: 'I am Inspector Lazaros. Shall we then speak English?'

Kapotas and Papa agreed and we introduced ourselves. Lazaros asked: 'Who found Professor Spohr?'

Sergeant Papa told the story.

'The door was not locked?'

'No.'

He frowned at that. 'Suicide is a private matter.' Then: 'Did you touch anything?'

Papa and I looked at each other. 'The door handle,' I suggested.

He nodded. 'How many guests now here?'

Kapotas said promptly: 'Fourteen.' There'd been a heavy

attrition rate in favour of places that had more than one dish on the menu and got around to making your bed before you got back in it.

Lazaros asked: 'And how many short-stay couples tonight?'

Sergeant Papa put on a puzzled look. 'I do not understand, sir—'

Lazaros's head jerked impatiently. 'Do not bugger about, Papadimitriou! I know this hotel, I know you. How many?'

'Two,' he mumbled. 'Rooms 115 and 117.'

'Thank you.' The inspector made a note. 'Now, did any of you know the Professor before tonight?'

We shook our heads in chorus, then I said: 'There's one other man who did: Ken Cavitt in room 206.' It was rough luck on Ken, but it was going to happen anyway.

'Do you think he came here to meet Mr Cavitt?'

'Yes.' I told about the daughter ringing up.

He made a couple of brief notes. 'They met this afternoon, in his room?'

'Yes.'

'There were four used champagne glasses.'

'I was the fourth. I brought him up the champagne, he invited me to have a glass. We chatted.'

'Did he say anything that tells you why he committed suicide?'

'Not a thing. He seemed reasonably chirpy. You don't have any reason to suppose he *didn't* commit suicide?'

He frowned down at his notes and let out a broadside of smoke. Then: 'I would have preferred a suicide note.' Then looked up. 'All right. Please wake Mr Cavitt. Now I will talk to the daughter.' And I think he gave a little shiver.

*

I rang Ken from the desk. And rang and rang. Then a blurry explosion of: 'Yes, *what* the bloody hell is it?'

'It's Roy – don't ring off—'

'For Jesus' sake—'

'Sorry, Ken: red alert, scramble, all fire warning lights on. The Professor's suicided and the boys in blue are here.'

For a long time there was just the sound of his breathing. Then: 'He's done what?'

'That's right. And they want a word and if you don't come to them they'll come to you.'

'Yes. All right.' His voice was calmer, quieter. 'I'll be down.'

The lights were on only at the bar end of the long room, a small patch of orange brightness that looked warmer than it felt and faded quickly into the dark cavern of the dining area. A few wisps of blue smoke from Sergeant Papa's cigar hung in the thick stale air. He was sitting with Kapotas at one table, Nina and the monkey-faced chambermaid at another. They waved the coffee-pot at me but I shook my head and went across to the bar.

Thunder rumbled distantly and made me realise how quiet it was. I poured myself a glass of soda water and sipped. After a time, Nina got up and came across and sat on the customers' side of the bar.

I said: 'Sorry about all this. Makes me wonder if I should ever have gone into the hotel business.'

She smiled sideways and little crowsfoot lines crinkled around her eyes; it was the first time I'd seen – or had time to see – her in a good light. She looked older, as all women do, but not that much. And she looked clean and smelled good. Maybe I was beginning to regret something.

She shrugged and her breasts bounced gently on the counter. 'It makes a change. And I dare say I got up later than most here.'

'Like a drink?' But she shook her head. 'I expect they'll just ask you to establish where I was and then you can go.'

'They did that already.'

'What about Suzie?'

'Ah yes. Well, I suppose they'll have to ask her the same about Ken.' And right then, Ken came in.

He'd shoved on the same trousers and shirt and was looking a little smeared and puffy around the eyes but moved smooth and steady enough. 'Christ, this is the time I wish I hadn't given up smoking.'

'Drink? There's coffee or anything.'

'Coffee and brandy. Did the old boy *really* kill himself?'

I said carefully: 'A pistol went off inside his mouth. It looked all right to me.'

Nina's eyes were suddenly wide. 'It looked *what*?'

'Genuine.' I beckoned the chambermaid with the coffee. 'It was a Walther PP in 9-mil. Luger. I saw the cartridge case.'

Ken shook his head slowly. 'He didn't have any reason to kill himself. He had a big thing going.'

I poured him a two-to-one mixture of coffee and local brandy. 'There's some angles, some loose ends, perhaps.' Nina was still watching and listening.

Ken gulped at the mixture in his cup and shuddered. 'Has anybody told Mitzi?'

'Yes. She's talking to Inspector Lazaros now. He seems quite a sharp boy.' I hoped Ken was getting the hint and Nina didn't know I was giving it; he could be called up at any moment. Anyway, he just nodded and hunched his elbows on the bar, brooding. After a while more, Nina gave me a cool look and walked back to the table, her little bottom twitching left and right under the short black skirt in real professional style. I tapped my glass against my teeth and sighed.

'When you last saw the Prof,' I said, 'what was he wearing?'

Ken didn't look up. 'Dressing-gown, same as when you were there.'

'Would he normally sit around all evening in one?'

This time he did look up – with a rather clogged contempt. 'Sure, he did all the time, in Beit Oren. Except dining-in nights, of course, when we wore white tie and tails.'

All right, so it hadn't been the brightest question of the evening. But then Ken put his face back down into his cup and muttered: 'If you mean was he the sort who liked comfort and class when he could get it? – then yes. I could see him wearing that until he changed for dinner, anyhow.'

'He didn't have dinner. He'd arranged to eat in his room anyway, to stay secret.' I thought about it for a moment. 'He took it off – the dressing-gown, I mean – to shoot himself. I can understand that, in a weird way; it was a nice gown. But then he put a shirt on instead; that, I don't quite get.'

He looked up again. 'Are you looking for rational behaviour in a suicide? They do the wildest things. Women put on their old wedding dresses; men build fancy machines to hang themselves with. I heard of an armourer sergeant once who spent months altering a dummy Vickers to shoot himself with and all the time he had a dozen real ones sitting around. Or are you getting the idea that perhaps it wasn't suicide after all?'

'Why should anybody make him change into a shirt before they shot him? But now listen, bright-eyes: when you get upstairs *don't* go stuffing that copper up with murder theories. He's doubtful enough already; if he gets convinced it's murder, we'll be stuck on this bloody island until the clock strikes thirteen.'

He cocked his head, then nodded. 'What I'll tell him, you could write on a flea's jockstrap.'

'And don't get him niggled, either, or he may stick his nose into the Queen Air just looking for some technicality to catch us on.'

'Christ, yes.' He'd obviously forgotten about my cargo problems. 'Okay, Roy, I'll treat him like a police officer and a gentleman. And I suppose we'll have a nice cosy chat about my last two years. Bastards. Oh well . . .' He looked at his watch. 'And twenty-four hours ago I was still safely tucked in the coop. Now . . .'

'You'll go on dreaming you're still there for a few days yet.'

'Yes, I did already. Your subconscious is a bit like a bloody met office, isn't it? – Just won't look outside to see what's really going on.'

'More coffee?' But just then a uniformed cop escorted Mitzi back in and looked blankly around the rest of us. 'Mister ... mister Cavitt?'

Ken got up. 'Ready and willing.'

'Please to come ...'

Mitzi had sat down at Nina's table. I went over, didn't sit. 'Just want to say how very sorry I am, Miss Spohr. If there's anything I can do ...'

She looked pale but dry-eyed; enclosed and introspective rather than openly sorrowing. She didn't look at me. 'Yes, please. If you can move my room.'

I nodded. 'Yes, of course.' The cops would be trampling around up there for probably hours yet. I went across to Kapotas and the Sergeant to arrange it, and after a bit of discussion we shifted her one down and a bit forward to 227, so she wouldn't be under the old rooms.

Then Kapotas asked: 'And what shall I tell Harborne, Gough, in London?'

'Whatever the police decide. What else can you say? People die in hotels all the time; it's nothing new.'

'But I must tell them what he was.'

'A Professor – whatever that means in Austria – and a medieval archaeologist.'

'But you knew him.' Slightly accusing.

'Only met him this afternoon. It was Ken who knew him; they met in jail in ...' From Sergeant Papa's expression I realised my mistake; I'd never mentioned that angle to Kapotas before, and he hadn't the Sergeant's eye for spotting these things.

'In jail?' he hissed. 'Both of them?' He stared around wildly. 'My God, now I'm running a brothel *and* a prisoner's aid society! Why don't we set up roulette wheels in the kitchen and sell marijuana at the desk? Or is that something else you forgot to tell me about?' And he glared at the Sergeant.

Papa stiffened and said with dignity: 'There are no drugs in this hotel while I am hall porter.'

'That's a small consolation, then,' Kapotas said bitterly, then looked at me. 'And I suppose *you* wouldn't be ...' Then he stopped because he'd remembered just what we'd discovered I *had* been doing. 'Oh God, I need a drink. And I don't care if it's after dinner or before breakfast!' And he headed for the bar.

Papa said calmly: 'He has not got the nerves to be a hotel manager.'

'He never expected to be one. And there must be hotels where it's easier.'

'Not much. Even the best hotels cannot really pick their guests; they can only keep out some who they know to cause trouble.'

'I suppose so ...' After that, we just sat in weary silence until a uniformed cop brought Ken back in and beckoned me up. Ken's expression was just on the contemptuous side of blankness, but I wasn't allowed to have a word with him.

After an hour and a half of Lazaros's interrogations, the atmosphere in 105 would have stopped flying at any airport in the world. The Inspector himself was still sitting on the same place on the bed, only now with two ashtrays crammed full of butts, some still smouldering. If he lost his job with CID, with his sense of smell he'd no chance of remustering as a police dog.

'Sit down, please, Captain.'

'Just mister.' I sat carefully on a sagging woven-cane chair, and he turned the pages of his notebook, sprinkling ash around an already grey patch on the counterpane.

'Did you know the Professor had been in jail?'

'I'd been told.'

'You did not tell me.'

'From me it would have been just hearsay. I knew somebody else would tell you.'

He looked up blearily. 'So you know something about the law and the courts?'

'A pilot my age is bound to. The air's got more laws than aeroplanes in it, these days.'

He seemed to accept that. 'Did you see the gun?'

I nodded.

'You have a good stomach. It made my sergeant sick.' It had taken a little finding: it had been in the bath itself, just about below the head.

'Same answer: a pilot my age has seen some messy accidents.'

He bought that, too. 'Gunshot suicide ... it is always too easy to arrange. And with the gun in all that blood, the fingerprints are gone. Why would it be in the bath, almost behind him?'

I pointed my right hand at my teeth. 'He sticks the gun in his mouth. The recoil blows it out again. If it stays in his hand for a moment, then it could swing his whole arm in an arc, right round to the side.' I swung my arm and clouted my knuckles on the next chair. 'Buggerit. So it hits the edge of the bath, the gun

72

falls inside, slides down to where it was. His arm flops back by his side. If I'd been faking a suicide, I'd've put the gun in a more obvious place. Anyway, can't you test his hand for powder marks?'

'It is being done.' He groped around on the bed and found a crumpled pack of cigarettes, then lit one from the stub of his last and found a parking place for that in one of the ashtrays. 'But whose gun could it be?'

'Doesn't the licence tell you?'

'I assume that is a joke.'

'In Israel he had a gun – so I'm told. That's what got him the year.'

He made a note. 'But his daughter said he had no gun now.'

I shrugged. 'Maybe she didn't know. Anyway, would she admit knowledge of a criminal offence?'

He nodded sagely; the question hadn't been too serious. 'And tomorrow all the relatives from Vienna will fly in and be very excited, and half of them will want me to prove it was murder because suicide is not respectable and the other half will prefer suicide because murder is not respectable, either.'

I grinned briefly. 'So can't you make it an accident? – while cleaning a gun?'

'He was licking the dirt out of the barrel, perhaps?'

'It's been done before. Isn't that how Ernest Hemingway died – according to the record?'

'I believe so,' he said gloomily. 'And people still compare national suicide rates. So – why did he kill himself?'

'Since when has guesswork been admissible evidence?'

'We are not in court, we are in a third-rate hotel bedroom and wishing very much we were home in bed.' His voice had a sudden edge to it. Then he paused, sighed, and joggled the loose flesh around his jaw as if he were trying to rub some life back into it. 'Perhaps I want it to be murder and I could solve it and become promoted. Suicide promotes nobody; there is nobody to blame except the world. What made him kill himself?'

'He was insane.'

He nodded. 'That is one of the best arguments in a circle that even you English have invented. Why did he kill himself?

– Because the balance of his mind was disturbed. How do we know it was disturbed? – Because he killed himself. Inquest closed. But why was he unbalanced?'

I took a pipe and peered at the crusted ash in it, but then lit it anyway. My tongue already felt like a new-laid tarmac road, so a few more puffs couldn't hurt. 'He'd spent a year in jail. In that time his wife might have walked out on him—'

'His wife died five years ago.'

'All right, but he could have gone broke, lost his academic status ... anything.'

He tilted his head and looked at me with rather worn curiosity. 'I find that our files have already heard of Professor Spohr. His academic status is ... somewhat past. Mostly he spends his time discovering relics and selling them, usually illegally.'

Cyprus is one of the touchiest places about the export of antiquities; the airport is plastered with notices forbidding it. I shrugged again. 'He obviously didn't belong to the jail-going classes, so just being inside might have shaken him up. But he could live through the year because he'd always got something to look forward to: getting out. And then he gets out and finds it's all flat and grey and no hope of that improving, so ... bang.'

'That is good,' he said admiringly. 'That is very sensitive and understanding. What did he talk to Mr Cavitt about this afternoon?'

I almost blew it – little though I knew anyway. With the rambling, late-night chatter and then the flattery, he'd done a nice job of easing me off balance for the important question. If I'd had less experience with coppers who were even bigger bastards, I'd probably have babbled of green fields. As it was—

I looked uninterested and shook my head. 'I dunno. I think it was just a booze-up with an old cell-mate. Anyway, Ken didn't tell me anything.' And I knew Ken hadn't told him anything, either. Drunk or sober, Ken's distrust of the Law was in far better training than mine.

He nodded vaguely. 'You see, perhaps Mr Cavitt was the last person to see him alive ...'

'Didn't his daughter? – Mitzi?'

'Ah yes, perhaps.' As if he'd forgotten her.

'Didn't you ask her why she thought he killed himself?'

'Yes.' He nodded again and his head went on waggling as if he were too tired to switch it off. Finally he said: 'Yes. She thinks it may be because he had incurable cancer and only two months to live.'

After a long time I said: 'And you still think it would be better if he'd left a suicide note?'

He smiled wearily. 'Yes.'

*

When I got downstairs again, Mitzi and Kapotas had vanished and Sergeant Papa was snoring steadily on a bench seat by the bar. Ken and Nina sat at a table, each with a small brandy glass, not saying anything.

I sat down. 'Did you know anything about the Prof dying of cancer?'

'Yep,' Ken said, a chopped-off sound. He went on staring at the tabletop. 'Mitzi told me just now.'

'Well, I suppose it must be true, and the post-mortem'll show it, but . . .' I shook my head helplessly. 'But if he'd only got a couple of months to go, it must've been pretty bad. Did he know about it in jail?'

'I'm sure he didn't. And the medical checks you got in there, they just about counted your legs and arms and no more. I remember he'd got this sort of hernia trouble, but that was right at the end and he said he'd wait and see a doctor in Vienna. Well, it turned out that was it: they operated and found a secondary cancer in his groin.'

'Where was the main one?'

'It was a . . . a melanoma or some word like that, sort of skin cancer in the middle of his back. Apparently it doesn't hurt, there. In fact, the docs said it wouldn't hurt at all until near the end and then you go down fast.'

Nina shivered and instinctively tightened her folded arms. I may have shivered myself, a bit. I'd stopped knowing what to feel about the Professor, but at least a 9 mm slug through the mouth sounded a bit more reasonable, now.

'If those buggers in Biet Oren had spotted it when he could still be operated on,' Ken said quietly, 'he'd still be alive. They bloody well killed him.'

'Well, not quite that,' I tried to soothe him. 'You should get back to bed; tomorrow's another day.'

'It looks like today from where I'm sitting.' Well, yes, since it was nearly three in the morning. But he suddenly slapped both hands on the table, levered himself upright and gave a long shuddering stretch like a cat. 'See you, kids.' And he'd gone.

Papa snored on. Nina looked at me with solemn eyes. 'Well?'

'I'll settle the account and you get off home, love.'

'I have to charge you for my time,' she said.

'I know. And I won't say I didn't end up with regrets, but . . . maybe another time. Right now I'd be as much use as a banana skin.' I started dealing pound notes from my wallet and grinned suddenly at what Kapotas would have said about Castle's money. At what he certainly would say, tomorrow, when I tried to prise some more out of him.

She said: 'I wouldn't have thought you needed us, usually.'

I let that go and kept on dealing. When I'd run dry, there were just sixteen pounds on the table.

Nina said carefully: 'I'll take Suzie's share, too.'

'I'd assumed that. Ken hasn't got any money anyway.'

'Well . . . we usually reckon on ten pounds each.'

I nodded and looked around. The bar takings would be locked up and I didn't fancy borrowing off Papa. Then I remembered the desk petty cash box; there just might be something left in it.

The only person left in the hall was a constable dozing in a chair opposite the stairway. He half-opened an eye and watched as I dishonestly appropriated property belonging to another with the intention of permanently depriving the other of it, or however they put it in Cyprus. The box had a pound note, a 500-mil., a new 250-mil., a few coins and even fewer stamps than I'd seen earlier. It came out at just over two quid.

'Can I owe you the last two? They'll have to pay me in a day or so if only to get rid of me.'

'Okay.' She collected up the notes, half turned to go, then turned back and said: 'Something about you and your friend Ken worries me.'

'What?'

'The way you don't take anything seriously, like being broke and this man shooting himself . . .'

'I thought Ken was taking that pretty hard.'

'The idea didn't shock him enough. It's . . . it's as if you were people in a war and you don't care about tomorrow.'

I frowned. 'That's a sort of shivery idea. I don't think it's like that.'

'People like you frighten me.' And she reached suddenly, pecked my cheek and bounced neatly out of the front door.

I watched the door wig-wag to a stop behind her, then slowly put the cashbox away under the desk and then just sat, too tired to do anything else. And too tired to feel anything, either.

Inspector Lazaros and his team came down at twenty past three. 'We are going now, you may lock up. Tomorrow I shall need formal statements from Papadimitriou and the daughter and you.'

'Not too early.'

'I hope not. Good night, Captain.'

'Just mister.'

I sat on for a while after they'd gone, then went in and woke Papa. 'They've gone, so you can lock up if there's nobody else left on a short-night. What happened to Kapotas?'

He yawned massively, showing a row of big, shabby teeth like a horse's. 'He rang up his wife and then went to bed in 217.' We locked the bar, put out the lights and went back into the hall, and I leant against a wall and watched him lock the front door and tried to think what was nagging at my mind.

He turned and saw me still there and stopped, smiling vaguely, just by the wooden postbox, like a big nesting-box, hung on the wall by the bus timetables and rack of airline brochures.

I said: 'Does the hotel have a key to that, or is it a proper post office box?'

He blinked, surprised. 'It belongs to the hotel. Once or twice a day somebody clears it and just posts the letters in the nearest proper box.'

That sounded like Castle's service with style, all right. 'Open it up.'

Now he really did look surprised. 'I think there is nothing in there . . .'

'So we'll check.'

He found the key on the big bunch and lifted the sloping lid. 'No, nothing.'

I looked for myself. 'All right, hand it over.'

'What?' The surprise was still there, but maybe a little fear behind it.

'The letter the Professor wrote. Hand it *over*!'

'But what letter?'

'That's why he put on a shirt. To come downstairs. And he bought the stamps off you and paid with a new 250-mil. note and it was too late for anybody to post it tonight but not too late for a fat vulture like you to remember it once the bloke was dead. I'll bet you'd have sorted out his room, too, if that chambermaid hadn't been there. Now either give it to me or stick around until I've got back Lazaros and told him my theory.'

'It is in my room,' he said shakily.

I jerked my head at the stairs.

He brought it down inside a couple of minutes: an ordinary long pale blue airmail envelope with a handwritten address to Pierre Aziz in Beit Mery, Beirut, Lebanon.

'I was going to post it in the morning,' Papa said, trying hard to get a little dignity back into his voice.

The envelope was still sealed so he might have been telling the truth except I was quite sure he wasn't. From its thickness, it probably only held one folded piece of paper. I stuck it in my shirt pocket.

'What are going to do?' he asked.

'Sleep on it. Behind a locked door.'

His expression got suddenly crafty. 'Now why should I not tell the Inspector that you have it?'

'Because you'd still involve yourself. And because, when the going gets rough, you scare easier than I do.'

After that, I knew our relationship would never be the same again. But then, it already wasn't.

10

Breakfast ran long and late the next morning. I got down around ten and Kapotas was already having his first coronary of the day over the desk cash box.

'They steal everything!' he wailed. 'Even a few—'

'Don't worry, that was me. I'll pay you back when you pay me.'

'I keep saying that I am not responsible for—'

'It's only money. And not even ours.' I ducked into the dining-room.

Ken was the only one I knew there; no Mitzi, no Suzie and there'd been no sign of Sergeant Papa. I sat down with Ken and ordered three poached eggs and enough coffee to swim in, then started on the last of Ken's coffee to bridge the gap. A half hangover, not the sort where you've got broken glass in your veins, always gives me an appetite like an opera singer.

Ken wasn't looking so hopeful of the day. His eyes were puffy and red – you *do* lose your alcohol capacity – and he was morosely scratching a new pattern in an old gravy-stain on the cloth.

'What's the matter?' I asked. 'Wasn't it like it is in the women's magazines? You're just getting old. Lucky to be able to—'

'Ah, shut up. I got my wick trimmed all right. It's Bruno.'

'You really liked him?'

'He was a pretty nice bloke, though the competition wasn't high, in there. I just don't see why ... and cancer patients just don't kill themselves, anyway. Once you know you've only got so long to live, it seems too sweet to waste. Have you ever heard of anybody committing suicide in the condemned cell?'

'Yes: Hermann Göring.'

'For God's sake ... he doesn't count. Anyway, he only beat the rope by a few hours, didn't he?'

'And he was a pilot.' I don't know why I was sounding so cheerful about it, except that it was too early to feel suicidal myself. Then my eggs arrived and I got noshed into them for a minute or two. 'Anyway,' I said finally, 'he wrote a letter last night. Posted it in the box in the hall and Sergeant Papa nicked it and I nicked it off him.'

Ken was staring at me with more than the puffiness narrowing his eyes. 'Who to? What's it say?'

'Bloke in Beirut. And I haven't opened it.' I nudged my jacket with my knife handle and the letter crackled in my pocket.

'Keep your voice down,' Ken said quietly. 'The bloke at the next table's a plainclothes jack.'

I didn't ask how he knew, just waited for a reasonable excuse to glance sideways. A nice clean-cut thirty-year-old in a fresh white shirt and not a hotel guest unless he'd come aboard this morning. Well, it figured. If I'd been Lazaros I'd have sent somebody around to drink a few cups of coffee and keep his ears wide open. The Inspector might not think there was something behind the Professor's death, but he'd be quite sure there was something behind the Professor.

I said gently: 'It could just be the suicide note the Inspector wanted him to have left. I suppose there's no law about posting one instead of sticking it on the mantelpiece.'

'To somebody in Beirut? When his own daughter's next door?'

'Are you looking for logical behaviour in a suicide?' I finished my last egg. 'I suppose it'd be more proper for Mitzi to read it than for Lazaros, and he'd certainly open it, but then again – if it *is* a suicide note, it might cause her unnecessary grief, right?'

'You're achieving new standards in logical hypocrisy.' He poured himself some of my coffee. 'So what now?'

'We wait until we're alone, Josephine.'

He half grinned. The puffiness was fading and his face was taking on the old lean, shrewd alertness. He nodded briefly and leant back in the chair. 'What happened to that girl at the Gatwick pub...'

*

It took five minutes before the cop decided he couldn't go on reading his future in the bottom of the little coffee-cup and wandered out. I twitched my chair to get my back to the glass doors and slid the envelope across the table.

Ken shook his head, barely a quiver. 'Pierre Aziz? Don't know him.'

'Nor me, though maybe I've heard something ... Anyway, Beit Mery's no refugee camp.'

'It's that hill with the fancy great hotel, isn't it? The Al Boustan.'

'That's the place.' I worked one fingertip in under the envelope flap. 'Well, jog my elbow.'

He grinned, reached and bumped my arm. The envelope ripped open. 'Dear me, it seems to have come undone ...' I unfolded the single piece of good-quality ten-by-eight writing paper with the single line Professor Doktor Bruno Spohr engraved across the top. No address; a professional travelling man. And underneath ... a big slab of type-written German, ending in two signatures, one of them Spohr's. I don't read German much beyond '*Bier*' and '*Flugplatz*' and I was pretty sure Ken still didn't either. The sheet had a slightly lop-eared, worn look; certainly older than last night. I shrugged and passed it across.

Ken frowned down at it. 'Oh Christ, why didn't we think of a German speaker writing in German ... *Das Schwert das wir in der Gruft in Akka entdeckt haben* ... Oh hell. Akka must be Acre, but what's a *Schwert* and a *Gruft*?'

'Dunno. What's the other signature?'

'Franz Meisler. The Prof's assistant, maybe, it's dated eighteen months ago; before Bruno got pinched.' He skimmed down the rest of the text. 'There's some dimension in here, too ... what does 1003 millimetres sound like?'

'Like just over three feet. Maybe it's a treasure map in words: one metre north-west of the lonesome pine ...'

'Well, a suicide note it ain't. And we'll have to show it to Mitzi. How do we explain how it got opened?'

'We blame the Sergeant, of course.'

'Stupid of me.' He held it up. 'You or me?'

'You know the lady best.'

*

But Lazaros and his band of merry men turned up before Mitzi did. They set up at a bar table and took our formal statements in chronological order: the chambermaid finding him,

Sergeant Papa confirming the finding, me arriving to reconfirm and tell Papa to get his finger out and into a telephone dial.

When I'd finished, I asked Lazaros: 'Was it cancer?'

He thought for a moment before answering. His shirt was clean now, but his long face still looked weary. 'Yes. The pathologist's preliminary report says it was well advanced.'

'So now we know.'

'Yes. Read the statement over, please, and sign if it is correct.'

Mitzi got back from wherever as I was reading, and Lazaros called her in. She was smartly but quietly dressed in a mid-length charcoal grey skirt, short-sleeved white blouse and what looked like a small antique gold coin on a chain around her neck. She gave me a polite, pale smile as we passed in the doorway.

Ken was leaning on the counter outside; Lazaros hadn't wanted anything formal from him. 'Half past eleven. When's it respectable to start drinking in this town?'

'When the cops are out of the bar. It's an old Cypriot custom.'

'I was thinking more of strolling round to the Ledra.'

'Well, unless you do it for the exercise, stop thinking. We're busted after last night. We can't pay for what we drink so we'll have to drink it here.'

Kapotas came out of the office in time to get the tail-end of that, and glared at me. 'It is all being charged in the end!'

'Sooner or later it's going to get cheaper to pay me and let me fly home.'

He waved a piece of paper. 'I can do nothing until Harborne, Gough tell me ... And what about the Professor? Will his daughter be able to pay? All that champagne and caviar!'

'Delicious it was, too,' I said, just to cheer him up. Then, to Ken: 'How was the Professor fixed, moneywise?'

He shrugged. 'Middling well, I'd guess. He didn't talk about it, but I'd say he was used to living well.'

'He'd had a year without income.'

'True, true ...'

A woman came up to the desk and said in an American accent: 'Good morning. Is this where Professor Bruno Spohr was staying?'

We all looked at her. After a moment, Kapotas said nervously: 'I am afraid the Professor is—'

'I know all about that. But I think he had his daughter with him; I was wondering if I could talk with her.'

I nodded at the bar doors. 'She's making a statement to the police in there, but she shouldn't be long.'

'Why, thank you. I'm Eleanor Travis.' And she held out a firm, slim hand.

She must have been about thirty-five, slim and a bit tall and with a general air of tautness. Something in the way the skin was pulled tight over the high suntanned cheekbones, the way she cocked her head and smiled, showing a lot of big white teeth, the cat-like precision with which she moved. Her hair was longish and blonde and a little likely to separate into straggles; she wore tight blue trousers – and had a bottom small enough for it – a blue denim shirt and a bright yellow silk neckscarf.

I said: 'Roy Case. And this is Ken Cavitt.' She shook his hand, too.

Then he asked: 'Did you know Professor Spohr?'

'I never met him, no, but I've heard a lot about him.'

'Oh?'

'I work for the Met in New York.'

'The which?'

'Metropolitan Museum of Art. I'm a medievalist.'

I said: 'Forgive me asking – but how did you know where the Professor was?'

Her whole body tautened another notch. But the smile stayed. 'It was on the radio this morning, the desk at the Ledra told me. I'd tried ringing him at a dozen hotels yesterday – including this one – and they'd all said he wasn't staying.'

Ken and I glanced at each other and he nodded about a millimetre. It sounded reasonable.

I said: 'He was trying to stay secret. I imagine a hotel guest is entitled to that. I suppose you didn't—' But then I said: 'Skip it.' I'd been going to ask if she'd played games with delivering those green envelopes all over town, but if she had she certainly wouldn't admit it.

Ken said. 'You really are from the Met, are you?'

This time the smile was long gone. Kapotas stood up straight and made worried twittering noises.

She said coolly: 'And who are you two?'

'He's an old friend of the Prof's,' I said quickly, 'and I'm an old friend of him. Sorry if we sound snoopy, but a man doesn't commit suicide every day.'

'I'd guess once is the most anybody ever did.' Her voice was quite calm. She reached into a big shoulder bag made of fringed white buckskin, rummaged around and handed all three of us visiting cards. It said:

Eleanor Travis
Metropolitan Museum of Art, New York. TR9–5500.

Instinctively I ran a fingernail over the lettering to see if it was engraved. I hadn't had cards of my own since I'd left the RAF, where all officers *had* to have them and they *had* to be engraved, to show we were gentlemen as well.

'It's engraved,' Miss Travis said, voice still freeze-dried.

Ken grinned. 'And you know? – I'd've said she was no gentleman.'

Her face twitched for a second, then she smiled outright.

I said: 'Sorry again. But ... other people were trying to track him down and I'm sure one did.'

Ken said sharply: 'When was this?'

'Last night. I found out just after I found him. Meant to tell you. Sorry.'

Miss Eleanor Travis, medievalist, asked: 'Just what is all this?'

'Perhaps you can tell us,' I said. 'You were looking for him, others were looking for him. You must have had a reason, so maybe they had the same one.'

She nibbled the idea like the first taste of some new foreign food. 'We-ell ... I've been researching in Rhodes the last two months and a rumour came through that Professor Spohr had been dropping hints that he had something interesting, and it sounded like he was trying to work up bids from the big museums, and I heard he was going to Cyprus so I called the director at the Met and asked if he wanted me to try and find out what it was all about.'

'And he said Yes?' I suggested.

She put on a slightly hesitant, artificial smile. 'Er ... how well did you know Professor Spohr?'

Ken said: 'I met him in jail, if that's what you mean.'

'Normally,' I said, 'Ken and I only move in strictly Blue Book circles, but you can't blame somebody for the people he meets in jail, can you?'

Her glance flicked back and forth between the two of us. 'Ye-es,' she said slowly. 'Well, this is what the director said.' She took a crumpled cable form from her Sitting Bull bag and passed it over.

Address and mistakes apart, it read:

GO CYPRUS IF YOU LIKE WILL PAY HALF EXPENSES BUT
IF WE BUY DIRECT FROM THAT OLD CROOK WILL BE
FIRST TIME KEEP US INFORMED.

Ken said: 'Yes, I see,' quite tonelessly, and then: 'So you don't know what he was hawking around?'

'I was hoping his daughter would know – unless you do?'

He shook his head. 'He never told me. But he had something, all right.'

Mitzi came out of the bar with Lazaros close behind. He came straight across and asked Kapotas: 'Did Professor Spohr post any letters here yesterday?'

It was a clever idea, but eight hours too late. Kapotas shook his head. 'No. I opened the box before I went home yesterday, and again this morning. Nothing.'

'Did he make any telephone calls?'

Now why hadn't I been that clever eight hours ago? Kapotas reached for the book beside the switchboard and ran a finger down the column. 'Room 323 ... yes, at 8.25 last night he spoke to a number in Israel, in Jerusalem.'

'Papadimitriou put it through, did he? Why didn't he tell me?'

'He probably forgot in the fuss last night,' I said soothingly. 'He was in a pretty panicky state.' And this was an angle where I didn't want anybody getting rough with fragile fat old Papa.

Lazaros grunted and looked half convinced. 'Just the number, no name, of course?' He wrote the number down, then stared at it. 'I can ask Papa; he probably listened in.' And headed off to the doorstep where the Sergeant was sunning himself.

Mitzi was standing just on the edge of our little sewing circle; now she leaned timidly forward. 'May I see the number, please?'

Kapotas shoved the book at her. She took a diary from her bag and copied it down. Ken asked: 'Do you recognise it?'

'No, but perhaps I can call it and ask what ...' her voice trailed off.

Ken indicated Eleanor Travis. 'This is Miss Travis from the New York Met. She wanted to meet your father. Mitzi Braunhof, *née* Spohr.'

Eleanor stuck out her hand and Mitzi shook it tentatively. 'I am sorry, but I cannot say anything about—'

Our Eleanor hadn't come all the way from Rhodes (paying half her own expenses) for that. She said firmly: 'I just wanted to see if the Met should put in a bid for whatever it was your father had turned up.'

When in doubt, talk money.

Mitzi frowned briefly, looked a little bothered, then shook her head. 'I am sorry I do not know ... I have not had time for his papers yet, you understand ... I only know it was *ein Schwert* ... a sword.'

Ken and I looked at each other; he recovered first. 'Look – maybe we could all sit down for a little chat.' He looked towards the bar, where Apostolos was just unlocking the grill, but still with a table-full of policemen comparing and arranging papers.

He turned to Eleanor and smiled his best smile. 'If you've got any money, we could all go and have a quiet drink at the Ledra.'

11

Miss Travis had a little trouble getting used to the idea that two grown men could be completely broke, right down to the point at which she had to pay off the taxi. I spent a little time explaining about the laws of receivership and none at all telling where our last mils had gone.

We were just ahead of the lunchtime rush at the Ledra bar, so we got a corner table by the french windows and the waiter came across and said gravely: 'Good morning, Captain Cavitt. It's been a long time.' And Ken said indeed it had and why didn't we all just drink whisky sours to make the ordering simpler? When Ken gets sparking, you don't find much room to argue, so we all had whisky sours; from Mitzi's expression as she sipped, it was the first she'd ever met.

When nobody was overhearing, Ken laid the folded paper on the table. 'Your father posted it last night, the Sergeant took it out and opened it. Roy took it off him.'

Mitzi's hand reached for it, then stopped, as if she were suddenly scared.

Slowly, hands trembling just a little, she unfolded the paper. 'Have you read it?'

I said: 'We don't read German.'

She skimmed it quickly, ending on a frown. 'But it does not say where is the sword.'

Ken lifted his glass and took a gulp and put it down again, face expressionless.

Mitzi said: 'Who was it being sent to?'

He gave her the envelope. 'Have you heard of Pierre Aziz?'

'I think my father . . . I think I have heard the name.'

'How about Franz Meisler?'

'Yes, he was working with my father in Israel. I think he is now in America.'

I glanced at Eleanor. But she shook her head. 'Say – d'you mind telling me just what that is?'

Mitzi looked down at the paper again. 'Only a . . . a description of a sword.'

'May we hear it?'

Mitzi sipped, cleared her throat and started. 'The sword which we . . . in the tomb . . . at Akka . . . have found . . . is of . . . made of steel. With a name . . . on the . . . blade . . . of Ufert.' She looked up doubtfully, but Eleanor nodded enthusiastically.

'Ufert, that's right. Twelfth-century German sword-maker. Go on.'

'With . . . double-edged blade . . . straight . . . guardpiece . . . some traces of gilding on the *Knauf*? The knob?'

'Pommel,' Eleanor said.

'Yes . . . which is of iron. With on one side . . . a gem of about 25 millimetres . . . perhaps a ruby.'

Eleanor frowned. 'That's odd.'

'Odd?' said Ken. 'A ruby 25 millimetres across? It's a sight better than odd.'

'No, I mean one set into a twelfth-century European sword. They hadn't picked up the idea of decorating swords much, at that time. Sorry, go on.'

Mitzi took another sip of her whisky sour, blinked and went on. 'On the other side of the . . . the pommel . . . a . . . an inlay of gold wire . . . and enamel . . . in shape of a shield . . . three gold leopards on red.'

'Three leopards!' There was a sudden light behind Eleanor's eyes – which were blue, I noticed for the first time.

I said 'So the owner kept a pet shop?'

'No – it means the owner was probably Coeur de Lion. King Richard the Lion-Heart.'

*

After a long time I said: 'I suppose that would make it quite interesting, historicalwise.'

Eleanor looked at me. 'Just quite.'

'I thought it was lions on the English whatsit.'

'No, three leopards was Richard's bearing. Lions came in just after. Mind, to a German sword-maker they were both as mythical as dragons.' She looked at Mitzi. 'Is that all?'

She'd been silently mouthing her way through the paper. 'No . . . then is the measurements of the sword, and then where it was found: in the ruins of the church of Sainte-Croix.'

I took out a pipe and started scraping it out. 'What is that thing, then? – a sales brochure?'

Eleanor said: 'No. Well, yes. Sort of, perhaps. A sword like that would only have a limited intrinsic value—'

Ken bent his eyebrows at her. 'With that ruby?'

'We-ell . . . there's rubies and there's rubies, particularly around that time. Twelfth-century swords aren't exactly common – most of them were still made of iron and rusted away when they didn't break, and I wouldn't believe in this one if it *hadn't* been found in a tomb where it might have been properly protected . . . But still, there's a few around and as works of art they're nothing and not great swords besides: the real European arms and armour came much later. But if you can tie that sword to King Richard *and* prove it's one he carried on his Crusade . . . Well, name your price.'

I said: 'I thought naming prices was your end,' and began to fill the pipe.

'Well – start at half a million and it could go as high as one.'

Ken started to say something but it jammed in his throat like a fishbone. Finally he said huskily: 'Dollars?'

'Sure.'

You can smell a million dollars; you can taste it. But I've never been able to do more.

Eleanor went on: 'The nice thing is, it was found at Acre: that's where Richard sailed home from. Probably he presented it to somebody, you know: "I must away but let my sword stand guard in Outremer until my return".' She looked a little abashed. 'They did say things like that.'

Ken said: 'I bet they also said: "Sorry I can't pay the ten ducats, but keep this until I've pushed through a tax raise".'

'Yes – the Crusaders were always in money trouble. You know, he *could* have found the tomb of Henry of Champagne.' She turned to Mitzi. 'Didn't he tell you anything about this?'

She shook her head quickly. 'He was good at secrets. Only he said that he had found a most valuable sword.'

I asked: 'Who was Henry?'

'He took over from Richard. He was quite a diplomat: kept a small kingdom going there without any military back-up. But he died a couple of years before Richard. Fell out of a window while reviewing some troops.'

Ken said: 'No wonder he's remembered as Henry of Champagne.'

'They didn't invent the wine for another four hundred years. Anyway, Henry was supposed to have been buried in Sainte-Croix. So, the regulation thing would have been to leave the sword in place and whistle up other archaeologists to witness the find.'

'And give it to the Israeli government.' Ken said. 'So instead, he wrote out this description, got his assistant to sign it, and hid the description in one place and the sword somewhere else. The real value comes when those two get togther again – am I right?'

Eleanor nodded. 'Something like that. The description's worth nothing by itself; the sword could be worth a few thousand – but the big museums wouldn't touch it without any documentation.'

There was a time while we just sat and thought. The barstools were filling up rapidly. A BEA captain I'd known in the RAF at one end, the usual bunch of journalists at the other, some Swedish officers in the middle.

Mitzi cleared her throat nervously and said: 'Then perhaps I should go and talk to this Herr Aziz in Beirut. Do you know how much it costs to go there?'

'Costs?' said Ken, appalled. '*Costs?* You're talking to two men who own an airline. You're our guests. However—' he looked at his empty glass and then Eleanor '— could you spring for another round?'

*

Kapotas raked a trembling hand through his hair. 'You want what?'

'Just the seventy-five pounds I'm owed already,' I said pleasantly. 'Only now, before the banks close. And, of course, tacit agreement to us using the aeroplane. I'm not asking for permission, you understand; only that you don't notice.'

'But you don't expect me to . . .' He seemed as much muddled as dazed. 'But this is absurd. What do you want to do with the plane?'

'We just want to pop across to Beirut on – what would you call it? A merchant venture, perhaps.'

'And you can participate,' Ken joined in. 'Don't get the idea that we're limiting your contribution just to the seventy-five that you owe Roy anyway. If you want to put in some more of your own, then naturally you share, *pro rata*, in the eventual profit.'

'Of which,' I added, 'we have every confidence.'

After a time, Kapotas said in a calm but slightly shaky voice: 'Have you been drinking?'

'A jar or two,' I admitted. 'But nothing noticeable.'

Ken said: 'Are you really trying to tell us that you're turning down this unique opportunity?'

Kapotas just looked at him.

I said: 'All right, but you'll be sorry. So just write me the cheque for seventy-five and I'll get round to the bank.'

'I keep telling you, I can do nothing until Harborne, Gough—'

'And we both know Harborne, Gough's reckoning they can screw me by waiting until I get so bored I'll fly the aeroplane home for nothing rather than pay my own fare. And we know the hotel's got money in the bank here and you must have some discretion about using it. So start.'

He just looked stubborn.

I sighed. 'Well, we'll get the girls to lend us the fare to Beirut and I'll ring my bank and they can cable through a few quid there.' I reached for my room key. 'We'll be checking out, then.'

'But wait . . .' Kapotas frowned at me. 'What about the plane?'

'It belongs to Castle. Harborne, Gough'll probably send another pilot down to fly it back. You can't expect me to stay on forever without pay, can you?'

'But . . . the boxes of champagne—'

He jerked his head in a small, significant nod at Ken.

'Don't worry,' I said cheerfully. 'You can speak openly in front of my partner; he's older than he looks. Those boxes? Do what you like with them. They're not mine.'

'But . . . what is in them . . .'

Ken said quickly: 'Does anybody *know* what's in them?'

'I don't,' I said. 'They haven't been opened.'

'The one we . . . I opened here . . .' Kapotas stuttered.

I shrugged. 'I don't know what happened to that box. But I'm sure that if there was anything, say, illegal in it, then you'd have reported it to the police.'

He glared. 'I can still report it!'

'Twenty-four hours late? And when you've had police crawling all over your hotel for half that time? Dear me.'

There was a long silence.

At last Kapotas said between his teeth: 'I call this blackmail.'

'It's certainly a fascinating moral problem,' Ken said thoughtfully. 'There's no doubt but that Roy is owed that seventy-five and that you've refused to pay—'

'As receiver,' Kapotas went back to his old refrain; 'I am not responsible for debts incurred before Harborne, Gough took over. Therefore, I am not strictly acting for the old Castle International board, who hired Mr Case, but for the new owners, the debenture holders.'

'But strictly,' Ken said, 'we aren't blackmailing *you*: it's not *your* money we're after. I suppose you might say we're putting the bite on your beloved debenture holders, but only by offering to help conceal what one of their agents – that's you – did while acting on their behalf: to wit and namely, failing to disclose the illegal importation of what may be twelve boxes of unlicensed firearms by Castle International or their agent. That's you,' he said to me.

I said: 'I admire the grammar, but I lost the moral in there somewhere.'

'I told you it was a fascinating problem. I bet they set it as a passing-out exam for Jesuits one day. And it gets better.' He looked back at Kapotas. 'You see, you don't propose yourself to have anything more to do with those boxes, do you? But in order to protect you completely, we can't be so negative. We have to act positively, possibly even commit a crime, by knowingly taking those boxes somewhere else.

'You see the difficult moral position you're putting us in?' he added.

'I'm putting YOU?' screamed Kapotas.

Ken nodded gently and said: 'And we haven't even begun considering your responsibility towards those boxes as assets of the company, which they must, *prima facie*, be assumed to be.'

'You're right,' I said. 'I hadn't realised how fascinating it all is.'

There was another long silence, except for Ken tapping on his front teeth and trying to make a tune by opening and closing his mouth while staring blankly at the switchboard.

I asked: 'What *is* that you're trying to do?'

Kapotas said: 'But legally, you understand—'

Ken said: 'Vilja, Oh Vilja from the Merry Widow. It's a difficult one, there's a jump of over an octave in the beginning there.'

'Ah, the Viennese influence, of course.'

'*Legally*—' said Kapotas.

Ken looked at him, seeming surprised that he was still there. 'Legally, you can go around and look up our old friend Inspector Lazaros and tell him you're sorry you're a day late but you've something important to confess. We won't stop you.'

I said: 'I didn't know anybody had done an arrangement of it for top third molars.'

Kapotas took a cheque-book from his inside pocket.

12

I phoned in a flight plan for takeoff at 3.45. We went out in a taxi, collecting Eleanor from the Ledra on the way, and she was pleasantly surprised to see me handling my own money again. I didn't bother her with the details of how I'd got it.

The others parked in the café while I arranged for refuelling. In fact, the Queen Air still had over thirty gallons aboard, which was enough to reach Beirut although not with legal reserves. But I was thinking well beyond legality: I wanted enough in the tanks for a fast departure if somebody blew the whistle on us. Back to Cyprus or further if the Lebanese got snotty, up to Adana in Turkey if the Cypriots asked for extradition. I didn't really expect either, but a good pilot is always flying a hundred miles or so ahead of his aeroplane.

Of course, one thing I couldn't be sure about was where we'd go if Harborne, Gough suddenly woke up and decided we'd stolen the Queen Air. Maybe Baffin Land had some pensionable openings in civil aviation.

Ken came into the Met office with me, just to remind himself. The map showed that last night's storm had been part of a cold front going through; it was now somewhere in Syria, with its low-pressure hinge up in Turkey. Beirut was reporting about three oktas – or eighths – of cloud and 20-odd knots of wind from the south-west, visibility five miles. Fair enough; it is a north-east wind that brings the dust and smoke from Beirut out across the airport. I made a few notes and then switched to studying the weather further west and likely to come our way sooner or later. I'd been out of touch for a couple of days myself.

We all make jokes about the Met boys, but most of their mistakes are matters of degree. A low gets deeper than expected, a front moves faster. But you can count on both low and front existing. And a pilot lives with the weather like living with a family. He watches the patterns of mood and illness come and go and, if he stays awake, he knows where he is in the pattern and doesn't get any nasty surprises. If the North

Atlantic has measles this week then Europe will have it in a couple of days; maybe more so, maybe less, but it'll be there. God doesn't wake up in the morning and say: 'Now what shall I give 'em today?' Except with hurricanes, maybe.

Bar a few gaps, I've lived with the weather myself for the past twenty years. I knew what Ken meant when he said not knowing made you feel cut off.

We got aboard at about half past three and the inside smelt like a hot oil well, so I left the door hanging down – the inside of it forms the steps – as long as possible. The interior of a Queen Air is about the height and width of a Volkswagen Microbus but there's no standard layout. Castle Hotels had chosen to have five largish passenger seats and had scrapped the lavatory in favour of extra luggage space just aft of the door. Now part of that space was filled with the two frontmost seats which had been pulled off their rails to make room for the champagne boxes stacked either side of the narrow aisle, behind the cockpit. It looked a bit clumsy, but it put them right over the centre of gravity. Anyway, I hadn't expected to be flying passengers until I'd got the seats back in place.

Ken was already in the right-hand pilot's seat when I squeezed through and started unpacking the checklists and Aerad guide from my briefcase.

'God, but you keep a shitty aeroplane when I'm not around,' he said. Well, I suppose the floor was just slightly smothered with pipe ash, used matches and crumpled pages off my navigation pad. I'd been meaning to do something . . .

I said: 'I got involved. Have you remembered which way is up, yet?'

He smiled, jerked his head back towards the stacked boxes and asked softly: 'How did you resist opening that lot?'

'If it's what we think it is, we've got no alibi at all once they're opened.'

'I suppose not.' He picked up the checklists and sorted them.

Both side windows were open and a bit of breeze was limping through, but it wasn't any snowstorm outside. Already my shirt was sticking to my back, and it would be nasty and clammy when we cooled off at 5,000 feet.

The hell with it. Let's get started. I went aft, whistled up a ground crewman with the statutory fire extinguisher, shut the door, made sure the girls were strapped in, then went forward and sat down.

'Let's go.'

Ken started to read the checklist. 'Brakes *on* . . . beacon light on . . . circuit breakers *in* . . . master switch . . .'

I turned the ignition key and the aeroplane began to wake with a gentle hum. Needles stirred sluggishly on the dials. A thin whine as the boost pumps came on, and now we were working. I set up the engine control, Ken watching my hand, memorising the moves.

'Throttle about half an inch,' I explained. 'Mag switch to "prime", you can see the fuel pressure drop, then pick up and you're ready.' I pointed to the port engine and the crewman outside nodded and aimed his extinguisher vaguely in that direction. I wondered if he'd remember to set it off if the engine actually did explode.

'Mag switch to *start* . . .' The propeller grunted around and I rammed up the mixture lever and it spun and howled. I set the run-up for 1400 revs, turned on the alternator, and did it all again with the second engine.

The crewman wandered dreamily away. Of course, he might really be suffering from disappointment.

We sat and watched the oil temperatures creep up; these engines are touchy about that. The radio came in on somebody from the aero club asking for takeoff. We watched the little aeroplane, half a mile away, run along and bounce into the air, wings rocking nervously. It wouldn't hurt to stay on the ground an extra few knots, with upcurrents like that coming off the hot tarmac . . .

Then I glanced at Ken and knew he was filing away just the same idea, along with his guess at the horizontal visibility, his own estimate of the wind, and whatever was happening around the airfield: that Piper Colt in the circuit, an Olympic 727 taxiing in that would bring a fleet of vehicles rushing out at any minute, a Trident loading but unlikely to move until we were gone.

I got taxi clearance and pressure setting and trundled us slowly down past the aero club and the RAF hangars and around to the run-up point for runway 32. The club Piper was weaving and twitching low on the approach. I ran up both engines, tested the magnetos and feathering. The Piper floated past our nose, bounced and settled down. You could almost hear the pilot's sigh of relief.

The tower said: 'Whiskey Zulu, line up and hold.'

I drove on to the runway behind the Piper. It scurried along and turned off. The tower said: 'Whiskey Zulu, clear to go.'

I looked over at Ken. He was sitting with his hands in his lap, face quite expressionless. I slumped and let go of the controls. 'Okay. Take her to Wyoming.'

He looked and grinned slowly and sat up. His hands trembled a bit as he settled them on the controls, then pushed the throttles smoothly forwards and we were both home again.

*

We levelled out at 5,000 feet – I'd elected to fly beneath the airways so that I didn't need to keep applying for changes of course whenever I wanted to dodge a bit of the cumulus cloud I expected ahead – and Ken steadied her on 155 knots indicated, then trimmed her to fly hands-off.

'She feels like a real aeroplane,' he said grudgingly. He didn't like the controls of most private aircraft and particularly not American ones. 'Bloody heavy on ailerons, though.'

I was sorting through the Aerad guide for the Beirut approach charts. 'They've got servo tabs working in the *opposite* direction.'

He stared. 'You mean they deliberately make her feel like a DC-3? Why?'

'Ask Beech; I only work here.'

He made a growly noise and went back to frowning at the instruments. I found the Beirut pages and set 351 kilocycles on the second Automatic Direction Finder compass, although we wouldn't pick up any signals just yet. The first ADF was already tuned to the Dhekelia beacon on Cyprus's south coast, and a moment later we went slap over the middle of it. You could tell by the way the needle shivered, uncertain which way to turn, before spinning round to face backwards.

Neat. He'd worked out our exact amount of drift and compensated for it in about two minutes, not having touched an aeroplane in two years and this one never before. The coastline and its fringe of vivid pale green water crawled away behind; I switched from Nicosia approach to the Flight Information Region and said hello, and that was about as much as I needed do for the next hundred miles.

Ken seemed happy enough without any chatter, so I unstrapped and went back to the girls. 'All okay?'

Mitzi nodded, Eleanor grinned – a quick expression that showed a lot of white teeth. 'Fine, fine. Is that our in-flight refreshment?' And she nodded at the boxes stacked a few inches ahead of her knees.

'Sorry, no.' The Queen Air isn't pressurised (which was why I was going around rather than over the weather) but we could talk by using stage voices. 'I'm just carting it around for a bloke until he decides what to do with it.'

Mitzi asked: 'The plane is for the hotel, then?' She'd seen the Castle insignia on the tail.

'The hotel group, yes. But they don't mind.'

Eleanor said: 'Something I wondered about: we've neither of us got visas for Lebanon. Does it matter?'

'Not a bit. You can buy 'em before you reach the immigration desk. Costs a few dollars, that's all.' But that reminded me of something. I looked at my watch. 'We'll be starting our approach on Beirut in about half an hour. Anything you want, just stick your head through and shout. Not that we've got anything.'

Eleanor grinned again and I wriggled back through the doorway and into my seat. 'How're we doing?'

'Just starting to get Beirut.' Ken pointed at the second ADF compass; its needle was slopping about just left of centre.

I put on the earphones and got a faint steady tone, with every now and then the identification letters in morse: B-O-D. 'That's it. But something I thought of: what about your passport problem?' Normally, each of us carried two passports so that we could keep the Israeli stamps on one, the Arab ones on the other. And the same sort of juggling with some African countries. But your second passport is only issued for a year, and Ken's would be way out of date by now.

He shook his head. 'No matter. My passport didn't get stamped going into Israel and for some reason they didn't bother going out. I'm clean.'

Well, perhaps that figured. I put a match to my pipe and the cockpit swirled with smoke.

Ken sniffed. 'Now I know I'm really home. When's your uncle going to sell the pig farm?' He stretched and licked his lips. 'You know – suddenly I miss not smoking. In jail it didn't matter much. I'd never been in the coop before, so one more difference you didn't notice. But in a cockpit . . . Maybe I'll start again.'

'More pilots lose their licences for heart trouble than anything else.'

'Ahh, that's just BOAC types overeating and worrying about the stock market.' A tower of cumulus cloud stood straight ahead, its top well over 10,000. Ken turned us 30 degrees right and started the stopwatch hand of his watch. Then nodded over his shoulder. 'That champagne—'

I looked quickly back, but though the little sliding door wasn't shut, the girls obviously couldn't hear.

'That champagne: was the paperwork good?'

'Very.' I took the sheaf from my inside pocket. 'Even this certificate of origin thing. God knows how they got that.'

'Did you have the papers with you, that night? – when you got mugged but nothing taken?'

'Yes.' I touched the corner of my jaw reflectively.

'Could it be they just wanted a look at the papers? To make sure you'd brought the cargo they were expecting?'

'It's possible.'

'I mean, somebody *is* expecting that load, and they'll have paid some in advance, maybe all. Had you thought they might start wondering if you'd sold it all for yourself and gone whoring on the proceeds?'

'No, I hadn't really thought that.' Somehow, I just hadn't had time.

'Hadn't you better start thinking it?' he suggested gently. 'I mean, besides sleeping with your back to the wall and your eyes open.'

'It's an idea. Only – why should anybody in Cyprus know what I was really carrying? It wasn't for them and you wouldn't exactly sling this sort of information around.'

He checked his watch; we'd been on our new heading just 90 seconds and the cloud was now behind the port wing. He turned us back 60 degrees to port and started the watch again. Another 90 seconds and a 30-degree turn and we'd be right back on our original track.

'You got thumped around midnight, yes? But the news that Castle had gone bust and the aeroplane's stuck at Cyprus must have come through about nine hours before. Plenty of time to catch a flight from Beirut. And they'd know exactly which hotel you'd be in.'

'There's that,' I admitted.

We made the last turn of the dogleg. After a while, he said: 'And you got hit on the chin. Couldn't you see who did it? You can hardly get bopped on the chin from behind.'

'You can if you try. He just spun me around and bomp. Anyway, it was dark. I just got the idea he was big and male.'

'I'm glad it wasn't small and female. But hell – nobody hits anybody on the chin except on TV.'

'So maybe he was trying to break into TV work. Damn it all, it just happened.'

'Well, next time try and remember to ask why.'

13

As airports go, Nicosia is just a country way-station where you can usually get permission to back-track down the runway after landing. But Beirut's something else. Not just the gateway to the East – or the West – but the main junction of the whole area. Where the north-bound routes from the Gulf and East Africa join the east-west traffic for Europe and the States and you may as well stop off for a few beers and a couple of barmaids between flights. Like what Cairo used to be and Damascus pretends it is.

So you slot yourself into a queue of big jets whose approach speeds are higher than your flat-out maximum and go hammering down the glidepath feeling their big snouts snuffling up your tail and praying the flaps won't tear off. In over the permanent bonfire behind the docks where they burn the old crankcase oil from the taxis (at least that's the story and I'll believe anything about Beirut taxis); slicing across the width of the city towards the sea again, parallel to the sudden suburban hills like Beit Mery that the locals insist are mountains – and finally you float half the length of runway 21 waiting for the speed to unwind before you drop her on. I did the landing; Ken would have done it better.

The radio told us to park on a ramp way down by the eastern hangars, which left us a long way to walk but out of sight of the terminal building, which might just help.

We trudged across the warm concrete sniffing the sharp smell of burnt jet fuel that I still find vaguely exciting because to me it still means fast fighters and not airliners. That dates me. Eleanor asked innocently: 'Is the champagne going to be all right in there?'

'Should be,' I said. 'The aeroplane's locked; anybody stealing stuff still has to get it through Customs . . . If we just forget about the problem, maybe it won't go away.'

Ken switched hands on two pieces of Mitzi's luggage – she had as much as the rest of us together – and let the girls get a few paces ahead, then said quietly: 'When *somebody* finds out that aeroplane's in town they'll bust the course record for corrupting a Beirut Customs officer.'

'Impossible. Anyway, they must have corrupted one in advance, just for this cargo. Then the handling agent brings it through when he knows that one's on duty. I'm rather counting on that. The agent daren't do anything until he's got these papers, and even if the Customs bloke recognises the aircraft he won't blow the whistle if he's still hoping for a payoff. Given the usual foul-up in communications, I'd think we've got most of twenty-four hours.'

'I hope you're right. Incidentally, the copper in Nicosia's going to be spitting blood, ours for choice, if we don't turn up for the inquest.'

I shrugged as well as I could with two handfuls of luggage. 'He didn't subpoena us. Anyway, he's only interested in Mitzi and maybe you.'

'Turn off the extinguisher, Jack, I've stopped burning, huh?' he said dryly. 'Well, maybe we'll be back in time anyhow.'

Ken took the girls through immigration and Customs while I made my number with control, paid my landing fees and generally sniffed the official air. It smelt calm. By half past five we were in a Ford Galaxie taxi going sonic down Khalde Boulevard. Beirut driving is terrible, but that's all. It doesn't get really aggressive, such as you find in Israel.

'Where,' Mitzi asked, 'are we going to stay?'

I knew what Ken would say – and he did: 'The St George. Is there anywhere else?'

'For God's sake come down to our price bracket. We'll stay at some small place in the same area and do our drinking in the St George.'

But the girls decided they, at least, would go for the St George itself. I think they were both just a little apprehensive about Beirut and felt that in a big western hotel there'd be less chance of anybody throwing them across the crupper of his Cadillac and galloping them off across the burning sands.

Well, things do happen in Beirut, if not quite that.

Anyhow, we made sure the girls got rooms at the St George, then took the taxi on and found ourselves a small place on the

Rue Ibn Sina, about five minutes' walk away but no sea view. We had a rendezvous in the St George for half past six, and Ken and I made it with just twenty minutes to spare.

*

The St George bar has the air of a London club-room that got a bit bleached in the sun. Not that much light gets in past the long drapes; if you want to do anything as touristy as get tanned, you sit outside overlooking the swimming pool. Real Beirutis prefer the leather armchairs, the unhurried waiters, the elegant pale woodwork, the incense of diplomacy and big business.

A waiter took our order, gave an unspoken opinion that our clothes belonged out by the pool if not in it, drifted away.

I asked: 'How did it feel – the aeroplane?'

'Nice to be back. But a bit small for our business. What d'you think we should get once we're back in the money?'

I shrugged. 'I was thinking something like a Britten-Norman Islander. Second-hand, you can pick them up for around £30,000 complete.'

Ken made a sour-smell expression. 'A third-level job? Little feeder-liner like that? Hell, it wouldn't carry more than a ton.' Our Scotches arrived and he stirred his ice with the plastic stick. 'I'll bet you can still get a DC-3 for ten thousand, four-ton payload and all.'

'And all those hungry horses to feed.' An Islander's engines churn out just 600 horsepower total, a DC-3 Dakota gives 2,400 – and the fuel costs are about in proportion, let alone your servicing bills. I could get you a four-engined jetliner, 80 seats and no more than fifteen years old, for just over £100,000, but if you wanted to stay rich you'd use it as a garden ornament instead of the concrete gnomes. It's when you start operating an aeroplane that you go broke.

'Well,' I said, 'maybe we could stretch to a Skyvan with a ton-and-a-half.'

'Still third-level,' Ken grumbled.

'Look, chum, third-level's the only place for small operators these days. Short field, rough field, stuff. Everything bigger's got jets flying into it. Nobody wants to ride in a DC-3 any more. That's one reason you can get them for ten thousand.'

'I wasn't thinking about people.'

'Nor strawberries nor monkeys?'

He finished his Scotch and clattered the ice in his glass. 'No, hell, but . . . what else do we know?'

'Jail?'

He took a deep breath and then nodded briefly and waved at the waiter leaning on the bar.

'By the way,' I said, 'what are we doing here?'

'Helping Mitzi track down her father's sword . . . Sounds like something out of a folk song, doesn't it?'

'What are we getting out of it?'

'I liked Bruno – and he pretty well promised me a piece of the action once we got out.'

'D'you think Mitzi accepts that as a debt against the estate? She might just say Thank You very prettily. Even if we find the bloody thing.'

'Look, Roy, she needs me – us – a private aircraft, just as much as her father did. *Nobody* can walk aboard a scheduled flight carrying a three-foot sword; the Lebanese would nick it and swear it had been found in Tyre or Sidon. It could just as well have been.'

'Have you been swotting up the Crusades?'

'What the hell d'you think Bruno and I talked about in jail? Women? Cold beer?'

'Sorry.' Then the girls arrived. Changed, of course, since women can't unpack a suitcase without putting on something fresh, but in Eleanor's case a good idea too: Beirut's a bit stuffy about women in denim pants. Now she had on a plain white shirtwaister with a wide pleated skirt showing a nice pair of slim brown legs. I wondered if she was sun-tanned all over and then wondered why I wondered it.

The waiter took an order for a couple of vodka tonics and the girls said their rooms were fine and how were ours and we said fine, although in fact we'd only hired one and it was lousy, and finally Mitzi said: 'We rang Mr Aziz—'

'Did you?' Ken was a bit surprised.

'There are many pages of Aziz in the telephone book. I would not have found his number without the address.'

'Big family,' I said. 'I thought I knew the name.'

Eleanor said: 'They can't all be one family. You should have seen how many.'

'Better word would be a "clan", like the Campbells or Stewarts. The clans run the country. Not so much Beirut, there's too many foreigners and foreign money here, but certainly the rest.'

'What did the man *say*?' asked Ken.

Eleanor was still looking at me. 'It sounds positively feudal.'

I said: 'No, it's all done through Parliament. In the Smiths' district you get a Smith standing as Conservative candidate, a Smith for the Liberals, a Social-Democratic Smith and so on ... the peasants get a free vote, and if that isn't democracy, what is?'

Ken snapped: 'What did he *say*?'

Mitzi said: 'Come to a party.'

'That's Beirut,' Ken groaned. 'Where and when?'

'At his house in ... in Beit Mery. After dinner.'

'I'm hungry,' said Ken.

*

It was dark when we started up the hill, which was probably good for the girls' nerves. But I knew what sort of drop there was beyond the low walls on the outside of the hairpin bends, and the taxi driver was – as usual – practising for his fighter-pilot badge. From the way Ken talked between clenched teeth, he remembered those roads, too.

'When we get there,' he asked Mitzi, 'what are you going to say?'

'I will tell him my father is dead and ask where is the sword he found.'

It was all right – the taxi driver didn't speak English. That's why I'd picked him out of the bunch that rush you whenever you step out of a hotel in that town.

Ken said: 'That sounds a bit sort of ... straightforward.'

'But why? He knows it is true, that he owes me the sword.'

It all sounded a bit straightforward and true to me, too, but of course I've never had the chance to play the bereaved daughter. The Lebanese can be sentimental about family ties. Their own, anyway.

Eleanor said: 'I wonder if . . .' and then seemed to change her mind and went on: 'Do you have any idea why Mr Aziz got involved in this at all?'

'My father needed some person to sell for him. He was an archaeologist, not a salesman.'

'But why somebody in Beirut?'

I said: 'I can guess at that. Anywhere else – Cyprus or Rome or anywhere – the Israeli government might get an injunction to stop the sale as an illegal export. They'd try, anyway. The Lebanon just doesn't recognise Israeli law.'

Eleanor grunted and sat back – the three of them were on the back seat, me leaning over from beside the driver.

Then Mitzi got an idea: 'He cannot have sold it already?'

There was a silence except for the roar of the engine and the squeal of the tyres. The headlights swept across a battered wall covered in rows of political posters, all showing almost identical confident chubby faces with a few lines of coloured script below. Only the colours were different.

Eleanor said: 'No, I don't think so. We'd have heard something. And like I said: it wouldn't go for half the price without the documentation that you've got. I guess that's why your father kept the two separate while he was . . . while he was away.'

That didn't exactly explain why the Prof had posted the authentication off to Aziz just before he died, though. But I didn't mention it.

Ken said: 'So, in a way, that bit of paper's worth as much as the sword itself.'

'In a way,' Eleanor agreed, 'Hell' – her voice got a little thoughtful – 'I'm in a kind of equivocal position about all this. Employees of the Met aren't supposed to go chasing about after illegal exports.'

'You mean they're not supposed to get caught,' Ken said dryly.

*

Aziz lived not quite at the top of the hill and not quite where the driver first thought he did, either. But we found it; a rambling modern split-level affair dug back into the raw rock hillside, and a drive-way jammed with big cars glistening in the warm orange light flooding from a dozen thinly-curtained big windows. But outside, there was a sudden sharp chill to the air. We'd climbed less than 2,000 feet, but that included the difference between the hot, cramped streets and an open hillside facing the sea. You should be here in summer to get the real contrast.

Eleanor and Mitzi were shivering slightly, but still looking out over the spread-out lights of Beirut below. It's funny how, down there, you never seem overlooked by the hills, but up here you seem to be staring straight down the city's cleavage.

Ken came back from bargaining with the driver and said briskly: 'Any city looks beautiful from up high at night. Let's get in where the booze is free.'

Eleanor murmured: 'I bet he writes fairy stories in his spare time, too,' but she followed.

It was a big room, with a higher ceiling than you'd expect in that shape of house, bright and white-walled and not looking full with over thirty people standing around sipping and chattering. As we came in at the top of a small flight of steps, most turned to look at us.

I'd known Ken and I wouldn't be contending for the best-dressed award, but I'd put off thinking about it. Now we stood out like two witches at the Princess's christening. Almost everybody else – they were mostly men anyway – was in a neat city suit and crisp white shirt. The exceptions were a character in the gold-embroidered white robes of the Yemen and a cove who'd had his length of blue pinstripe cut into a normal jacket and a calf-length skirt; arab head-dress and sandals, of course. I'd seen the mixture before but it still gets me.

The door-opener in the white jacket was still wondering if we'd come to collect the garbage when our host bustled through the crowd with hand outstretched.

'You must be Mademoiselle Braunhof-Spohr, of course. And Mademoiselle Travis. Eleanor Travis of the Met? You don't know me but I've heard of you. And also ...?' He looked at Ken and me and held the smile with an effort.

He was shortish, with a comfortable round body in a dark blue-green silk suit and a surprisingly bony square face. It was as if forty-five years – I guessed – of good living had all sunk into his belly and left his chin and cheeks untouched. His hair was thin and dark, shading to pure white over his ears.

Ken said: 'Case and Cavitt. We fly aeroplanes. We brought the ladies to Beirut and they brought us up here. I hope we're not intruding.'

'Of course not, messieurs, naturally not. All friends of Ma'mzelle Spohr ... You must have a drink ...' Another white jacket materialised at his elbow with a tray. 'Champagne or gin and tonic for the ladies. And for the gentlemen ... ?'

'Scotch,' Ken said. 'I never know where I am with champagne.'

Aziz didn't get it, thank God, but smiled briefly and turned to Mitzi. 'And how is your dear father? Did he send you to see me?'

It wasn't long and it wasn't quiet, but it felt like a long silence to me. Eleanor stiffened, Ken froze, Mitzi's eyes sparkled darkly. She said calmly: 'My father died last night.'

It took a moment to sink into Aziz, and then, oddly, his first reaction was anger. He snapped his head from side to side. 'Why was I not told this? It must have been reported?' Then he recovered and turned back to Mitzi, taking her elbow protectively. 'But my dear, this is most terrible. You must sit down, tell me what happened ...' And he led her out through an arched doorway filled with a bead curtain.

Ken sipped and frowned. 'That boy's got class. Of a sort.' He grinned at Eleanor. 'And Miss Travis of the Met, I presume?'

She smiled automatically and rather artificially. 'Yes. If he knows the Met's staff that well ... he's no little grave-robber. You can see that anyway.' She nodded at the wall beside us.

It was long and plain white – most Beirut houses go in for more décor – and packed with alcoves, each holding some antiquity: a Greek vase, a curved sword, an amphora on a metal stand, a green-crusted bronze helmet.

'They mostly aren't medieval so I can't tell, but they look pretty valuable pieces. I don't know ...' she frowned and her voice trailed off.

The conversation around us had got buzzing again, together with some appraising glances at Eleanor. She might not know it, but her blonde Nordic good looks put her up with the Swiss franc as hard currency in Beirut. I planned on sticking by her; alone, I'd be ignored. Ken seemed to have the same idea.

A couple of minutes later we had a discussion group of a man from a pipeline company, a manager of an Italian bank branch, somebody to do with hotel management and a vulture in blue spectacles who said he was the Minister of this or that.

'I'm afraid I didn't quite gather what our host does,' I said to the hotel management, who was staring past me at Eleanor's chest.

'Some of everything,' he said without shifting his eyes. 'But the main family business is arranging and leasing concessions, you understand?'

'No.'

He glanced at me, a little impatiently since he'd rather be talking to Eleanor's cleavage. 'If you want to make Coca-Cola in the Yemen or build a Hilton in Aden, he will do the arrangements. Hilton know he will pick only good men to finance it, and the financiers know he will get good terms from Hilton. Then he puts in a little Aziz money for good faith and takes out a lot as his fee. Very simple.'

I nodded. 'All you need is to be a big man in a big family with a reputation going back five generations.'

He smiled briefly and maybe sourly. 'That is all.'

'I heard they were opening a Castle hotel out here ...'

This time his grin was quite genuine and satisfied. 'That is gone; busted. Pierre was not involved in that; he is not a fool. The English end let them down, and my poor friends who put money in do not know what to do. They were buying the name Castle and now it means failure.'

If his poor friends had fallen into the pool of the sacred crocodile he might have been happier, but only might.

I tried to make the next question sound vague and disinterested. 'Was a man called Uthman Jehangir involved in that?'

He looked at me sharply. 'Jehangir? Do you know him?'

'Met him in Cyprus once. He mentioned the Castle.'

He shook his head. 'He is not big enough. He is a sportsman – no, you would say playboy. A gambler. Perhaps they asked him to run the opening night party, to bring a film star. He

109

knows such people. But he would not put money in a long-term affair, even if they let him.'

I nodded and said: 'Uh-huh,' as if that finished Jehangir for me, too. And, nice man that I am, I gave my friend his reward: 'Eleanor, have you met Mr umm errr from the hotel business?'

On the edge of the crowd I found a waiter with a tray and prised another Scotch out of him and then stood there admiring the vast antique chandelier that didn't really fit with the modern teak or white furniture. But in Beirut you have to have one; it's as much a status symbol as a Rolls-Royce is to a pop singer. It was nice to know that even after five generations of success you don't get immune to it.

Ken drifted up beside me. 'Met anybody who knows God personally?'

'Not unless He's in the hotel business.'

He jerked his head at the archway. 'They're taking their time in—' But just then Mitzi and Aziz appeared. She looked pale, big-eyed and serious; Aziz just serious. He saw us, came over, and said in a low voice: 'Messieurs – if you could kindly help us . . .'

'Eleanor too?' Ken asked.

Aziz looked over to where she was under siege and smiled faintly. 'No, I think she seems busy enough. And – as yet – this does not concern the Met.'

He led the way back through the arch.

14

The husk of the house may have looked sharp and modern, but inside it had the thick cool walls, the stone floors and heavy doors of the traditional Middle East. We turned left at the end of the corridor and almost immediately through another arched doorway into a smaller, lower-ceilinged room.

If you wanted to pick it apart, it was an odd mixture of east and west: pottery jars turned into shaded lamps, embroidered leather cushions scattered over solid, square-cut Scandinavian furniture, Afghan rugs on the floor, a leather-topped antique French desk in a corner. But there was nothing self-conscious about it; the man himself was this mixture. So is Beirut, but not usually in such good taste.

He waved us to sit down, and I parked my glass on a hammered brass table top. Mitzi sat upright on the edge of her chair and said: 'He won't give me the sword.'

Aziz sighed gently and perched his wide backside on the corner of his desk. 'I have been trying to explain to Ma'mzelle Braunhof-Spohr that, until this evening, I had not heard of this sword. I did not know it existed until I saw this.'

'This' was a small sheet of paper covered in handwriting. Ken got up, took it, read aloud: *'Das Schwert das wir in der Gruft . . .'* I looked over his shoulder and saw it was a piece of St George's Hotel paper.

So our Mitzi hadn't taken any chances. She'd copied it out and put the original . . . ? Without the Prof's signature the paper was worthless, but Aziz would recognise the description as real.

Ken handed it back, his face quite calm. 'So?'

Aziz said: 'You were a friend of Professor Spohr?'

'We shared a cell in Beit Oren.'

Aziz smiled. 'Some of the best friendships of this century are formed in prison. However . . . did he talk to you of this sword?'

Ken shook his head. 'You don't talk about things like that in jail.'

'I understand. So now you are helping Ma'mzelle to track down . . . her inheritance, one might say.'

Mitzi burst out: 'My father found that sword! It is his . . . memorial!'

'Unhappily,' Aziz said gently, 'he found it with my money.'

*

Ken had his head cocked on one side, as if he was trying to identify a distant sound. Or idea, maybe. 'Say again, please. I didn't quite follow.'

Aziz opened a cedarwood box on the desk and took out a long thin cigar, then remembered his mànners and gestured the box to us. I shook my head, but dug out a pipe and started filling it. He struck a match, then looked at Mitzi. 'If Ma'mzelle does not mind . . . ?' He lit the cigar.

'An archaeological dig is, you must understand, a slow affair and therefore expensive. At times, one digs with a spoon, not a spade. And all the time, one must live, one must have assistance – these things cost money.'

'My father was not poor!' Mitzi snapped.

'You must know best, Ma'mzelle, but . . . he lived well. And a dig is also a speculation. Naturally no man wishes to sink all his capital into an affair that may have no return at all. So he treats it as a business matter and – one might say – issues shares.'

'You mean,' I said, 'the Israeli government let him dig there on money coming from the Lebanon?'

'Oh no.' He smiled. 'No, it was from a foundation in America. I have quite forgotten what name I invented . . . Birch . . . Birchwood . . . Birchbark . . . it does not matter. Most digs are backed by foundations, universities, museums, even governments.'

Ken said: 'And they all want a return on their money, too?'

'Not so much in the same way – but Professor Spohr was finding it a little difficult to get governments and museums to back him, by then.'

I glanced at Mitzi but she didn't seem insulted. Not happy, just not insulted.

There was a time of silence while everybody else thought and I lit my pipe. The smoke drifted away on a gentle current of air from a hidden air-conditioner. The only windows in the room seemed to be just above head level on the wall behind the desk, behind a length of heavy curtain.

Then Aziz got off the desk and waddled over and opened a wall cupboard full of bottles. 'Please help yourself, messieurs. Ma'mzelle?' And Mitzi held out her glass to be refilled.

Ken said thoughtfully: 'Bruno didn't contact you after he got out of Beit Oren?'

'No. I was a little sad, but I thought I would give him time.'

I'd expected Ken to follow that up, but he just said: 'Well, that seems to be that. You don't have the sword – that's it.'

Aziz said quickly but quietly: 'But no, not quite. You will understand – as a return on my investment, I want the original of the document.' And he held up the piece of St George's paper.

*

'You see?' Mitzi said bitterly. 'He must have the sword already.'

'No, no, no. That document itself is worthless until you have found the sword. But *then* – it ensures that I share in the profit. That must be fair, no?'

It sounded like it – assuming you believed the man, of course. I looked at Ken to see how he was taking it, and he was frowning uncertainly.

Then he said: 'But that cuts out Mitzi completely if you find the sword yourself.'

'I am hardly likely to, am I?' Aziz spread his neat pudgy hands. 'But I will also promise that she shares in the profit in any case. Half and half.'

We all looked at Mitzi, still sitting rigidly upright. She said: '*Scheisse.*'

Aziz stiffened where it hit him, then sighed and picked up the desk phone and said a few words.

Ken looked at me and I stayed slumped in the low chair. I had a good idea of what was coming and no idea at all of what to do about it.

It came in about twenty seconds. The heavy door jerked open and a man the shape and size of a concrete gatepost walked slowly in. He had dark emotionless eyes in a square jowly face, sleeked-back dark hair and a greasy grey suit that bulged where it touched him, which was most places.

'This is Pietro,' Aziz said, almost apologetically. Then he told Pietro something in Arabic and Pietro took out a fat stubby revolver and just held it, not pointing anywhere special.

Still with a hint of apology, Aziz said: 'Pietro is going to search you.'

Pietro did. First Ken, then I stood up for it. He did it efficiently, knowing what he was looking for. He passed all my papers to Aziz, now behind his desk, who just glanced through the documents about the Queen Air and its cargo and then stacked them neatly.

Our shoes, too. I was careful not to catch Ken's eye, partly because I didn't want to see what he was feeling, but mostly because I hadn't any bright ideas to pass on and I didn't want him to think I had.

Then Pietro turned to Mitzi.

She stood up with the slow, quivering stiffness of any angry kitten. 'If you make that ... that creature touch me, I will scream until—'

I said: 'Look, love, women have screamed before in this house and it hasn't done any good. Just relax.'

'Please, Mr ... er, Case,' this time Aziz looked really hurt. 'This is just a matter of business.'

So Pietro searched her, just as efficiently, running his fingers down here, squeezing there, feeling for the crackle of paper. It was about as sexless as being kissed by an alligator, but I don't suppose she enjoyed it any more.

When Pietro stood back, Aziz – who'd been searching her handbag – sighed again and said: 'I expected nothing, but ... one has to be sure. Now please, everybody sit down.'

So we sat while he dialled an outside number on the phone, then started giving what sounded like orders. I thought I heard the name 'St. George'.

Mitzi sat and steamed like a leaky pressure cooker, Ken was slumped almost horizontal, chin on chest but staring out from under his dark eyebrows at Pietro's gun. It had a thick short barrel, a long ramp foresight and the generally oversized look of a magnum calibre.

Ken muttered. '.357 Combat Smith.'

I nodded; he was probably right. The end of the butt sticking out of Pietro's fist had the typical Smith & Wesson shape, otherwise it could just as well have been a Colt to me. A pretty daft gun, mind you. In a two-and-something-inch barrel a bullet just doesn't have the time to work up the m.p.h. that a magnum cartridge can give, and you can hire somebody to whack your hand with a crowbar much cheaper than .357 ammunition costs.

For all that, Pietro looked as if you could mount a siege gun on him and he'd absorb the recoil.

Aziz finished his phoning, stood up and smiled tentatively at us. 'Now I really must join my other guests. I hope it will not be long before I have good news and you can go, but meanwhile . . .' he shrugged delicately and gave Pietro more orders. 'I have told him that you may help yourself to more drinks – but only one person to stand up at a time. You understand the problem, I am sure.'

He smiled once more, went out – and locked the door behind him. The click of the big key made me wince – and then I realised what it must do to Ken.

His face was pale, the muscles at his mouth and jawline bunched in white knots and his hands squeezing the sharp chair-arms.

I had to say something. 'Nice comfortable place we've got here,' I gabbled. 'All we want to drink, for free, feminine company, plenty to read, we'll be out of here in half an hour and I've spent longer waiting to be served in some bars.'

He took a deep breath and relaxed a fraction.

Mitzi said: 'But how can he do these things? We should go to the police straight away.'

I shook my head. 'This is the Middle East, love, and he's an important man. We're small-scale; we've got no family behind us.'

'They cannot have gangsters like *him*,' and she flicked her hand at Pietro.

'A bodyguard. Everybody who's anybody has them. Aziz must have three or four; they're as much status symbols as chandeliers. This is a gun-toting area. Your father knew that.'

'But they searched me – and locked us up!'

Ken stiffened again. I said quickly: 'They'd say they searched us for guns, of course. It may not be an offence anyway. As for

115

shutting us up – so prove it. Like another drink yet?'

She shook her head and relapsed into broodiness. When we were all quiet, Pietro walked across and sat down behind the big desk and laid the pistol in front of himself, within easy grab.

I said: 'Is your name Aziz or do you just work here?'

It took him a moment to realise I was speaking to him. Then he just grunted. I'd been pretty certain he didn't speak English, but wanted to be sure as I could.

I stood up carefully; Pietro put his hand on the gun – not nervously, just as a gesture. I waved my empty glass and looked thirsty and he nodded at the cupboard, and I went over and found myself a Scotch and a vacuum flask of chilled water.

That put me about ten feet from the desk, and the size of the desk itself made it another five feet to Pietro so I wasn't going to try throwing a drink in his face.

I just said conversationally to Ken: 'Nice big desk that. You could play table tennis across it.'

He looked up and there was a tiny light in his eyes. I went back and sat down and sipped. And studied the situation.

The desk was planted diagonally across a corner and well out from it. Ken was sitting a bit in front but almost in line with its length; nearly in line at the other end was the drinks cupboard and floor-to-ceiling shelves of expensive-looking books.

I left it for ten minutes and the room grew quiet and cool, almost cold, around us. Ken had his eyes shut and looked as if he was dozing.

Then I stood up, and Pietro put his hand back on the gun. I said: 'Can I get a book to read? Book – livre – libro—' I pointed at the shelves. 'What's the Arabic for "book"?'

'Koran?' Mitzi suggested uselessly.

'For God's sake.' I walked over and patted a row of books. 'May I?'

Pietro frowned slightly, as if he was thinking, then nodded heavily. I smiled graciously and began reading titles. It seemed to be solid history of the Middle East, and I do mean solid. A lot was in English, the rest in French or German, but I was picking for size rather than language. I took one or two down, pretended to glance at them, then chose a nice leather-bound volume a bit smaller than the average encyclopedia format. I think it was about Schliemann at Mycenae; anyway, it was in German. I opened it up and turned around.

As I moved, Pietro put his hand on the Smith, then took it away again. I didn't look at him. 'Hey, listen to this,' I said to Mitzi, and peered at the title page. 'I am not going to say Go or anything like that, but go when I shut the book. How d'you like that?'

'*What?*' She genuinely thought I'd got my brain caught in the wringer.

I grinned at her, slammed the book shut and skimmed it across the desk top. Ken was moving as it left my hand; he hit the floor on his knees and caught the revolver in mid-air. I heard the hammer come back with a firm snap.

Then Ken was back in the middle of the room to give himself space and Pietro was lifting slowly to his feet with a disbelieving expression. He took a step and looked at Ken and then another step.

Ken just spread his feet slightly and waited, the gun cocked but pointing loosely at the floor. Pietro took another step around the desk and his mouth worked a bit and he was walking through mud into the barbed wire and machine guns. Ken didn't make any move and he had no expression. A machine gun doesn't need one.

Pietro took a pace and there was suddenly a glitter of sweat across his forehead. The room was as quiet as an icicle but Pietro could hear thunder. His mouth came open and he tried to move his foot and did – by millimetres, like a man learning to walk again after a stroke, while the sweat bulged out on his forehead and dribbled down his face. And then he locked solid. For a moment his face showed he was trying to move forward, then some part of him snapped and he just stood there.

Ken lifted his left arm slowly and pointed to a chair and Pietro turned and took two exhausted steps and collapsed into it. Then, like a contracting muscle, his big square body turned slowly on its side and drew up into the foetal position.

He was no friend of mine, but I think that's the part I'd rather have missed.

Ken said: 'Touché,' and let the Smith's hammer silently down.

*

The door was impossible. It was built of seasoned timber at least a couple of inches thick and stiffened with ornate iron-work like an old castle. It was probably just Aziz's passion for the past – he could hardly have planned his study as a dungeon – but it came to the same thing for us.

Ken was behind the desk finding the cords to the strip of high curtain and pulling it back. Sure enough, there was a shallow window there but no way of opening it.

'We could stack up a few things and bust out through that,' he said.

'What's the rush? Don't you want to wait and talk to the nice Mr Aziz again, like he promised?'

He grinned and started jerking at the desk drawers. 'Okay, I'll stay if you think he'd be offended.'

Mitzi was just standing there, a little dazed by what had happened. 'But how,' she demanded, 'did you know that Mr Case would—'

'All those years on the halls,' Ken said. 'You never heard of Cavitt and Case, Astounding Telepathic Acrobats? ... The un-trusting bastard's locked most of these drawers.'

'Don't bust 'em,' I warned. 'And don't leave prints. We don't want to give him any legal squawk at all.'

He bounced the heavy pistol in his hand. 'You think he'll worry about that?'

'The most you can do is kill him. He'll still be a big man in a big family.'

He looked down at the gun and said sadly: 'Yes ... they don't change things as much as you think.' He glanced at Pietro, then laid the pistol down and started sorting through the one drawer he'd got open.

Mitzi said: 'But must we wait? Why do you not shoot at the door to make it open?'

'And spoil the party?' I asked. 'Anyway, that only works on T.V. Ken tried it once in Isfahan.'

He chuckled. 'Yes – bloody thing jammed the lock so solid they were still trying to open the door by its hinges when we left town.'

'Which admittedly wasn't all that much later,' I added,

The phone rang.

'No,' I said quickly, and Ken took his hand off it. 'He'll probably take it on an extension somewhere – and anyway, we wouldn't understand a word. But good news or bad, he'll come in here after.' The ringing stopped and we all stared at the phone.

Then I said to Mitzi: 'My guess is somebody's been searching your rooms at the St George. Will they have found it?'

She hesitated a moment, then shook her head slowly. 'No.'

'Is it in the hotel safe?'

Again a hesitation, again: 'No.'

'Well, I doubt if they could have got that opened, but probably they'll know you didn't use it. And I don't think they've had time to find where Ken and I are staying . . . Now he's got to come back and ask again.'

The phone tinged once. Ken stood up and said softly: 'Places for the Second Act, please.'

*

We should have thought of Aziz bringing a second man – another bodyguard – if the next step was to 'ask' us again. For those sort of games you need two.

But it didn't make much difference. As they froze in the doorway, Ken was up on his feet, the Smith held in both hands and sighting down it at Aziz's belly. 'Step inside and tell your friend to close the door.'

The new bodyguard was taller, leaner, older, but his sports jacket and trousers had the same greasy shabbiness of Pietro's suit. Some sort of caste system, I suppose. He glanced at Aziz, who told him something – the right something, since he pushed the door shut and just stood there.

Ken said: 'Tell him to give his gun to Roy. And if he wants to try and be clever, that's fine with me.'

Aziz passed it on, part of it, anyway. I walked across behind Ken and took the second gun. This cove was a little more humble about his personal artillery: all he had was a standard Colt Police .38 with a six-inch barrel, which was very much more my idea of a gun to hold if the voting got noisy. Not too easy to conceal, but they don't bother too much about that in Beirut anyway.

Aziz was staring puzzled at Pietro, who was still curled up and if he wasn't quite sucking his thumb, he might as well have been. 'What happened to—'

Ken said quietly: 'You locked me in.' The Smith was back pointing at Aziz's middle.

He may have gone a bit paler. 'I assured you it was only a temporary—'

'You locked the door.' Ken's voice was still quiet but his hands were white on the gun.

Aziz said: 'But of course, it was only—'

'You locked the door.'

'I am *telling* you—'

'You locked the door.' The statement had gone beyond meaning, now. Aziz twitched his head side to side, looking for help, a way out, just an explanation.

I said: 'Hold it, Ken. Let me talk to him. I'm loaded, too.'

For a long moment Ken just stared fixedly down the gun at the fat man's stomach. Then he let his hands drop. Aziz let out a shaky breath.

I said: 'We'll be leaving soon, so you'd better organise a car to get us down the hill.' I jerked my head at the telephone. 'We'll have to trust whatever you tell them, but you'll come out to see us off, so if you want to arrange a shoot-out ...' I shrugged.

Aziz nodded and went to the phone and gave a few brief orders, looked up at me.

'When we're out of here,' I said, 'You're back in charge again. What sort of deal are you offering Mitzi now?'

His thin face ran through a kaleidoscope of expressions: relief, suspicion, amusement. Then he spread his hands. 'Just as before: a fifty-fifty share, as I arranged with Professor Spohr, when you find the sword. But meanwhile, I must have the document for security.'

Ken snapped: 'You'll get it shoved up —'

'Hold it, hold it.' Then I shook my head at Aziz. 'No, I'm sorry. I might have voted for that before, but then you changed your way of doing business. You got a bit too crude and insensitive ...'

He winced; that must be one of the worst insults you can

hand a French-angled Lebanese. Let him suffer.

I went on: 'I think we're prepared to accept that you *did* back the Professor—'

'I can prove it,' he said. 'Of course, the documents are not here, but ...'

'Let's just say we accept it. And so, when and if Miss Spohr finds the sword, she will make sure you are fully refunded and, on top of that, properly rewarded.' I looked at Mitzi. 'Okay?'

At that moment, her ideas about proper rewards were running to lighted matches under fingernails, but she managed a brief grunt of: '*Ja.*'

I looked to Aziz and he looked back almost pityingly. 'You cannot expect me to accept that, when I have the original agreement signed by Professor Spohr which—'

'I haven't seen that agreement,' I said, 'but it must at least imply a conspiracy to commit a crime in another country, namely Israel, and namely the illegal export of an antiquity. In a Beirut court you might get that agreement to stand, you being the Aziz ben Aziz, and you might even make it binding on the Professor's heirs. But outside of Beirut, and depending on the texture of the paper, I very much advise you to use it to wipe your arse.'

There was a long strained silence broken at last by Ken's chuckle. 'You been studying for the Bar while I was away?'

'Only in them.'

Aziz said coldly: 'Do you expect me to trust you, then?'

I shrugged. 'We had to start off by trusting you.'

Ken said: 'Confucius he say: when pistols come in door, trust jump out of window forgetting trousers.' So he really was feeling calmer. But I still didn't want to leave him alone with Aziz.

'The car should be ready by now,' I said. 'Go and collect Eleanor.'

He looked doubtful, or maybe disappointed. 'Can you manage ...?'

'Of course. Get weaving.'

He went out. Aziz and the new boy looked at me, and after a time Aziz asked: 'Why was your friend so very angry?'

'Yesterday morning he came out of jail after two years. Every day they locked the door on him. So then you did, too.'

'*Mon Dieu.*' He went a bit paler. 'That was, as you say, insensitive of me. But what else could I do?'

'If you can't think of another way of doing business then you'd better get used to being on the wrong end of a gun.'

He thought this over, then said slyly: 'What would you do if I told Emile to take his gun back?'

'I've shot men before; one gets used to it. I mean me, not them.'

He didn't say anything more, and Emile had never looked as if he was in a volunteering mood anyway.

Then the door opened and Ken hustled in a rather bewildered Eleanor. 'What's all the rush about?' Then she sensed the stiffness in Aziz's and Emile's attitudes – and saw the gun in my hand. 'Great Jesus, has the rodeo come to town?'

'Just an old Lebanese business custom.' I reassured her.

'We're leaving by the back door,' Ken said. 'And like now. Ready to move?' He took his gun out of of his pocket.

'Emile stays here,' I told Aziz. 'You come with us, so I should advise him not to sound the sirens.'

Aziz told him something, then looked at Pietro, still curled up, eyes closed and far far away. In time, too. Instinctively, he lowered his voice: 'What did you do to him?'

'Nothing,' I said. 'He just wanted to take his gun back off Ken.' I locked the door behind us and gave Aziz the key. As we headed down the dim corridor away from the noise of the party, I said: 'Treat him gently. He may not be much of a bodyguard again, but I think he sort of died back then.'

15

The ride down the hill, in a big metallic-grey Mercedes, was a lot smoother than the journey up. And no problems, either. I'd wondered if Aziz might call the police and have us picked up for carrying illegal firearms, stealing a car, kidnapping a chauffeur and everything short of barratry and mopery. Then I'd decided he didn't want us in jail any more than we wanted to be there, and for once I was right.

Nobody said much until we were standing on the steps of the St George watching the car flow away in the cold lamplight. It wasn't even very late; not yet midnight.

Ken stretched and said: 'Well, one final jar before the dew falls?' He looked around us and Eleanor and I nodded.

Mitzi said: 'I think I will go to bed, please.'

'Your choice,' Ken said, and we walked up into the hotel – which was still as wide awake as high noon. 'But just as a matter of professional interest: where *is* that paper?'

Mitzi turned to Eleanor. 'You still have it?'

'The document about the sword? Sure.' And she dug in her big handbag and passed it over.

'Je-sus,' Ken said softly. 'If the bastard had only known ...'

'Was that what it was all about?' Eleanor asked.

'An animal searched me,' Mitzi said bitterly, stowing away the paper and then heading for the desk to pick up her key.

Ken looked at Eleanor. 'Didn't anybody try to take off *your* clothes?'

'Didn't they hell.' She looked a little warm. 'Enough of them *implied* the idea, though I don't think they were looking for bits of paper. You know there was another room, smaller and darker, where they had a little brazier thing burning?'

I felt a smile crawling on to my face and tried to frown it down.

'Did they?' said Ken innocently.

'They suggested I should stand over it, kind of; it was supposed to be ... well, aromatic.'

Ken grinned wickedly. 'And which one of us'll you have first?'

She blushed, really blushed.

'And modern science,' I said, 'proves there's no such thing as an aphrodisiac.'

She stared firmly at the lift doors while her blush faded. Mitzi came back with her key to say goodnight.

Ken said: 'For God's sake be careful with that piece of paper. Why not the hotel safe now?'

I said: 'No,' without quite knowing why except that it was an obvious place and I didn't think Aziz needed any help in thinking of obvious places.

'I will keep it okay,' Mitzi promised. Then she smiled, rather demurely. 'Thank you for being so brave, like knights.' She turned away into the lift.

Ken looked at me and raised his eyebrows. 'Gadzooks and forsooth.'

'Just show me the nearest dragon and stand aside.'

'Oh come on,' said Eleanor impatiently. 'She was just trying to say you smell like horses. Who's buying me a drink after dragging me away from all those lovely sexy men?'

As we headed towards the bar at the end of the lobby, Ken murmured: 'I can tell you of one quote maiden unquote who'd better not get immured in any foul dungeons if she wants to get rescued by Christmas.' We sat down and he thumped the table. 'Ho, varlet: two foaming goblets and a gin-and-moat for the damsel.'

'For goodness' sake,' said Eleanor, a bit embarrassed. 'What really happened up at the house, there? I didn't know you two had guns.'

'We didn't,' Ken said. 'We borrowed them off Aziz's body-guards.'

'He got a bit simplistic about wanting the authentication of the sword,' I explained.

'And he searched Mitzi?' She frowned. 'Well, I suppose there was nothing else you could do.'

It hadn't seemed quite that easy at the time, but Ken just said gravely: 'Not without turning in our keys to Camelot's executive washroom.'

The waiter appeared and we ordered; I switched to vodka, lime juice and soda, which doesn't taste of much but hasn't wiped its boots on your tongue the next morning.

'Aziz said one thing,' Ken said. 'That he'd financed Bruno's digging in Israel. D'you think that's true?'

'It's likely,' Eleanor agreed. 'I'd wondered if that was the connection. It isn't just the money, it's that governments don't give permission to one-man-bands. An archaeologist needs some sort of endorsement. What did Aziz do – set up some phoney foundation?'

Ken nodded. 'In the States.'

'That figures. So now he wants his cut, does he?'

'That or the whole cake.'

I said: 'Mitzi's still convinced Aziz has the sword. Question: is she right?'

They thought about this while I looked around the bar. About half the seats were occupied, mostly with Beirut residents in standard dark suits (but not Lebanese, who don't use even the best bars much; these were Europeans and Americans) plus a few tourists in brighter gear. None actually looked like Aziz's boys, though he could well have planted one. He might want to know where Ken and I were staying.

The waiter brought our drinks and, when he'd gone, Eleanor said: 'Now we know Aziz is really involved, that he wasn't just looking after the sword while Spohr was in jail – then I'd say No, he doesn't have it. It's a guess, but I just think we'd have heard something before this.' She glanced from Ken to me and back, her blue eyes very serious.

Ken nodded slowly. 'If he *has* got it, then Bruno didn't know he had. There'd be no point in involving me and an aeroplane. Aziz is big enough to get the sword out of this country a hundred ways without my help. I say he hasn't got it . . . Buggerit,' he added.

That made it fairly unanimous. I said: 'So the poor bastard was being honest, in his own way.'

Ken looked up sharply. 'It's that *way* of his that I didn't take to.'

'Quite so, quite so. And I think he's going to spend the night thinking up his next move rather than fasting and praying to change for the better. And if he hasn't got the sword, is there any reason to think it's in the Lebanon at all?'

'If it is,' Ken said gloomily, 'we stand damn-all chance of finding it compared with him. I see what you mean; fingers out and wheels up.'

'Huh?' said Eleanor.

I said: 'You seem fairly fireproof so you can make up your own mind, but Cavitt and Case announce their departure for Cyprus as soon as possible tomorrow. And I think Mitzi'd be a fool to stay, so if you can persuade her the sword isn't here . . .'

'If I can't,' she said dryly, 'I'm sure I can convince her that her parfit gentil knights have suddenly gotten dragon-shy.'

'It's quite a nice face,' said Ken, 'but she ought to get the mind broken and re-set.'

Eleanor just grinned. Then: 'But if the sword isn't here, where is it?'

That brought down the glooms like a cloudburst. Ken's face shut tight, then he finished his Scotch with a quick jerk of his head and stood up. 'That was today. Coming, Roy?'

He walked out.

Eleanor stared after him. 'What did I *say*?'

'Israel – or almost.' I swallowed my own drink. 'That's the one place he can't go back to. When they let him out of jail they deported him.' I stood up. 'We'll be round here about eight. Be packed if you're coming.'

*

It was a five-minute walk to our hotel, but we did it in ten to make sure nobody was following. The night clerk stopped picking his teeth long enough to hand over our key and, as an afterthought, a message: *Ring Uthman Jehangir not after 2 a.m.* It gave the number.

'Who in hell's he?' Ken asked.

'Met him in Nicosia. He wanted to buy some champagne off me.'

'Ah. D'you think . . .?'

I shrugged, looked at my watch: only half past midnight. 'I suppose I'd better ring him, since he knows we're in town.' Probably he'd asked for me in Nicosia and then followed on the evening flight. He could have found out our hotel from the control tower: you always let them know where you're staying.

But now I certainly hadn't got the twenty-four hours' grace I was hoping for.

Ken said: 'I'll go on up and kill a few spiders,' and went. There weren't any room phones so I made the call from the desk, with the clerk no more than a yard away and his breath a lot closer.

Jehangir himself answered.

I said: 'It's Roy Case: you left a message . . .'

'Of course! Delighted to hear from you. Very glad you could get to Beirut.'

'It was a last-minute decision. I got a sort of charter . . .'

'Fine. But now we can get down to business. Why don't we meet at the races tomorrow afternoon? You know the track?'

'Yes, sure . . .' I didn't want to meet Jehangir, not in his own town, but we'd made enough enemies for one night. 'Okay, then. About two-thirty?'

'Just fine. Until then.'

I rang off and the clerk carefully wrote the item down on our bill.

I was careful to say 'It's me,' before I went into the room; sure enough Ken had the gun half pointed. He was stripped to his shorts – once gaudy red-and-yellow stripes, now faded and torn – and his body looked bony and pale.

'What was all that about?' he asked.

'Business. I said we'd meet him at the races tomorrow afternoon.' I locked the door behind me.

'What?'

'Just keeping him happy. I can forget.' I began to undress.

It was a small room, maybe ten by eight, but even then the two beds weren't big enough to crowd it. The Castle rooms had been old-fashioned and worn; this place had started cheap and nasty and worked its way down. Ken climbed in between the patched grey sheets that felt like damp sandpaper and sighted the Smith at the ceiling light.

I said: 'There's less noisy ways. Are you going to sleep with that bloody thing?'

'Probably.'

'Couldn't you borrow the clerk's teddy-bear? – at least it

wouldn't blow my head off when you have a bad dream.' I climbed into my own bed. 'Are you going to hang on to it?'

'I don't take off my coat in the rain. Aren't you keeping the Colt?'

I shook my head. 'I've got enough problems in this town without getting caught with a gun, too. Anyway, nobody wants us dead.'

He propped himself up on one elbow. 'Your funeral. But I tell you what, give me those three-eight rounds.'

So I fished the Colt out of my jacket and shook out the cartridges. A .38 will fit a magnum .357 – it's identical calibre, really – but not vice versa: they make the magnum rounds too long to fit into, and probably blow up, an ordinary .38. I passed them over and he stuffed them into the big Smith.

Actually, it wasn't a bad idea. Now, with a heavy gun and a – relatively – light cartridge he'd be a lot more accurate for not much loss of power and far less kick.

I lay back again. 'Happy now? Glass of water? Bedtime story?'

'Stuff it.'

I turned off the light. 'If you dream anything good, ask if she's got a sister.'

*

He dreamed, all right, but not that. I woke as his feet thumped on the floor, and snapped on the lamp. He was sitting on the bed, head down almost on his knees and his whole body covered in sweat as if it had rained on him. His right hand was locked, white-knuckled, around the gun.

He was swearing to himself, just a long rhythmic mumbling curse.

I said gently: 'You were back inside?'

He lifted his head slightly, wiped the hair back off his forehead. 'I was back. Shit. I'm not going back. I'm just not going to go.'

'Was it bad in there?'

'Ahhh . . . not like some you hear about. They didn't treat us like animals, just like things. We just had to be there, to be counted at the stock-taking. You knew you could never *decide* anything; you'd wake up in the night and think "Tomorrow

128

I'll—" and then remember you couldn't. It was the nights – and the walls. I'm not going back to that.'

He waved the pistol in a gentle, meaningless gesture. But it was something he could control, could use to control events. Maybe sleeping with it made a sort of sense, after all.

Then he asked: 'We don't have a bottle, do we?'

'Sorry.' I wished I'd thought of it, even at Beirut prices for Scotch.

'I'll be all right.' He stood up shakily, found a rag of hotel towel and wiped the sweat off. Then lay down, looking at the ceiling.

When he spoke, his voice was normal again. 'It's funny – when you come out you want to shack up in some place like the Ledra or a Hilton. But you know something? – even this bed's too soft for me. Bloody silly.'

After a pause, he added: 'Mind, in every other way I've had enough of crummy joints like this.'

'We've stayed in worse as often as better.'

'We were younger. There was still time for the good times to come.'

'Stop feeling your age; you'll make it fall off. That's just three-in-the-morning talk.'

'Maybe.' He rolled over and shoved the gun back under the pillow. 'Sorry, Roy. I'm okay.'

Perhaps. Anyway, he didn't wake me again.

16

The morning was clear, blue and calm, though that meant a sea breeze later if it stayed sunny. It's the best time of day in the Middle East, before the dust and smells and tempers have begun to rise. You feel even a taxi would only run you down by accident.

We checked out and, with only hand baggage, walked around to the St George, losing my Colt in a dustbin on the way. The doorman gave us a friendly salute and we went straight on up to the third floor. The girls had rooms looking inland, back over the front door, and in shade at that hour, so they were break-fasting on Eleanor's balcony.

She'd thought to order four cups and an extra pot of coffee, which did a lot for Ken's mood. I'd matched him drink for drink the day before and it had been well spread out, but I think he'd woken with a touch of the little green men. But at least the 3 a.m. mood had passed.

'That's real New World hospitality,' he said cheerfully, pour-ing us both cups. 'Who but an American would have thought of it?'

'A Viennese,' Mitzi said coolly. She was slumped in a wicker chair wearing a frilly nylon house-coat that wasn't quite tran-sparent but gave me the idea she was fairly well dressed under-neath it.

Which was fine; I didn't want to hang around longer than we had to.

'Have you two ever visited the States?' Eleanor asked.

'Sure,' Ken said. 'We did the whole works, when we were in the RAF. We saw Offutt Air Force Base, and Scott Air Force Base, and Edwards Air Force Base, and Maxwell Air Force Base, and what was that place in Alaska? and the Lockheed plant in Georgia . . .'

'And the Body Shop on Sunset Boulevard,' I added.

'That's right, they left the cage door open that night and we were off before they could rouse the National Guard. We've been around, kid, we've seen the whole deal.'

Eleanor grinned. 'You should write a book, like everybody else.'

'See volume four of my memoirs.'

Mitzi gave a little sideways smile and said: 'I did not see a man get drunk on coffee before.'

I held up my wrist and stared obviously at the watch. 'The countdown has started. Who's coming?'

Both girls stood up in chorus. Mitzi said: 'I will finish in a minute,' and zipped out.

I said: 'Any word from the old man of the mountain?'

Eleanor shook her head. 'Nothing. I'll just close up my case and call a porter.' She went back into the room.

Ken poured the last of the coffee. 'I don't like it.'

'You mean it's quiet out there?'

'Yes. Too quiet.'

In fact, the Rue Minet Hosn below was anything but: just now it was a whirlpool of whining, squawking traffic. But there was so much of it and it was all so ordinary and self-centred that Aziz's finanglings seemed pale and feeble, a ghost in daylight.

I said: 'Perhaps he just ran out of nasty ideas.'

But he hadn't.

*

'What exactly does that say?' Eleanor asked.

She can't really have meant that since the document was written in both Arabic and French and a lot of legal pomposities besides, so I gave her the quick-lunch version: 'It's a sort of court order – a *saisie-conservatoire* – attaching the aeroplane. Freezing it here.'

'So we don't fly?'

'Not in this aircraft.' I looked at the deputy airport manager – we were sitting in his office – and asked: 'Does this affect any of us personally?'

'Not that I know of.' He was a thin, good-looking man with a sharp widow's peak of black hair, and a half-apologetic, half-intrigued attitude to our troubles.

I looked back at the document. 'It's bloody silly. He claims Miss Braunhof owes him money so he gets an order seizing somebody else's aeroplane.'

The deputy manager spread his hands in mock surrender. 'Please, it does not help to tell me. You must tell the court.'

'On Saturday?' Ken said.

I said: 'Aziz obviously wasn't keeping court-room hours. He got hold of some judge at home—'

'There was one at the party,' Eleanor chipped in.

'Easier yet. And he convinces him he's got a claim and he gets an *ex parte* order.'

'What is that?' Mitzi asked.

'Without the other side needing to be there,' Ken said. 'But hell, a court won't give an injunction or order unless there's a proper case being brought.' He looked at Mitzi. 'You haven't been served a summons or something like that?'

She shook her head.

I said: 'It seems that doesn't work in French law. This *saisie-conservatoire* lapses in five days *unless* he's started an action *de recouvrement de dette* by then. Is that right?'

The deputy manager nodded gently. 'Our civil code is still mostly the French pattern.'

'But is it going to stick?' Eleanor demanded.

He smiled sadly at her chest. 'I am afraid I have to enforce it.'

Ken said: 'It's a plain bloody swindle.'

I stood up. 'Come on. Let the man get on deputy managing. We've got time for coffee now.'

*

So at takeoff time we were sitting in the airport café finishing a second breakfast, Eleanor frowning over a xeroxed copy of the order. 'As I see it, we just get hold of some lawyer to represent us—'

'On Saturday?' Ken said again.

'—and then get hold of this judge. I guess that's his signature at the bottom—'

'And he'll have gone fishing.'

'—and get the order lifted.' She gave Ken a stiff look.

I nodded and began lighting a pipe. 'That's how it would go in London or New York, and Aziz would get his balls in solitary confinement for making a fool of the court – forgive the legal language. But this is Beirut. Aziz knows what he's doing: he wants us stuck here. We can run around until we turn blue and I bet we get no action for five days.'

'What will he have done by then?' Mitzi asked. She looked a little pale, and I wasn't blaming her. She was the one Aziz was after; Ken and I were just obstacles and, on the morning's showing, not much of that.

I shrugged. 'I dunno. He must already have tried to get you arrested—' she went positively white; '—but even a Beirut judge probably wouldn't wear that.'

Eleanor was back studying the order. 'At least it shows how much he lent your father.'

'How much?' Mitzi asked shakily.

'Twelve thousand dollars, US.'

It didn't sound much, not in one way. In another, it sounded like the cost of space flight. 'Even if we'd got it, it isn't really what he wants. It's that document. Except if we could pay twelve thousand into the court they'd free the aeroplane.'

Ken suggested: 'Why not put up Eleanor as a bond? In Beirut she must be worth—'

She straightened her back, chin and breasts pointing a broadside at him. 'And why not your own mother?'

I said: 'Oh, he traded her in years back, when she still had some mileage left on—'

'For God's sake be serious!' she snapped.

I slapped my hands on the table, tilted back my chair and said: 'Right, one serious thought coming up. We catch the lunchtime flight for Cyprus. Let him have the aeroplane – it isn't ours, anyway. In a way, that order's our safe-conduct. It implies he'd settle for the aeroplane, so if we give him that . . .'

Ken shook his head. 'Hell, no, Roy. I just hate to let go of an aeroplane – and it won't look good on your reputation, bugging out so easy.'

He had a point there. 'So, let the girls take the flight. We stay here and see what we can do. It'll be more without you hanging on our sword arms.'

Eleanor looked momentarily wistful, then resigned herself. 'I guess that's the best idea.'

Mitzi still looked worried. 'Herr Aziz . . . he will not stop us leaving?'

He might try. One thing he'd almost certainly do was have a man sitting around the airport to see what we did next.

I slapped the table. 'Third great thought coming up. We give you back to the deputy manager; he'll get the tickets for you on the quiet. May I?' I leant across and undid another button on Eleanor's blouse. 'Now he wouldn't hand you over to God or the Gestapo.'

*

Ken and I lunched in one of the little Arab cafés up on the Corniche de Chourane by the new hotels built by and for the gulf oil sheikhs. It isn't the European end of town, but we wanted to stay clear of obvious places. We hadn't been followed from the airport, but they could have been so bad that they'd lost us by accident.

'After all,' I said, 'Aziz isn't a mobster. He doesn't have real professionals on his staff; he's just improvising with what he's got.'

'There's some hard boys around Beirut, and I don't mean those jazzy guerrilla groups.' We were eating a cold *mezze* sort of thing: spicy olives, pickled cucumbers, houmus, sliced Kafta sausage and other cold meats. It was pretty good, though maybe not as much as Ken thought it was. Anything that wasn't served with four stone walls around it still tasted like the day you lost your virginity.

'They're there,' I agreed, 'but Aziz himself wouldn't know them, and he might be careful not to know the people who do know them. He's doing all right in straight business and he'd screw himself if he went in for the narcotics and prostitution and stuff.'

He looked up from his plate, unconvinced. 'How d'you know he isn't in already?'

'Because he's too vulnerable. The boys in those trades don't believe in competition, and the easiest way to get rid of him would be to send out a whisper that he *was* involved. He's got to talk to people like Hilton and Sheraton and Coca-Cola and any smell of dope-peddling and white-slavery would rub off on them. They'd be looking for a new contact man as from yesterday.'

Ken stuck an olive in his mouth and chewed it with grudging agreement. 'All right, so from nine to five he loves small animals and big children. What was he doing after hours last night?'

The café doors swung open and a couple of well-built characters in bulging lightweight jackets stood looking coldly around. The waiters froze in a relaxed, familiar way, and everybody else gave one glance and then looked at their plates.

The bodyguards' eyes fixed on us, the obvious strangers. Ken's right hand crawled on the table.

I hissed: 'Keep still. You know the form in this town.'

He nodded and relaxed. A small, tubby man in a blue silk suit and Arab head-dress walked in between the tough guys, and the proprietor made a small gesture towards a reserved corner table. The bodyguards watched us warily as they followed him across.

The room quickly got back to its normal murmuring and clattering. 'Cheap millionaire,' Ken commented. 'What were you saying about Aziz?'

I shrugged. 'He turned rough when he thought he was getting cheated. You know what these types are like: they'll lose thousands on some crazy gamble, they give it away in handfuls inside the family – but you cheat them out of a penny and they feel you're trying to castrate them.'

Ken finished his plate-load except for the houmus. 'Who was cheating him, then?'

'We were – in way. If we'd let the post go through, and Sergeant Papa had, too, that authentication would've gone straight to Aziz.'

Ken grunted. I went on: 'And before that, the Professor himself was.'

'Oh, come off it, Roy.'

'Well, I'll give you odds Aziz thinks so. Look: the Prof found the sword over a year ago, right? Some time before he got arrested, anyway, because he had time to get it hidden and have that authentication drawn up. Yet he never told Aziz anything, not then, not after he got out of jail and that was six weeks ago.

What d'you expect Aziz to think? He's got twelve thousand dollars on this horse and the jockey cuts him dead in the street.'

Ken shook his head. 'You're trying to have it both ways. You can't say Bruno was cheating by not sending him the authentication when we know he was.'

'So he changed his mind. We know he changed it enough to shoot himself: suicide isn't long-term planning.'

'Or is, if you look at it another way,' Ken said gloomily. 'You still prefer a suicide verdict?'

I shrugged. 'I'm not the coroner. But posting that letter sort of fits. Irrevocable step and all that.'

'It's still bugger-all use if it doesn't tell you where the sword is. And you're only taking Aziz's word that Bruno didn't contact him.'

'I suppose I am.' And I began wondering why I was.

'Still,' he perked up and snapped his fingers for the waiter, 'that isn't our immediate problem. We've got to get the aeroplane out of hock.'

I looked at my watch. 'They should just have taken off – but we don't make any move until we've confirmed they got on that flight.'

'Agreed.' He did a quick check of the bill and dealt some scruffy notes on to the table. 'Then what?'

'Should we try for a lawyer?' I asked.

'Hell, no; the length of a lawsuit increases by the square of the lawyers involved. Aziz'll have enough already. Anyway, this town doesn't work on law, it works on pull. We need some pull.'

'And where do we find that on a Saturday afternoon?'

He looked slyly happy. 'At the races? We never cancelled that date there . .'

17

Beirut Hippodrome is a fairly standard sort of course for that end of the world: an oval sand track with a fancy colonnaded wooden stand on the south side by the finish, an open-air café next to it and the ring and stables and stuff somewhere behind that. Two things make it different: you come in through the north gate so you have to walk clear across the track to reach the stand, and most of the middle is a forest so that spectators can't see the north side and most of the last turn to home.

Some say this is so you won't notice what's happening on the back straight, others that it's a bluff to make you think something's happening there instead of it all being arranged beforehand by *le Combine* with its go-go and stop-stop pills. Oddly, the locals don't seem to get angry about this: *le Combine* is just another factor to consider along with the jockey, recent form, hard or soft going, distance, whether Orion is in Venus and whatever else racegoers worry about.

Me, I have no opinions bar one: that the first time I bet on a Beirut horse it'll be because I saw a tout in a vision and he had nail-holes in his wrists and ankles.

We just missed the first race, so by the time they let us across the track people were drifting back from the rails tearing up tickets and calling for another jar. The stand looked about half full, the café area more so, with Jehangir at a front table, his tin leg stuck stiffly out and his smile gleaming in the sunlight. He waved us in and I introduced Ken and we sat down.

'Three more beers,' Jehangir called, and a crumpled old waiter took off at a hand-gallop. For once, our style of dress – if that's what it was – didn't seem too far out of place. Royal Ascot this wasn't, though there were still a number of city suits around. But Jehangir himself was in candy-pink trousers and striped shirt, and a lot of the crowd had had similar ideas.

'You see that man in the glasses?' Jehangir pointed inconspicuously. 'Seventeen years ago, he assassinated the President of Syria.' He seemed pleased by the thought, like a man recommending a horse. The man looked fiftyish, but still lean and hard; a policeman wearing a carbine that had gone green, I mean *green*, around the breech wandered up, saluted the assassin smartly. Jehangir nodded approvingly.

Our drinks arrived. Jehangir said: 'Now we can drink beer and talk champagne. But first, you must let me mark your cards for you.'

We hadn't even bought race-cards, since they come only in Arabic – which tells you about how many tourists come here – but Jehangir bent studiously over his own. 'I know nothing about the second, but in the third and fifth, ah . . .'

I said: 'On her death-bed, my mother made me promise never to take sweets from strangers or advice from friends.'

Jehangir grinned. 'You will die rich.'

'I'm sure half of that's true.'

Ken asked: 'Are you feeling lucky or knowledgeable?'

Jehangir shrugged deprecatingly. 'A little of both. But surely you don't believe all these stories about *le Combine* that one hears from losers?'

'I knew a man here who bought an ex-racehorse, just for some exercise, and he swore it wouldn't get up in the morning without him shouting "The joint's raided!"'

Jehangir grinned automatically. 'Who wants to hear stories about honest dealing and hard work?'

'Not me,' Ken assured him, and both of them smiled.

I said: 'Were you doing any work for Castle Hotels when they were still in business?'

He bent his head gracefully. 'They asked me to be host on the opening night – and bring a few friends from Rome. Some say I run the best non-political party in Beirut.'

I nodded. So the 'champagne' would originally have been delivered, maybe not direct to him, but certainly close to him. I glanced at Ken and knew he was following the same thought-prints.

Jehangir looked at his fingernails. 'Am I to take it, from your arrival in Beirut, that Mr . . . er, Kapotas is no longer an interested party?'

Ken said: 'He's a busy man, a lot of things on his mind. We don't want to see him overworked. You know how it is?'

'Oh, I know,' Jehangir said softly. Then, to me: 'So, if all the documentation is still complete, one might just go ahead as if nothing as heart-breaking as Castle's failure had happened?'

'One *might*,' I said.

'Apart,' he added, 'from the matter of the delivery charge?'

So then a tall young black man in blue jeans came up to the table and gave Jehangir a wad of money the size of a club sandwich. Ken stared. 'Jesus. Was that the first race?'

Jehangir flapped the wad casually. 'It looks more than it is. But you haven't met Janni, have you?'

The Negro shook hands and gave me a quick, slightly uneasy smile showing a lot of very white but uneven teeth. He was very dark, with a bluish sheen on his skin but a sharper nose than you'd expect; East Africa, somewhere, which went with a Muslim name. That apart, he had shoulders like a bulldozer blade and a chest like a concrete mixer, but carried his weight lightly.

'Gentlemen,' Jehangir said gravely, 'you have just shaken hands with the next heavyweight champion of the world.'

Now I could see the thin pale scars above and below the eyes. Janni smiled again, but not until we looked at him.

Ken sounded impressed. 'Are you a fights manager as well?' It fitted, of course: horses, Via Veneto parties, boxers – they went together. And boxes of guns, too?

Jehangir lit a cigarette and waved it. 'Only for the best. Janni boxed on the Ethiopian team at the Olympics, but went down with flu in the second week. I was the only one who'd spotted him by then. If he'd gone through and won, of course, the Americans would've got him. And given him ten fights in six months and ruined him.'

I asked: 'What's the score so far?'

'Fourteen fights in two years, and we've won the last nine in a row, mostly inside the distance.' I love that 'we' you get from managers, just as if they'd been in there, too, throwing left hooks with their cigars. 'Next month to Rome, and once we've won that, the Sporting Club in London.'

'Tomorrow, the world,' Ken murmured, looking at Janni.

Jehangir nodded. 'But Janni hardly speaks any English yet. And why rush it? So far he can't understand what stupid questions sports writers ask nor what rubbish they write.' Nor read account books where somehow the boxer ends up with minus ten per cent of the take.

The crowd stirred and several people stood up from tables around us: a line of stubby, sawn-off horses was walking out between us and the stands, jockeys in the driving seats, one in green silks who could have switched weights with his horse and the records book would never have noticed a thing.

Jehangir hauled himself upright, said: 'Excuse me, gentlemen, just one moment,' and walked stiffly off to get a closer look. Janni went with him, carefully blocking people from bumping the master's left leg.

Ken said: 'Give me five pounds to put on that fat jock. There's no way he can be honest.'

'My mother's dying words were: "If you lend money for gambling it's a hundred to six you'll never get it back".'

'Gabby old bat on her death-bed, wasn't she?' Then, with no change of voice, he went on: 'I'd said nobody hit anybody on the chin except on TV. I forgot about trained boxers.'

I rubbed my chin and nodded. 'And Jehangir knew I'd got all the documents. Well, if the kid ever makes world champion I'll remember to feel honoured.'

'Not in a million years. Not if his eyes get cut like that at this level of competition. Two real fights and he'll be learning English by Braille. What are we asking as a delivery price?'

'Let's see what he suggests about shaking the aeroplane loose.' I lit a pipe and leaned back comfortably. The sun was pleasantly warm but no more, and the air smelled only faintly of horses. A young waiter hurried around putting fresh charcoals on the pans of the hubble-bubble pipes that stood beside half the tables; you just plugged in your own mouthpiece and took a drag. Simple; I keep on meaning to try it sometime.

By and by the horses cantered off to the start, Janni hurried away to the Tote and Jehangir came and sat down again.

Ken said: 'I thought you didn't know anything about this race?'

Jehangir grinned and shrugged. 'I can't resist any race. Now – we were talking about a delivery price, I think.'

I said: 'There's a snag: the aeroplane's been sort of confiscated.'

Jehangir went stiff and expressionless.

'Only a tiny bit sort of,' Ken reassured him, and passed over the copy of the court order.

The crowd grunted the Lebanese version of 'They're off,' but Jehangir went on reading. Even when the rest of us got up and stood on our chairs to watch the finish, which was nicely choreographed into a tight bunch with our fat friend in front by a nose. Mind, his horse could have dropped dead twenty yards before and they'd still have won on combined inertia.

The sand cloud settled and Ken shook his head at me. 'The next time you get your mother on the ouija board, pass her a message from me, will you?'

Jehangir looked up. 'How did you get on the wrong side of the Aziz family?'

'Do they frighten you?' Ken asked.

'Only like a big truck: no problem if you can see it coming.'

Ken grinned. 'It's a frame, of course. Mitzi – the lady mentioned there – her father *may* have taken twelve thousand from Aziz to finance an archaeological dig, but that's nothing to do with us anyway: we just gave her a lift to Beirut.'

Jehangir nodded gently. 'Of course. I heard about her father's suicide in Cyprus.'

I'd forgotten he'd been in Nicosia perhaps as late as we were, and I rather think Ken had, too.

Ken said: 'She's on her way back to Cyprus now, so we can't count on any help from her ... Any steps you think we should take?'

The line of horses walked back past us, led by the fat boy, who at least had the decency to look a bit uneasy. Jehangir just sat frowning at the paper.

At last he said: 'This is a nuisance. I hoped to be able to unload this evening. I suppose I could try talking to Aziz himself ... point out that the lady has gone, that by keeping the plane here he's only causing you unnecessary trouble ...'

'I don't think,' I said, 'he much minds about that.'

Jehangir raised an elegant white eyebrow. 'Ah – it's gone that far, has it? Well, I'll try ringing him anyway. I might persuade him to release the cargo, at least.'

Ken said: 'I've just thought of a much simpler way: you give us twelve thousand dollars as a delivery fee, we give it to Aziz – and bingo, everybody's happy.'

Jehangir was staring at him, mouth drooping. Then he closed it with a snap and swallowed. 'Actually, that sounds to me rather a complicated way – as well as making for somewhat expensive champagne. Let me see . . . at a thousand a box that would be . . . er, just over $83 a bottle. I know champagne's been going up quite frightfully these last few years, but . . .' And he smiled appraisingly at Ken. He'd only been talking to give himself time to think.

'It's a rather special champagne,' Ken said quietly. 'And in fact it isn't twelve boxes any more. One got opened in Cyprus by mistake.'

'Ahh,' Jehangir nodded; but by now he'd been expecting something like that. 'What happened to that box, do you know?'

I said: 'The man who opened it, he doesn't really appreciate that class of wine. So he – laid it down, as it were. His grandchildren's grandchildren might find it, but not until then.'

Jehangir's mouth twitched, but he said gravely: 'Splendid. If one doesn't understand these rare vintages, one shouldn't touch them. I suppose we *are* talking about Mr Kapotas?'

I nodded.

Jehangir went on: 'But that makes things even more expensive: we're up to . . . to ninety dollars a bottle, now. I hope and believe that I'm a good trader – so does everyone in Beirut – but that's going a bit high for even my customers.'

'The trouble is,' Ken said, 'that nothing less than twelve thousand is any practical use to us.'

'Just to get your plane out of the pawn-shop? If you wait a few days it'll fall back into your lap. The court can't keep up the pretence of this order for long. It may cost you a couple of hundred dollars in legal fees, but you might well recover that, too. Or were you wanting to get Mr Aziz out of Miss Braunhof-Spohr's affairs entirely?'

'Something like that,' Ken admitted.

'It's very noble of you.'

Ken smiled bleakly and said: 'I was thinking that you wouldn't be buying just the stock but also, as you might say, the goodwill.'

'Ahh.' Jehangir nodded slowly. 'That puts it very nicely. But you don't seem to have considered that I've already bought quite a lot of goodwill in connection with this cargo. Possibly more than you have. I don't think my name is on any of those documents Mr Case carries?'

He looked at me and the best I could do was shrug.

Jehangir beamed at me. 'I thought not.' Then Janni came back with a sombre expression and no wad of notes. Jehangir waved him to a seat. 'You can't win them all, can you?'

He was looking at Ken, but I said: 'That's what my mother told me. What d'you suggest now?'

'That I contact Mr Aziz and see what we can work out. Then I contact you. Will you be at the hotel?'

'We'd better be, hadn't we?'

'Good. Would you care to leave the manifest and so forth with me? – It might speed things along.'

'I'm not in that much of a hurry.'

Jehangir gave me one of his quick grins. 'Now, I must think about the third race.'

I stood up, but Janni was on his feet first. His English might be lousy, but he was a good enough fighter to smell the change of mood. He just stood there, shifting his weight from foot to foot.

Ken stood up slowly, his face clenched tight. Jehangir grinned at him, too, and said: 'You will still have a delivery fee, of course. It will cover a few days in Beirut and any legal fees. And you will get the plane back – unless Castle does, first.'

Ken said quietly: 'What happened to your leg?'

Jehangir tapped his thigh gently, getting a muffled tinny noise. 'They do a very good job, these days. Light alloy with a glass-fibre socket moulded exactly to your stump so it can be held on by pure suction; brilliant. I actually had this fitted in England, at Roehampton. Oh yes – I lost the original to a bit of stray firing in the 1958 troubles.'

Ken nodded. 'Not something that's still going around, then.'

'Oh no.' Jehangir looked at him carefully. 'No, I don't think so.'

143

As we walked away I said: 'Never try to blackmail a gambler: he's accustomed to risking the odds.'

'Who told you that? No, don't say it.' His face was still stiff. 'The bastard. The swindling sod.'

'Hell, you said yourself the guns had probably been mostly paid for. Why should he spring another twelve thousand?'

'You took all the risks without being paid for them. I was just standing up for your rights.'

'Yes? Well, if my rights happen to feel tired, you just leave 'em lay. D'you think we should let him have those guns?'

'Why? – d'you want them for yourself?'

The gate to the path across the course was open so we walked out through the men raking the sand smooth again, along with a few punters who'd seen the light after just two races. But there were still twice as many hurrying in the opposite direction.

I said: 'I'd trust me with them more than I would him. Anyway, if he doesn't unpack the things fast, it wouldn't be much of a trick to trace them back to us.'

Ken shrugged: 'He's just another middleman. He's not charging up El Hamra shouting "Liberty!" with an M3 and a tin leg. They probably aren't even for this country.'

We reached the main gate just before they shut it for the third race, and stood on the pavement waving at taxis.

Ken said thoughtfully: 'What d'you think he *will* do next?'

'Talk to Aziz. He's got to.'

'And we just wait?'

'No, we ring Aziz first.'

'Us? Ring Aziz?' He stared at me. 'And what do we tell him?'

'Promise not to laugh? Why not the truth?'

18

It was six o'clock, almost sundown, when we met Aziz by the souvenir counter in the airport lounge. I suppose we shouldn't have expected him to come alone; the party of the second part was a short, brisk fifty-year-old with a big beak, gold-rimmed spectacles, tufts of white hair sticking out like awnings over his ears, blue suit and smart black briefcase. He could have gone a step further and worn a placard saying LAWYER around his neck, but he didn't need it.

. Aziz was in weekend dress, which to him meant a grey silk suit and a cravat instead of a tie. He introduced us to the lawyer, keeping an expressionless expression on his face.

The lawyer – I hadn't caught his name – said: 'I have told Monsieur Aziz that this is highly irregular.'

Ken said: 'It can't be too irregular for a man to see some property he's had the court attach. There must be a legal presumption that he could get to own it.'

Aziz grunted, shrugged, and said: 'Enfin, let us go and see it, then.'

I said: 'I want to make a short statement first.'

'Who is your legal adviser?' the lawyer asked.

'I'm advising myself and if that means I've got a fool for a client then you should worry. Statement: the aeroplane and its cargo belong to Castle Hotels, not to Mitzi Braunhof-Spohr, not to her father's estate, not to me. She didn't even pay me for the ride here, so no money's involved. She's already flown out and there's nothing to stop me going, too, and then you can fight it out with Castle and good luck. Statement ends.'

The lawyer consulted himself on how much of this to believe and what to advise if so. Aziz was staring blankly at a case of that filigree white silver and turquoise jewellery that you find all over the Middle East; he hadn't shown any surprise at hearing that Mitzi had gone.

Finally the lawyer said: 'You wish to disassociate yourself from these proceedings?'

'I'm disassociated already. Now I'd like to show Mr Aziz the property he's had attached.'

Aziz looked at the lawyer with a slight shrug of Why Not? So we showed various papers and passports to the Immigration control and got ourselves let out airside through a back door.

As we reached the hangar by the Queen Air, Ken said: 'I think Mr Aziz might find he wants to stop being legally represented from here on.'

Both of them stared at him, the lawyer with legal steam coming out of his ears. I said quickly: 'Let's say we show Mr Aziz first and he can call for legal advice as soon as he wants to.'

Aziz and the lawyer looked at each other, suddenly smelling something more than the jet exhaust drifting down the breeze.

I said: 'I can't exactly hijack him, can I?' and walked over and unlocked the Beech, climbed up into a sauna bath atmosphere, opened another button on my shirt and sat down in the rear seat. After a few moments, Aziz climbed in behind me.

'Well, there it is,' and I waved a hand at the stacked boxes.

He moved carefully forward, a little alarmed at the way the small aeroplane swayed under his feet, and lowered himself gently into a seat facing the boxes.

'But you must not leave such wine in a heat like this!'

'I wouldn't know, I just fly these things around. Unloading and Customs and so on isn't my business—' Ken came past me – 'but if you like, we'll see how it's getting on.'

I found my pipe-cleaning penknife, opened the sharp blade, and passed it to Ken. He got the top box clear of the tie-down straps and slashed the paper-tape bindings, then ripped open the staples.

Of course, if it wasn't sub-machine guns we were going to look right bloody fools. And it wasn't. But we didn't.

We got eighteen assorted types of automatic pistol plus spare magazines and ammunition in screws of newspaper.

'Oh dear me,' Ken said in a tea-party voice. 'This wine really has gone off. Changed completely, wouldn't you say?'

I said carefully: 'I saw those boxes loaded aboard, already sealed, of course, at Rheims. I've got all the paperwork, certificat d'origine and so forth, all clear and complete. As I say, I just fly where people tell me.'

Ken said: 'A man must want this sort of stuff pretty bad if he goes as far as slapping a court order on it.'

'Mad keen, he must be. I'm glad I'm disassociated.'

'Me too. Somehow it doesn't seem quite nice, does it?'

Aziz was up on his feet, crouched under the low ceiling and having throat attacks because that was where his heart was. At last he managed to sputter: 'You knew what was there!'

'Not precisely true,' I said. 'But anyway, I've advised myself not to say anything until I've consulted with myself and as it's Saturday I've gone fishing.'

Aziz glared, and the sweat was trickles, not drops, on his face. 'You are trying to blackmail me!'

'Everybody says that to us,' Ken complained. 'D'you want your lawyer in now?'

Aziz plumped back into his seat and the whole aircraft shuddered. But his voice – and his thinking – were under control again. 'All I need to do is report this to the police and pfft – you are in jail.'

'There's much in what you say,' I agreed. 'But the police will never believe Ken and I were doing this freelance, on our own. The money's too big, the paperwork's too good. They'll be looking for somebody at this end, in Beirut.'

Aziz said: 'But I am not connected with this at all. They know—'

'Except for that court order,' Ken said. 'When a real court takes a proper look at that, what'll they find? – that you got an injunction on an aeroplane *and cargo* that had nothing at all to do with the debt you claim Bruno Spohr owed you.'

Aziz was getting a little warm again. 'By its nature, an interim injunction is a delaying tactic; this is understood. It is to create time, it is not expected to be a final judgment.'

'Oh sure,' Ken said, 'but the court's still going to ask you what all this was about.'

I said: 'And you're going to say: the sword of King Richard, Coeur de Lion.'

'And the court will say,' Ken took it up, ' "You mean *not* about these dozen boxes of modern weapons we see before us?" '

I said: 'And then the court will hand down its verdict.'

'Which will be ha-ha-ha,' Ken said.

'So we'll see you at the six-in-the-morning slop-out,' I said. 'And meantime, give our regards to Messrs Hilton, Sheraton and Coca-Cola, will you?'

Gradually it grew quiet; it was a slack time at the airport. And dim; the sun was probably down by now, though that was behind the hangar from us. Inside the Beech was a gentle twilight, cooling now as the breeze drifted through.

Then Aziz said softly: 'Yes, it is blackmail – but very good blackmail. I will get the order lifted immediately – as soon as I can contact the judge.' He looked at Ken's suspicious eyebrows. 'An hour, or less.'

I said: 'Fine. And the deal stays the same: when and if we find the sword, you get at least twelve thousand dollars and I hope much more.'

Both were staring at me, but Ken spoke first: 'Where did you get that idea? Hell, where did you get that money?'

'It's still what Mr Aziz is entitled to.' I nodded to him. 'You carry on. I'll look after your interests.'

He stood up carefully. 'I believe you will. I think you are a man of honour.' He edged back and down the steps and away.

Ken said: 'And *I* think you're a man who's left his mind in his other suit. We're not giving that conniving bastard—'

'Always leave 'em laughing. Once he lifts that court order he's just about proved his innocence – but we've still got the cargo. It just needs one anonymous phone call to the Customs here – or Cyprus – and . . .' I shrugged. 'I'm just trying to make him believe he could still have something to lose; a vague promise on twelve thousand is the most he'd believe from me. We'll never see that sword, anyhow.'

He nodded slowly, then chuckled. 'What I like about you as a man of honour is you don't bring work home at weekends. What now?'

'File a flight plan and take off as soon as we're cleared. Let's get the stuff back in the boxes.' The pistols were heaped on one of the passenger seats in a foam of torn paper.

Ken picked up a Browning 9 mm and worked the slide: nothing in it. 'It still doesn't add up. We've got five or six makes of pistol here, three or four calibres. I just don't understand it . . . What d'you say we open one more box? Just to see?'

'Oh Jesus, no.' But of course I was interested, though I'd far rather have sealed boxes than heaps of handguns littering up the aircraft.

I said: 'Well . . . just one. Only one.'

He grinned and picked up my penknife.

*

Why should I have been surprised that the next box had two French sub-machine guns and nine revolvers? Plus the usual minimum of ammunition, the whole weighing – I was sure – just 50 lbs. The revolvers weren't all the same type, of course: Colts, Smiths, a single Luger and two J. P. Sauers. Add that to automatics by Colt, Walther, SIG of Switzerland, Beretta, Browning and MAB, and you had Christmas in Dallas when everyone's opened their presents.

Ken said slowly: 'I thought bringing those M3's down here was daft, but *this* dolly-mixture . . . there's eight calibres of ammo here and nine boxes yet to open. Even a guerrilla group needs some sort of standardisation.'

I said: 'Give me a revolution to run and I'd swap you all the pistols for a few bazookas and Kalashnikov assault rifles.'

'Sure . . .' He dropped a SIG back on to the seat and rubbed his hands together: they were sticky with gun grease. 'I mean, it doesn't seem as if the supplier's cheated or anything. It's all good stuff, none of the cheap Spanish junk, and just about all of it's new. No more than proof fired, I'd guess. And there's *some* ammo for each type . . . You'd be better off starting up a shop than a revolution with this.'

Suddenly that made sense. 'Well, why not? We didn't think Jehangir was the revolutionary type anyway, just a middleman. A shop-man.'

'A shop where you buy a gun with just two loads, throw it away after because there's no more ammo?'

'It suits some customers.'

He got up slowly and stretched as far as he could in a crouched position. 'Yes, you forget there must be some non-political pistols out here. You mean banks?'

'The last I heard there were eighty different banks in Beirut and I'm not talking about branches. The hold-up-gun concession on that could be worth having.'

149

'Ye-es ... if you shoot anybody you've got to sling the gun away anyhow, haven't you? Same way, you don't want to risk a used gun that might tie you to somebody else's killing, so it has to be new stuff. And nothing bigger than a sub-machine gun – you could hide any of it in a car.' He shook his stooped head in admiration. 'Lovely, lovely Mr Jehangir.'

I stood up. 'Let's get it out of sight.' I started shoving guns back into the boxes. 'D'you still want to let Jehangir have this lot?'

'I suppose not. But a hundred and twenty new pieces ...' he shook his head again. 'That's *capital*, boy.'

'It's six years in Sand; they wouldn't believe *we're* loyal Palestinians.'

He started to help me.

*

I filed a flight plan at the tower and got a provisional okay for when the injunction was lifted. Aziz and his lawyer were still up in the deputy manager's office, probably trying to raise the judge.

Ken and I had another coffee – he'd had to come back to collect his bag and clear customs and so forth – and it got to be seven o'clock. Ken galloped his fingers on the table. 'I should have started smoking again.'

'Try a pipe.' I had one of mine going, after only three matches.

'Any time I want to make the match business rich I'll send them a cheque. You look like the old lamplighter on piece rates.'

I struck another match, then shook it out as Aziz's lawyer and the deputy manager came up.

The lawyer gave us both a nasty look and said in a controlled voice: 'I think it is all arranged.' I don't know how much Aziz had told him, but obviously not all.

The deputy said: 'I understand you are not legally represented?'

I nodded.

'In affairs of this sort, an agreement between the lawyers of both sides, saying the case is settled, is usually enough. But I suppose you can agree for yourself ... sign here, please.'

I signed something.

'Good. I am happy it is satisfactorily concluded.' He smiled at the lawyer and got a stare of stony hatred in return. A bad loser, that man – though that probably made him a good lawyer, of course.

I got on to my feet. 'Thank Monsieur Aziz for us, please. And tell him that our agreement stands.'

So I got a look of fresh-cut loathing, as well.

19

It was dark when we got outside again and the field was a maze of grounded stars: the yellow-whites of the runway, the greens of the threshold, the dim blues of the taxiways and occasional red obstruction warnings. And back and beyond, the rich windows of Beit Mery and the other hilltops twinkled lazily in the rising air.

It had turned busy, too; the air was full of burnt paraffin and the heaving roar of taxiing jets. We kept close to the buildings: it's when you get noise all around you that you can walk into something, though there aren't as many spinning propellers as once, thank God.

I left the Queen Air's door open so I could go out and check the navigation lights, turned them on, let Ken finish off the cockpit check while I put the straps back around the champagne boxes.

I felt, rather than heard, the first foot on the steps. Before I could move, Janni was up and inside, grinning from a fighting crouch that was more from choice than the height of the cabin. I backed off a step and turned sideways to keep my chin to myself.

More scuffling, slower this time, and the aircraft tilted a little as Jehangir came aboard. A slim automatic glinted in the dull cabin light.

'Good evening,' he said calmly. 'Are we ready to start unloading?'

More swaying and a third person stuck a sharp moustached face around the edge of the doorway. Beneath it was a customs uniform.

I said: 'Monsieur Aziz won't like it.'

'No—' he shook his head firmly '—that's done with. I tried to ring him, only to find he was here at the airport. So I realised you must have rung him yourself. And I hurried down.' Pausing only to change out of the pink rig into dark trousers and shirt, a short dark jacket. The total effect was almost black – maybe intentionally.

He leant a forearm on the rear seat back and pointed the gun across it. 'How, by the way, did you persuade Aziz to lift the order?'

Over my shoulder, Ken said: 'Truth. Faith moves mountains but truth moves financiers.' He was close behind me and I hoped he'd remember where he was – in a small, fragile aeroplane – before he started a gunfight. Also where I was, of course.

'Ah,' Jehangir smiled. 'I really didn't need Aziz poking into my business.'

I said: 'Your name didn't come into it. Yet.'

'Well . . . Now let's get on with it. Stand aside, please.'

I turned, stared hard at Ken, and sat down in a seat facing forward at the stacked boxes. Ken shrugged briefly and sat on the other side of the gangway.

Janni came forward, undid the straps, and hunched his way aft with a box. He dumped it in the doorway, came back for another. A third. The aeroplane settled a little on the main wheels.

'Three is one-fifty pounds,' Ken said softly, 'and two blokes back there is another three hundred and Janni must be nearly two hundred himself. Six-fifty already. One more?'

'Could be two. Mind if I go first?'

'I was going to suggest it.'

Janni came forward and lifted the next box, then spotted that it had been opened and called to his boss. Jehangir took a step forward and peered.

'Oh dear, so you had to get inquisitive.' He glanced back at his tame customs officer.

I said: 'We did say it was the truth that moved Monsieur Aziz.'

Jehangir suddenly chuckled. 'I wish I could have seen that little prig's expression. Never mind. A diligent customs officer would obviously open some for a random check. Janni!'

He stepped back and Janni moved past us with the box. As he went the aeroplane tilted up behind him like a seesaw. 700 pounds aft of the centre of the main wheels and nothing ahead of it was just too much. The nosewheel lifted and the tail headed for the tarmac.

I threw myself into the cockpit, ramming myself on to the

controls, as far forward as I could get. Behind me there was a crash as Janni dropped the box, a crunch as the door-steps touched the ground and a scream as the customs officer fell off them.

Maybe he made the difference, maybe it was also Ken backing in behind me. She slowed, the tail bumper touched gently, then the whole caboodle swung back on its nosewheel with a slam that lifted my gold filling.

But nosewheels are built for slamming; tails aren't.

Ken shouted: 'Drop the gun! *Drop it!*'

He had both hands on the Smith, pointing straight up the gangway between the seats. I couldn't see what at.

Then he fired.

Inside the aeroplane, the noise was like a grenade. I leant over Ken's shoulder. At the far end – about eight feet away – Janni was picking himself off a scatter of champagne boxes, Jehangir was clinging to the last seat, looking as surprised as hell.

As I watched, he lurched and his left leg slid eighteen inches out of his trouser cuff. He stared at it. The leg rolled a little, the foot at an impossible angle.

Ken said: '*Now* lose that gun!'

Jehangir let it fall, lowered himself on to the seat-arm, grabbed his leg and hauled it back into his trouser. 'You know what this will cost me?'

'Would your stomach have been cheaper? Now get the hell off this aeroplane.'

Janni was on his feet, giving Ken a vicious glare, then helping the master up. Holding his leg more-or-less in place. Jehangir shuffled to the door. Janni helped him on to the steps.

Jehangir turned for one last word. Ken took it instead: 'I'll tell you something: I was so rushed back then, I couldn't remember which leg was which.'

Jehangir vanished. When we felt their weight go off the steps, Ken moved back to watch them. 'Wind her up. I'll do the chocks and pitot head.'

I was calling for taxi clearance before I'd got the second engine started.

*

Ken dropped into the right-hand seat as we turned across the front of the main terminal. 'I got the cargo back forward but not tied down. Shouldn't be bumpy tonight, though.'

'How's the door?'

'Bit bent at the top, but it latches.' He shook his head. 'I didn't expect his damn leg to come right off. Wonder what it counts as? Can't be grievous bodily harm, can it?'

'I expect the French have a word for it.' We got to the run-up area off runway 18 as a big jet started its takeoff. The line of lights crawled, walked, ran and slanted steeply into the dark sky.

'Whiskey Zulu, request takeoff.'

'Whiskey Zulu, hold at run-up.'

I'd been listening to the tower long enough to get a picture of what was going on around, which included a Pan Am flight established on the approach. They'd let us go after that had landed.

I ran up the engines briefly, did a perfunctory mag and pitch check. Out low beyond the city two new stars sparkled alive; Pan Am's landing lights.

The tower said: 'Whiskey Zulu, cancel takeoff. Return to parking ramp and shut down.'

Ken glared at the little cabin speaker. 'The hell with *that*. Just Jehangir pulling one of Aziz's tricks.'

I flipped off the brakes and pushed open the throttles. 'Beirut Tower, Whiskey Zulu: your transmission faint and intermittent but understand clear to takeoff. Rolling.'

The Tower screamed: 'Whiskey Zulu, *negative*! Return to ramp!'

'You're still indistinct, but thanks and good night.'

A deep but tense American voice broke in: 'What the hell's going on down there? Is that runway clear or not?'

'Stand by, Pan Am,' the Tower soothed him. 'Whiskey Zulu, return to ... no, where *are* you, Whiskey Zulu?'

'Whaddaya mean, *stand by*? D'you think I'm in a Goddamn *balloon*? I'm past the outer marker!'

The Queen Air broke ground, I snapped up the wheels and banked steeply right, over the sea, and left them to sort it out between themselves.

*

I levelled out at 5,000 and put in the autopilot; it could have done the climb for me, but I was still new enough to this aeroplane to want to handle the controls more than was strictly necessary.

Outside, the night was dark, moonless, crystallising as we got away from the dust and haze of the coastline. And still: no cloud, just a southwest wind with no sense of ambition.

Ken said: 'Nicosia in time for a late dinner, then. What after that?'

'Back to the Castle. Then either Kapotas gets the okay from London for us to fly the aeroplane home, or we cable the bank and buy our own tickets.'

'Tomorrow's Sunday.'

'So we're stuck there till Monday anyhow.'

After a moment he said: 'What about Mitzi – and the sword?'

'What about it? We haven't a blind idea where it is except probably still Israel. We did our best for Mitzi, but now it's time to resign from the crusade and get back into something profit-making.'

He was quiet for a while. Then: 'Did you know I was deported from Israel?'

'The Consulate said.'

'I meant to tell you myself. So we couldn't go to Israel anyway . . . but I'd like to have found King Richard's sword.'

'Me too. And the Holy Grail and Henry Morgan's treasure and King Solomon's mines. Not necessarily all in the same week, though.'

'Screw you, too.' But when I glanced across, he was grinning. 'I suppose really it wasn't our type of weapon, anyway.'

'One sword, king-size, only one previous owner . . . Mind the store for me?'

'Where are you going?'

'Back to dump the cargo.'

He sat up. 'Oh Christ no. I tell you, that stuff's *capital*.'

'It's jail bait. We've been lucky so far, mostly because we've kept ducking and weaving, but lucky besides. Just think how many people know by now: Jehangir and Co., Aziz and Kapotas and anybody they've told, then Kingsley and God-knows-who in Europe.'

'Yes, but it's still—'

'And when we reach Nicosia we're due for a bollocking about that takeoff from Beirut – they're sure to have complained. If just one official gets snoopy, then kiss me good night, head warder.'

'Well, maybe, but . . .' he sounded wistful. 'I mean, those pistols are all new. Average £50 apiece just on a legal sale across the counter. That's a thousand quid before we open another box.'

'Ken, we can't *arrange* a legal sale. We aren't arms dealers. We were never the bright boys who fix for stuff to go from A to B and somebody called C to carry it. We were C, pig in the middle. But at least we insisted on honest manifests and end-use certificates and all.'

'An honest end-use certificate? We knew bloody well that half the stuff we carried was going to wind up in some other country.'

'I'm not talking about morality, dammit, I'm talking about getting caught. Those certificates were protection.'

'Were they?' – sourly.

'Mostly. And you only did two years. If they'd thought you were a freelance smuggler . . .'

He nodded but said doggedly: 'It's still *capital*. Like something I've been investing the last two years . . . a chance to get started again. There must be *something* we can do with it – more than the fish can, anyway.'

It's tricky to argue with that, particularly when you agree with most of it. The fact that the load probably belonged to Jehangir, at least legally or morally – or come to think of it, not quite either – wasn't bothering me. I wriggled back out of my seat. 'Okay. The champagne papers'll see us through for the un-opened boxes. But the opened stuff goes out. Are you keeping the Smith?'

'Just in case comrade Jehangir hasn't switched to breeding lovebirds.'

He had a point, there. I slid the cockpit door behind me before turning on the cabin lights.

The escape hatch is the last full-sized window on the starboard side, just behind the wing and opposite the door. It came loose easy enough, with a blare of engine noise and wind, and the aeroplane twitched with the increased drag. I threw the submachine-guns first.

By the time I was down to tearing up and feeding out the cardboard boxes themselves, I was frozen rigid: any air comes cold at 170 knots. Putting the hatch back in was no fun at all and once I almost lost the whole thing and how would I explain *that*?

Then I went looking for any damage done by Ken's shot. And I couldn't find a sign, so probably it was still in Jehangir's tin leg and it didn't bother me if it rattled as well. But I did find the gun he'd dropped: a Mauser HSc with one up the spout, so he'd been seriously ready to shoot. But I wasn't going to open up the hatch and refreeze just for one gun. I put on the safety and jammed it up the backside of the rear seat, in among the springs. Then shivered my way back to the cockpit.

20

Nicosia did its usual speedy job of prising the landing fee out of me, then looked severe and said: 'There has been a complaint about your departure from Beirut.'

I looked surprised. 'What for? I had a clearance.'

'They say—' he glanced down at a sheet of telex paper '—they say the clearance was cancelled and you took off without permission.'

'I was flying below the airways; don't see how they can cancel that sort of clearance.'

He looked at the paper again but it didn't seem to help. 'I do not quite understand . . .'

'If they want to fill in a form 939 and send it to our Civil Aviation boys, then I'll answer it. Until then they've got no blasted business libelling me all over the Mediterranean.'

He frowned. He was pretty sure I'd done something, but he didn't want to stick his neck out on behalf of what he probably regarded as a bunch of hysterical Arabs.

So he coughed and nodded. 'I will tell them if they ask. Are you staying at the Castle again?'

'Where else?'

He went away and I finished up the paperwork and went outside to find Ken.

It was a quiet taxi ride into Nicosia town. Halfway there, Ken roused himself enough to ask: 'How are we cashwise?'

'Not terribly fit.' The Beirut hotel hadn't cost us much, but the flight and the bar of the St George had caused severe financial bruising. In various currencies, I had just about thirty quid left.

Ken grunted and left it at that.

Sergeant Papa wasn't on duty, so we walked straight in and turned left for the bar/dining-room. At the far end, a handful of families were finishing dinner; closer up, Kapotas was sitting at a bar table working over some account books with a glass of something beside him.

I said: 'The phrase you're looking for is "Welcome home". Is that whisky after dinner again?'

He looked up and his shoulders sagged a little. 'I haven't had any dinner yet. I thought you'd be in Beirut much longer. Welcome home.' ,

'Why, thank you. We haven't had dinner ourselves, yet. Is it edible?'

He dropped his pen and rubbed his eyes. 'I doubt it. And with you two back, my accounts will mean nothing – again.' He got up and took his glass to the bar.

Ken was already leaning on it, and Apostolos, smiling gently, was pouring our two shots. He touched up Kapotas's glass as well and we said 'Cheers' and drank.

Then Ken asked: 'Didn't the girls get back here?'

Kapotas shook his head, and Ken and I looked at each other. Then he said slowly: 'The Ledra, then? I mean, if you've got money you wouldn't come . . . I'll just check, I think.'

He went out. Kapotas watched him blankly, then nodded me away to the table, where Apostolos couldn't overhear. Then he whispered: 'What happened over there?'

I thought about it. 'We went to a party, we went to the races, we met some interesting new people. I suppose that about sums it up.'

'You brought back the plane?'

I stared. 'Yes, of course.'

'But not the cargo?'

'We-ell . . .'

'Oh *God*!'

'It's down to just nine boxes, now,' I said helpfully.

He had his hands over his eyes. 'But I thought that was what you were *going* for!'

'Sorry, it wasn't.'

He looked at me with haunted eyes. 'Do you know that a senior partner of Harborne, Gough is coming from London tomorrow to look at everything personally?'

My first thought was: with only thirty quid, where the hell can we get off this island *to*? Turkey, maybe? I said: 'I didn't know. But he won't want to open champagne boxes and count the bubbles, anyway.'

'He will want to count the boxes.'

That was a point. 'Well ... tell him you imported three boxes here and sold them off. Why's it worth his time to come here?'

'He is not coming only here: he will go on to the Lebanon to see about the new hotel there. But if I say I've sold them, he will want to see the money in the books!'

'So put it in the books. How were you going to explain it if I'd dumped the lot in the sea anyway?'

He studied the tabletop as if it was the Book of Kells.

I said grimly: 'I see: just another example of pilot error.'

He went on watching the table. An obviously British couple walked past from the dining area and I called: 'What's the dinner like tonight?'

The man looked at his wife, his shoes, the ceiling, finally said: 'I suppose I'm not used to this Cyprus cooking, yet.'

I said: 'Thanks,' and turned back to Kapotas. 'The only thing the British hate more than being cheated is hurting the cheater's feelings. I suppose we can get some sandwiches?'

Kapotas looked up balefully. 'It is not my fault this place is ... Oh God, if only I could get the plane away somewhere.'

'We'll take off for Britain any time you say the word; the word is "money", by the way.'

'How much does it cost to run that machine?'

I shrugged. 'In direct operating costs – that's the extra expense you get by putting it into the air – you won't see much change from £30 an hour. And that's not touching annual costs like pilot salaries and insurance and so on.'

'My God! It uses so much petrol?'

'Fuel's still not the worst of it. Most of your hourly cost is saving up for replacement parts and overhauls.'

He shook his head. 'How can a hotel chain afford it?'

'I thought we'd proved this one can't. Wait till you see the running costs of a private jet. That'll turn your hair white and your politics red.'

Ken came back in, picked his glass off the bar and walked across. 'Yes, they're there. I talked to Mitzi: she's not too happy about it all, but what can we do?' He sat down.

I said: 'She's got the document. It'll be worth a lot in the long run. A fair bit in the short run – Aziz would buy it now.'

Ken nodded. Kapotas didn't know what we were talking about, but Mitzi's name had rung a bell. 'The Inspector Lazaros – he was very surprised you had gone. He said you should call him.'

I suddenly felt weary. 'Tomorrow. Or some other month. What have you got in sandwiches apart from octopus?'

'*Or,*' Kapotas said firmly and not too unhappily, 'I must telephone him as soon as you get back.'

*

Lazaros wasn't at the station but they said he'd call me back and he did – inside a minute. He made it simple: 'If you will stay in one place for five minutes, I will be there.' So I promised.

Then I went through to the kitchen and talked them into a plate of cheese and ham sandwiches, chargeable to the staff account. There were just two cooks, no sign of Sergeant Papa, and the place certainly hadn't been cleaned up since I was last there. Mind you, the cooks weren't anything to dry your hands on.

I took the sandwiches back to the bar and Ken ordered two Keo beers to go with them. 'Somehow, whisky and sandwiches don't go together.'

'You picked up some strict etiquette up in Biet Oren.'

Kapotas winced at being reminded he was sheltering a fresh-hatched jail-bird, so I changed the topic. A bit. 'Did you find any real fraud in there?' I pointed half a sandwich at the account books.

'No. But then, nobody made the most basic mistake of fraud: to try and pay money back.'

'How's that again?' Ken mumbled, his mouth full.

'If you defraud money to – let us say – go to the Beirut races, and if you then win, remember never to try to become honest again by paying it back. You will have found a clever way to get the money *out* of the books, but who thinks it is twice as difficult to get it *in*? Any company expects some small un-explained losses; more money gets lost than is found. But a big mysterious payment in – that starts an investigation.'

'Let that be a lesson to us all,' Ken agreed. Then Lazaros walked in. Ken added: 'Join the night school. The subject is how to work a fraud – you might learn something.'

Kapotas paled, Lazaros just smiled wearily. He looked as tired as he had two nights ago, but at least he'd changed his suit: this one was a snazzy gun-metal-blue affair in some man-made fibre, with lapels most of the way out to his shoulders and lots of raised seams. The middle button had come off.

He said: 'Mia birra Keo,' to Apostolos, sat down and lit a State Express. 'Now: I know you went to Beirut. Why?'

Ken said: 'Well, there was this race meeting . . .'

'I hope you won.'

Ken and I looked at each other. I said: 'I'd guess we came out about even.'

'Good. Of course you did not think we could not have the inquest, without even evidence of identity?'

'Oh, come off it,' I said. 'You weren't going to have an inquest on a Saturday.'

'Did we have a choice? But why did his daughter go as well? Not for the races.'

Ken said carefully: 'No, but you know how it is? She wanted a break from sad memories and all that. And there was a bloke in Beirut she wanted to see – a friend of her father's – something about his affairs. So we gave her a lift . . .'

Lazaros watched him thoughtfully, twiddling the cigarette in his stained fingers. Apostolos put the beer down in front of him and he nodded and took a gulp. Finally: 'She came back with you?'

'She's staying at the Ledra Palace this time.'

Lazaros nodded. That was a lot more sensible than suspicious. So I asked: 'Did you get the Viennese relatives rushing in?'

'Not yet one. Just a Nicosia lawyer saying he has been appointed from Vienna to represent the family. No more.'

I glanced at Ken, then said as delicately as possible: 'Well . . . the Professor was an old man. No parents left, probably no brothers or sisters – and the cousins and such might not want to get too close to a man with a criminal record. It must make it simpler for you, anyway.'

It didn't make it happier for him, though. He took another gulp of beer, another long drag on his cigarette.

Ken said casually: 'Do you know yet who he'd been ringing in Jerusalem that night?'

'Yes. Our consul found out for us.' He looked hard at Ken. 'Do you know Israel? – but of course you do. Do you know a man called Mohammed Gadulla?'

'A fine old Yiddish name,' Ken said sourly. 'No, I don't know any Israeli Arabs bar a couple that were in the coop with me. What's Gadulla do?'

'He has a shop for ... an antiquities shop, in old Jerusalem.' Ken just nodded.

Lazaros went on: 'But of course Professor Spohr would know many such dealers. It need not mean anything – except that the call was made that night, just before ... before he died.'

Ken got up and went to the bar to get another beer.

I said: 'Do you really want the inquest to find you a verdict of unsolved murder rather than simple suicide?'

He looked irritated. He could certainly run around saying that cancer victims don't suicide and that suicides always leave notes, and drag up some dirt from the Prof's past – and Ken's and mine, if it came to that – but if all he achieved was a murder with no murderer, then his promotion board was going to cut him off the Christmas card list.

Ken came back and sat down. All this time Kapotas had been sitting quiet, doing nothing except go pale again when I mentioned murder. We were the only people in the bar, sitting in a lonely pool of orange light, the dining end of the room dark, now. Just like the night the Prof had died.

Then Lazaros said: 'Has Papadimitriou come back yet?'

'Sergeant Papa?' Ken asked. 'Where's he gone?'

Kapotas's face sagged. 'He rang today – to say he is resigning.'

'He has left for good?' Lazaros demanded.

I said: 'He'll never get another hall porter's job. Not at his age.'

Kapotas shrugged. 'He has not been paid for so long, so perhaps I cannot blame him, but ... with a full partner coming in tomorrow from Harborne, Gough ...'

Ken nodded at the ledgers. 'Maybe there's something in there he's afraid the partner will spot.'

Kapotas glanced at the stack of books. 'No. I am a good

164

accountant. I do not say I would want to be Sergeant Papa on Judgment Day when those books learn to speak, but now they are dumb. However he cheated, he kept it small and regular . . . That is also good advice, if you want to juggle account books.' He took a long sip at his whisky.

Lazaros looked stern. 'You should have told me he called you.'

Kapotas shrugged again. Ken asked: 'What did you want him for?'

'Don't you think he listened to that call to Jerusalem?'

'Ye-es ... Bruno didn't speak much Arabic ... I suppose Gadulla would speak English, running a shop like that ...'

I said: 'Don't you know where Papa lives, then?'

Lazaros nodded. 'He owns a ... a guest house just by Kyrenia. He makes his old mother be the housekeeper there.' That sounded like our Papa's well-known way with women, all right.

Lazaros lit another cigarette and stared at his beer. Ken asked: 'But why resign? – he may not have been paid, but he was still making money here.'

I said: 'Maybe his dear old mum finally got the staggers and he has to run the place himself.'

'Maybe he had a big inheritance,' said Kapotas gloomily. 'With his luck, he might.'

Ken looked at him sharply.

Then Lazaros said: 'Damn, I shall drive over and see him. Now.' He stood up.

'Why not ring him?' I suggested.

His long face tightened into something like a sneer. 'To give him time to invent some good lies, perhaps?' And he went out. We heard the glass front doors swing shut.

Ken took a deep breath, seemed about to say something, then didn't. Kapotas finished his whisky, collected the account books and stood up. 'I will just see that everything is secure and the cooks have not stolen the breakfast.'

'Are you staying the night?' Ken asked.

Kapotas nodded sadly. 'Without Sergeant Papa ...'

'Can I make a phone call?'

'Help yourself. You will, anyway.' He went out.

'Who to?' I said quietly. 'Papa?'

He nodded. 'There must be some staff book with their private numbers.' He went and began routing under the counter in front of the switchboard.

I carefully poured the last of Lazaros's beer into my own glass, which seemed to need it, and started lighting a pipe. It still wasn't much past 9.30 and the sandwiches had mopped up most of my weariness.

I was still only on my third match when Ken came back in, looking thoughtful. I asked: 'Did you get him?'

'Yes, but ... something odd. He sounded a bit strained, like. I don't think he was alone. I didn't say what it was about, but I said the Inspector was coming ... rather wish I hadn't. Hell,' he shook his head in a mind-clearing gesture. 'Let's get over there. We can use Kapotas's car.'

'What can we do that Lazaros can't?'

'Get there first. He's got to go the long way round. *Kapotas!*' he shouted.

21

I'd forgotten that aspect of the routes to Kyrenia. On the map, it's on the sea about fifteen miles due north along an easy road that runs over a pass in the coastal range. But from Nicosia to the pass is all Turkish-Cypriot territory: no Greeks wanted today, thank you. So Lazaros would have to take a forty-mile swing out west, around the end of the range through Myrtou or Larnaka, and back in on the coast road.

We went north. It took us a while to untangle from the Saturday night traffic, but then we were out in the dark, with big notices saying we were welcome to *free* Cyprus skimming past at the fringe of the headlights. On a clear straight road, the Escort station wagon got the wind up her tail. From the mileometer I'd guess she was only just run in, which might account for some of Kapotas's reluctance in lending her – but either we were getting faster at talking him into things or he was getting defeatist by now. Anyway, I reckon that if a car will do sixty on that sort of road then it *should* do sixty.

After a while, I said: 'When you say "scramble" I'm old enough not to ask why – but now d'you mind telling me why?'

'Sure. I've just been admiring your driving.' He sounded just a little breathless.

'Thank you. Do you think the Prof really said something in that call to Jerusalem?'

'I'm bloody sure he didn't. Bruno wouldn't even give his right name on an open line to a Jerusalem Arab.'

'D'you think the Israelis would—?'

'It doesn't matter what they would; it's just a risk he wouldn't take.'

'So ... ?'

'So the phone call was just to make sure Gadulla was still there, or something like that. So there had to be a letter to follow it up.'

'Two letters. Damn. And I only got one off Papa. Sorry.'

The station wagon hit a rut on a bend and its unladen rear end got slightly airborne. I twitched the wheel here and there and we got back to straight-and-level. I let the speed drift down to fifty.

Ken said: '*Thank* you ... I suppose Papa would choose the Jerusalem letter because it related to the phone call. Bruno may have dropped some sort of hint – and anyway, if the call was in English the letter would be, too.'

The road began to climb, then hooked right, riding up the shoulder of the hills. Raw rock and splashes of sand glowed in our lights. We'd done over ten miles by now; just over the pass and we'd be in sight of Kyrenia itself.

Suddenly, almost too suddenly, we were at the Turkish 'frontier', just a sentry box and an armed Turkish National Guard waving us down sharply. I suppose we were a bit suspicious, at that speed and at that time and in a car that didn't look as if it belonged to a tourist.

A dark wary face with a big moustache peered in at me.

I said: 'Evening. We're a bit late for a party in Kyrenia. D'you want to see my passport?' It didn't matter much what I said: I just wanted him to get my pure English accent.

He grunted and flashed a torch past me at Ken, who was already holding up his passport. 'Is your car?'

'No, our hire car broke down and the hotel lent us this one.'

He swung the torch and searched the back of the car, then grinned vividly. 'Hokay. Have good party.' He waved us on with the Thompson – without a magazine in, thank God.

I steamed off at a gentler speed. Now we were in a sort of no-man's-land, theoretically patrolled by the United Nations when they weren't throwing punches at me in the Atlantis Bar and Grill. Tonight, we didn't see a thing, and probably wouldn't until almost Kyrenia; the Greeks don't usually bother to man their own roadblocks.

I asked: 'Any idea where Papa's house is?'

'Out west, a bit up the coast.' He picked a road map off the plaited cloth atop the dashboard and turned it over to look at the town plans. 'Go in as far as the Town Hall and turn left for Lapithos.'

We came over the crest and started down in gentle swirling curves towards the twinkling lights of the coastline. No lights nearer than a mile, maybe—

—except the lights of a parked car. Instinctively, I braked. Our own headlights swung across a bright blue Volkswagen.

Ken said: 'I've seen one like that parked by the hotel.' Maybe I had myself; I braked down to a stop and slipped the lever into neutral. A gun flashed and cracked in the Volkswagen.

Then we were out on the road, rolling and scrabbling for the back of the Escort. Another shot. We huddled in cover, Ken untangling the Smith from his inside pocket.

Without any fuss, the Escort began to roll gently away from us.

On hands and knees, we scuttled after it, heading towards but past the Volkswagen.

'This'd be a great idea if we'd intended it,' Ken grunted. The Escort got faster, and we shifted to a crouching hop, like playing monkeys.

The gun banged thinly.

Then the Escort ran off the road, dropping a wheel into a shallow ditch with a groan and a twang. Its headlights stared into a bush; the Volkswagen had become a dark hump behind its own pale parking lights, perhaps fifteen yards away.

Ken leant the Smith and an eyebrow around the rear end of the Escort, the tail light glowing on the side of his forehead and the exhaust huffing in his ear. I heard the hammer click back.

I whispered: 'Hold on. I don't think he's shooting at us.'

'He picks his nose damn loud then.'

But I was pretty sure I was right. You can hear a bullet that's meant for you, and it isn't a whistle but a *crack*: a miniature supersonic bang, in fact. All I'd remembered hearing was the pistol itself – fairly distant. Not even a shot crunching into the Escort, which he could hardly miss.

Ken said: 'He's in the Volks or behind it.'

'I think he's bugging out.'

'Well, I'll take the Volks.'

'Don't let's rush into things.'

'If you don't think he's shooting at us, what're you worried about?'

'Being wrong.' Either side of the road, the rocky, bushy hillside staggered in blurred shapes up to meet the starlight. You could hide a battalion out there, I said: 'Anyway, militarily I'm stark naked.'

'So distract him.'

I crawled around to the front of the Escort, took a deep breath and stood up in its headlights and shouted: 'Come out of there!' – and threw myself flat into the ditch.

Ken's gun banged twice, the glass in the Volkswagen went *spang*, and he was zigzagging across the road, firing once more, ripping open the driver's door.

A heavy body slumped out on to his feet. Ken jerked aside into a crouch.

Far down the hill a pistol snapped, like a last farewell. Ken pointed the Smith into the dark, then jerked it down angrily.

I reached into the Escort, switched off the engine and lights, and walked across to look at Sergeant Papa.

*

'You didn't kill him,' I said. 'Not unless you ricochetted one to come in under his ear. With nice close powder burns, too.' Papa was still warm and limp and there was a tang in the air that was partly powdersmoke and partly something stronger.

'Did I hit him?' Ken asked tonelessly. He was standing guard beside us, looking somewhere else.

'You hit him.' There was a starred hole in the Volkswagen's windscreen and a frontal shot had ripped away a lot of Papa's left cheekbone. But the bone glittered white in my match-light, with no more than an ooze of blood. His neck wound was something else, on both sides. It isn't like a gun in the mouth, but it's still a messy way to go. Quick, though.

Being careful where I put my hands, I rolled him on his back and started on his pockets. 'I'd guess somebody beside him in the passenger seat, holding a gun to his neck.' The passenger door was slightly open.

Ken said distantly: 'Papa would have to be under the gun to drive up here at all. As a Greek he'd know it was a dead end for him.

'Sorry,' he added.

'That makes it a nice quiet place for an execution.'

'He wouldn't plan to leave Papa here.'

'Papa maybe, the car no. He'd want that – I assume it's Papa's car – to get down the hill again. To his own car, probably.'

He looked down to the lights of Kyrenia, glittering as calm

as the stars. 'So the bugger's down there somewhere, running like—'

'Nothing we can do.' I finished with Papa's pockets, then turned his head gently to look at the back of his neck.

Ken said: 'You think he was shooting just to scare us off?'

'That's my bet. Even if he knows us he couldn't recognise us by this car. We just stopped; if we'd passed on, then nothing.' I stood up.

Ken turned, glanced quickly at Papa in the starlight, then at my hands. 'Did you find the letter?'

'Now, what do you think?' Papa had put on a nice fresh dove-grey suit, regimental tie, clean black lace-up shoes. And he'd filled his pockets with the usual keys, coins, banknotes, identification . . . and maybe other things.

Ken waved the Smith at my hand. 'What did you take?'

'Some of his money.' I shoved it in my hip pocket.

After a moment, he shrugged. 'Why not? So what now?'

I peered into the Volkswagen at the space behind the back seat. Nothing. Then wrapped a handkerchief around my hand, pulled the bonnet hood release, walked around and lifted the lid. Crammed in above the spare wheel were two suitcases. When I prodded them, they felt full.

'What next?' Ken repeated.

I slammed the lid. 'What does your average honest citizen do when a body falls out on his feet?'

He considered. 'Stuff it back and get out at the speed of a tiger-fart?'

'Correct. But we aren't average or honest. We don't even stuff him back in.'

*

The Escort came out of the ditch without, apparently, a scratch on her. Ken scuffed the roadside to wipe out any tyre marks and climbed in. 'Home, James?'

'Not through Turkish territory – that guard saw us once; I don't want to give him a reminder. And while we're at it, dump the gun.'

He looked at it regretfully.

I said: 'It's almost empty anyway.'

He nodded slowly, wiped the gun clean and threw it up the

171

hillside. 'Naked again. Champagne for breakfast?'

'For Christ's sake.' I started us rolling downhill.

*

Kyrenia's narrow streets were bright but quiet. In a week or two they'd be busy and the harbour-front cafés and bars would be swinging. But we turned west before the seafront and headed out on the coast road.

As we cleared the town again, Ken said: 'Papa's house should be out here soon.'

The seaward side of the road was a straggling wide-spaced line of small hotels, holiday homes, closed cafés and Coca-Cola signs. I slowed down. 'We can't stop there – hell, his mother may be home.'

'I doubt it. No, I was thinking: if somebody finds out we were over this way anyhow, we'd better have a reason.'

'We could go back to Kyrenia and get offensively drunk.'

'That's an idea – hold on, there's the house.'

I stopped. The only clue was a small signboard, a carefully irregular 'rural' shape, saying: Grosvenor House. A stony drive stretched away towards the sea.

I backed the car diagonally to throw our headlights on the house itself, fifty yards up the drive. It was a square modern stucco box, painted a streaky cream and with all the architectural charm of a rat trap. The metal-framed windows looked small and mean, and you could tell there was a garden because there were some plants and bushes that couldn't have died in that climate without some help. But not a light showed anywhere.

'Jesus,' Ken said, instinctively whispering, 'to think a man could live in Cyprus and want to retire to a place like that. *And* call it Grosvenor House.'

'D'you want to go and press the bell so we can say we did and nobody answered?'

'If we're sure they won't ... Well, it's an alibi of a sort.' He got out.

'Don't rush: Lazaros should be along in anything over ten minutes.'

I parked a bit past the house, on a track on the inland side, and left the car facing away from the road. It looks less suspicious, somehow; people don't think they're being watched by the *back* of a car.

The sea muttered on the rocky coast beyond the houses, the countryside made all those creaking and groaning noises that are so much louder and less reasonable than city noises. I found my half-smoked pipe and lit it, then remembered to switch the interior light so it wouldn't come on when I opened the door. A few cars went by on the road, all fast.

Then a quarter of an hour had passed. No lights had come on in Grosvenor House. How long does it take to find a bell-push? Hell, the silly bastard wasn't trying to burglarise the house, was he?

I got out of the car and stood listening and not getting anything new. Then, down the road to the west, a car's headlights, moving jerkily, like somebody looking for an address . . .

I started to run, then remembered not to. Just briskly across the road and up the rutted drive of stones, with the headlights creeping step by step in on my left.

It took me perhaps two seconds to find the bell and morse out a quick SOS on it. Nothing happened, but I'd pretty much expected that, by then. I started around the side, away from the headlights, my rubber soles crunching in the stones, and me wondering why I hadn't picked out a Colt for myself from the collection I'd sprinkled into the sea so freely. I could use the comforting feel of heavy metal in my hand, the sense that one trigger-pull could cause instant fire and noise and death. It's a helpful way to get around a dark corner, even if you're flattering yourself about causing 'instant death'.

I put one hand against the wall – flakes of old paint, wet with dew, pulled off on my fingers – then took a wide step around the back of the house. And almost fell over Ken.

He lay on his face on the concrete patio that stretched out flush with the drive and with a lot of stones spilled over on to it. For a moment I thought . . . well, a lot of things, but my fingers were already feeling for a pulse in his neck. Before I found it, he said: 'God bugger it. That *hurts*.'

'Sorry.' So he'd been put out with some neck grip, on the carotid arteries, I think it is. 'How d'you feel?'

'That's a bloody stupid question,' he grumbled, lifting carefully to a sitting position against the house. 'Did you get him?'

'No. Who?'

'*I* don't know.' He put both hands under his chin and lifted gently. '*Jesus!*'

A car revved in low gear and tyres bit into the driveway. I stepped close to the house. I whispered: 'That'll be Lazaros. D'you want to meet him?'

'Only one person I want to meet—'

'Then on the feet, *hup.*' I got him effectively upright and we staggered across the patio towards the sea, keeping the house between us and the glow of headlights brightening in the driveway. There was no garage, no outhouses, no cover bar a few scruffy ornamental bushes before the ground began to crumble towards what Papa had probably described as a 'deserted beach'. True, but the sand had deserted it, too.

I helped Ken collapse behind one bush, then found my own. We waited.

Lazaros took his time. He rang the front bell, and again, then walked slowly round the house and tried the french windows that led on to the patio. Then he poked at a few windows, and even gave a drain-pipe a shake. Then he lit a cigarette and stared out seawards and we stopped breathing.

But at least there weren't any other buildings to snoop into, and Lazaros wasn't actually expecting people to be parked behind bushes, so he stood there and puffed and probably wondered what the hell else he could do to justify an eighty-mile round trip. Eventually he must have thought of something, because he went back and the car door slammed and the engine started.

I said: 'Stay there,' and ran around the other side of the house. Lazaros's car – a small blue Mazda – hesitated at the bottom of the drive, then pulled away towards Kyrenia itself. I waited until the noise had faded.

When I turned back, Ken had reached the corner of the house by himself and was leaning on it for a breather. 'He's gone into town,' I reported. 'I was a bit scared he'd just sit and put a watch on the place. Now let's get weaving.'

He looked longingly at the house. 'The letter might still be in there.'

174

'For God's sake. If it is, you'll never find it. And Lazaros has probably gone to make his number with the local coppers. When Papa gets found, this place is going to get as lonely as Piccadilly on New Year. Let's *go*.'

So we went.

I didn't say anything until we were halfway along the coast road towards Lapithos. Then: 'How's it feel now?'

'Bloody sore.' He moved his head carefully.

'How did it happen?'

'I was just snooping around, trying doors and windows – he must've come up behind me. God! – I'm getting slow. I shouldn't have been caught like that.'

'You weren't expecting trouble—'

'I *should* have been—'

I over-rode him. 'So we're dealing with a man who's queer for necks.'

'Yes, it must've been the same man . . . but what did he come back for?'

'Something he hadn't found on Papa.'

'So the letter *could* be still—'

'No. Look: we know Papa was travelling and it could only have been to Israel. There's plenty of boats go from Limassol to Haifa, and they sail at all sorts of times. So he'd either take the letter or burn it; left behind, it's just evidence he fiddles with the mail.'

He thought for a moment. 'He'd need passport, tickets, money, traveller's cheques . . . I suppose they got pinched, too.'

'I imagine. But he missed one thing: Papa had a hundred Israeli pounds in with his cash. That's the maximum you can take into Israel.'

'*That's* what you took. And I thought it was just your pension plan. So that's another bit of evidence we've concealed.'

'They'll find out. It'll be routine to check with his bank, but they won't bother till Monday.'

The car hit a bump and Ken winced. I said: 'Sorry,' and slowed, but not much. If Papa had got found, they might just try a roadblock on the coast route; once we were round the corner of the mountains there were too many roads to make it worth while.

The road forked and I stayed with the coastline, passing the lights of Lapithos on the left.

Ken said: 'So what *did* he come back for? He can't have planned on coming or he'd have pinched Papa's keys.'

'Maybe he didn't have time. One thing I didn't mention: Papa had been tortured. Cigarette burns on the back of his neck.'

'Jesus! So *that* was the smell.' After a pause. 'So he wanted Papa to tell him something ... d'you think he talked?'

'Not enough. I think he killed Papa because we stopped. That was the first shot.'

'So we got him killed.'

'Balls. He went up there to get killed. We just speeded things up, before the torture was finished, before he thought of taking the keys.'

There was suddenly a sign for Kondemenos, an early rough road over the end of the coastal range rather than around the end. But I took it, just to get off the coast road.

It was narrow and winding but now I didn't need to hurry. What I could see in the headlights was lonely moorland, and beyond, the black hills against the stars. A bit like the road where Papa had died.

For a long time, Ken said nothing. I knew that, absurdly but understandably, he felt worse about shooting a dead man than a live one. And the wrong man besides. And then getting jumped from behind ... It had been a bad night, though how you balance those factors – but I don't think he was doing much balancing.

At last, he said calmly: 'Papa must've known this character. Thought he was a friend, or partner.'

'Likely enough. He wasn't fool enough to think he could do a million-dollar deal all on his own. He'd need help.'

We were over the top, weaving downhill; ahead, the flat central plain stretched away into the night, pinpricked with tiny lights.

Ken rubbed his neck carefully. 'I wonder why the bastard didn't kill me, too. He could've done by just pressing a bit longer.'

'Perhaps he's managed to cut it down to one a night.'

22

Breakfast struck at half past eight.

'What the hell am I doing up at this time?' Ken asked sourly.
'I must have gone to bed sober or something.'

'Happens to everybody sooner or later.' I stabbed my poached
egg with a fork, but it didn't mind. 'How's the neck?'

'Stiff. Does anything show?'

'No.' He had his old brownish Paisley-pattern silk scarf
folded as a high choker; the same scarf I remembered him
wearing . . . well, two years ago, and it didn't look as if it had
been washed since. Funny how a man can change his shirt and
underclothes as often as he can afford it, and still wrap his neck
in a piece of silk that's been used to plug an oil leak.

He grunted: 'What's the weather?'

From habit, I'd already rung the airport. 'Clear today but
there's a low south-west of here. We could get a front through
tomorrow.'

'Umm.' He mixed more instant coffee. 'What odds that we get
Inspector Lazaros in here before lunch?'

'No bet. I suppose we say we spent the evening boozing?'

'As long as they don't test our blood-alcohol level. What I've
got in mine wouldn't keep a flea's mind off his mortgage.' He
looked at his watch. 'I wish they'd hurry up and find him. Once
we're told he's dead, there's a few questions we can ask.'

So right then we got Lazaros, well up on schedule but only
by missing out on sleep. If he'd looked tired last night, this
morning he looked exhumed. His face was fat and thin in the
wrong places, his eyes were puffy red slits and his suit drooped
like stale lettuce.

'You look like it was a night to remember or perhaps forget,'
I said cheerfully. 'Coffee?'

'No, thank you. I have had more coffee last night than . . .'
his voice died off, he dragged out a cigarette and lit it with
hands that shuddered from sheer tiredness.

'You had a night out with Papa?' Ken suggested.

Lazaros looked at him. 'No. He was murdered.'

Ken said: 'Christ! ... oh *no*,' and I said something but not quite as ring-of-truth.

Ken asked: 'You found him at his house?'

'No. He was in his car, on the short road from Kyrenia to here. A United Nations patrol found him after midnight, and I was called out just when I had got home to bed.'

'How was he killed?' I asked. We *had* to remember to get told these things.

Lazaros swung his thin bleary glance at me. 'He was shot. Twice, with two different guns. Probably to make the impression it was done by bandits – or the Turks. But one shot was already after he was dead.'

'Two guns,' I said, just to make it quite sure.

'Yes, so two men. One in the car with Papadimitriou – he would not have gone up there until he was compelled – and one driving the other car to take the murderer back.'

Ken said softly: 'How very logical.' And it was. So now we'd got them chasing two men instead of one.

I said: 'We were over that way last night. In Kapotas's car.'

Lazaros's eyes got almost open. 'What time? Why?'

'Oh, half past ten, maybe.' Deliberately late. 'We were sort of drinking around and thought Kyrenia—'

'Shit!' His eyes were definitely open by now, but no prettier for it. 'You went to warn Papadimitriou I was coming. You knew you could take the short—'

'There's the telephone,' Ken said. 'If we really wanted to warn him.'

Lazaros blinked and got a better idea. 'Or maybe you were the two men.'

*

After a while I said: 'It works, you know. We could just get over the hill and grab Papa, in the time.'

Ken's bony face wrinkled in disgust. 'And then stand there blasting away with two guns, waking up every sheep and United Nations patrol in the hills? Give me a jack handle and I'd beat his head in as quiet as a lullaby.'

'Oh, I like that,' I said. 'But I insist on doing something more creative with the body. Drive his car back down and dump it out *east* of Kyrenia, way off our route.'

'But that's quite beautiful,' Ken said. 'It's a pleasure to do murder with you.'

Lazaros said: 'Now just shut up and—'

'But why,' I asked, 'do you insist on a jack handle?'

'I'm not insisting at all,' Ken said reassuringly. 'Spanner, tyre lever – one has to keep an open mind, don't you agree? I'd say half the world's troubles—'

'Be quiet!' Lazaros shouted.

'—come from not keeping an open mind.'

Lazaros reached under his jacket and took out an automatic and pointed it between us. 'You are arrested.'

Ken said: 'Browning 9-mil. Double-action, so he might get it to go off.'

Lazaros stretched and slapped the gun down on Ken's hand. Or tried. Ken's hands shifted like a card sharp's, Lazaros jerked back, the gun twizzled loose on the table.

Ken's expression was plain disgust. 'Tough Paphos Gate copper. Just preserving that station's reputation, I suppose. Better keep the gun.' He pushed it across and Lazaros caught it before it hit the floor.

Then straightened up slowly. In the silence we heard the phone ring in the lobby.

In a carefully controlled voice: 'You are still under arrest.'

I asked: 'Are we allowed the traditional phone call?'

'To who?'

'I was thinking the superintendent at Kyrenia who's in charge of the case.'

Ken said, almost to himself: 'Of course. It's Kyrenia's murder. And murder's a Super's job. I wonder how he likes his witnesses? – just lightly antagonised or given the full Paphos Gate treatment?'

The chambermaid – Papa's 'niece' – came in and told Ken the phone was for him. He stood up. 'Do I get an armed escort?'

'Take it,' Lazaros said impatiently, holding the gun out of sight. Ken and the girl went out; Lazaros sat down again.

'Have you told her yet?' I asked.

He shook his head. 'It is not my case.' He sighed and put the Browning back under his jacket. 'Did you see his car – the Volkswagen – on the road?'

'Not to notice.' Who remembers a car he saw five minutes ago, let alone ten hours? 'But on the way over, we didn't pass anybody coming from Kyrenia.'

It was a small crumb of evidence, but he licked it up gratefully.

I went on: 'Why was Papa killed? Robbery?'

'They think not.'

'Had anybody busted into his house?'

He looked at me sharply. 'I do not think so. I went in with the Kyrenia police later and . . .' he shrugged. 'His mother is away, we think.' He leant his elbows on the table and rubbed his palms into his eyes. 'Forget about being arrested. I will tell Kyrenia what you said and where you are. And then I will sleep.'

Ken came back looking thoughtful – no, disbelieving.

'Bad news?' I asked.

'No-o. Good, I think.' He shook his head slowly. 'The Israeli Embassy – they've cancelled my deportation.'

*

Half an hour later we were sitting in a small, cool, sparsely-furnished café down Ledra Street sipping gritty-sweet Turkish coffee and me sounding like an elderly uncle.

'You're just the bloody bird dog,' I told him. 'Now the Professor's dead, they think you could be the only one to sniff out the sword. So they let you back in, you find it, then clang! The dog never gets the bird; he ends up back in the kennel eating tinned rabbit.'

'They don't know there's a sword.'

'They know there's a something. They know the Prof's reputation as a grave-robber – and maybe they overheard a hint in jail. They could know about our runaround the last few days. Enough other people seem to.'

He nodded calmly. 'I think you're right.'

'That's good.' I finished my coffee except for the sludge at the bottom. 'So now let's forget about the sword, concentrate on keeping our noses clean here and get back to England, home and booty.'

'But that's no reason not to go on to Jerusalem,' Ken added.

I slapped my cup down with a clang that made the tubby proprietor look at me wide-eyed. 'Now look, Ken: if you go back there you'll confirm everything they believe – that there's something hidden and you know where. They'll be sleeping in your pockets.'

'Maybe, maybe not.' True; how well a surveillance works depends on how experienced your target is. And Ken was.

'All right, so you find Gadulla and say: "Here, O swarthy foreigner, hand over King Richard's sword." What does he do? D'you think he's even got the thing?'

'It doesn't seem too likely,' Ken admitted. 'I mean Bruno trusting anyone that much. More like, the letter told him how to find it—'

'Fine. So whoever's got the letter doesn't need to go near Gadulla. He goes direct for the hiding-place.'

'The letter can't be everything,' Ken persisted. 'It can't have been complete, somehow. That's why he was torturing Papa, why he was snooping back at the house.'

There was something in that, but: 'That still doesn't help you. And, incidentally, Lazaros didn't say anything about the torture, so we don't know. Remember that.'

'Ah. That's the hold-out, is it?' Every fancy murder case brings in false confessions from nitwits, so they always conceal one piece of evidence, something only the real murderer would know, to use as a cross-check.

He finished his own coffee and looked at his watch. 'Gadulla's still the only lead we've got.'

'For God's sake, leave the damn sword alone. Tell Mitzi about Gadulla and then leave it lay – you can't afford to go to Israel, anyway. We've got a business to start up again.'

He smiled wryly. 'The same one?'

'I don't know . . .' I stared at the tabletop. 'We're sort of running out of time on that, I think. But now – we know a lot more about air cargo generally; we can cost a job properly. We don't have to go for the big margins and risks.'

He shrugged. 'If you say so. You're the boss on the business side.'

'Oh hell, Ken—'

'No, you always were. I'm a better pilot, but how often does that matter? – twice, three times a year? You're the one who knows how to bring in business; that matters all the time. I'm not complaining. But – just try and keep off strawberries and monkeys.'

I grinned. 'I'll try.' So maybe, after – how many? – three nights out of jail, he was cured. We could get back to work.

He stood up. 'I'll drop over and see Mitzi. Back at the Castle for lunch, no?'

*

I mooched about the town staring into closed shops and listening to church bells until noon, then back to the hotel for a first beer with Kapotas.

He was looking fresh and smart in a non-Sunday tie, but also gloomy and nervous. Then I remembered Papa *and* the partner from Harborne, Gough coming in that afternoon.

'Cheers. Have you got the books balanced?'

'On a tight-rope. You know about Papadimitriou?'

'I heard. Tell me – when we were in Beirut, was anybody here asking for him?'

'Would I know? Papadimitriou was the first person anybody coming here would meet, most of the time.'

I nodded. It was also possible that Papa had gone looking for a partner instead of one finding him.

'Somebody was asking about Professor Spohr,' Kapotas added.

'Who? When?'

'On Friday evening. Only by telephone. It was the Israeli Embassy.'

'Are you sure?'

He shrugged. 'The voice sounded . . . well, right.' There's already a clipped, dry tone you could call an Israeli accent just so long as you don't expect all Israelis to have it. 'I said I knew nothing and put Papadimitriou to speak to him.'

'This was Friday evening? After dark?'

'Yes, why?' Then: 'Oh, of course,' as he got the point.

Naturally no Israeli Embassy can be strictly religious; they'd break the Sabbath, all right – but only on important business. Dead or alive, Bruno Spohr couldn't stand very high on Israel's list of problems.

'What happened then?' I asked.

'I don't know.' He took a mouthful of beer and tried to think. 'Papa went out soon after, and . . . and I never saw him again,' he suddenly remembered. 'Perhaps I should tell the police.'

I nodded. God knows what they'd make of it, but at least they'd have the authority to check with the embassy. I'd get told to go and unleaven my head.

I changed the subject: 'Has Papa's niece been told?'

'She is off duty now. I gave Inspector Lazaros her address.'

A waiter – I mean *the* waiter – came in and started clattering about leisurely, laying the tables behind us. I went to fetch two more beers.

Then Ken came in, bouncing like a frisky cat. He saw the glasses in my hand. 'Lay off that stuff, boyo – you're aviating.'

I put the glasses carefully back on the bar. 'I'm what?'

'Doing the ever-popular intrepid birdman act. Private charter to Israel.'

If the glasses hadn't been out of my hands they would have been anyway. 'To *where*? On whose money? And with that . . . that . . .' Apostolos the barman was watching me; '. . . with that . . . load?'

Kapotas was on his feet by now. Ken grabbed both beer-glasses and shooed us back to the table, out of range of the bar. He shoved one glass at Kapotas and gulped at the other. 'The girls'll pay the charter, they've agreed. They think Gadulla's our only chance, and if it comes right we need the Beech. Now *you*—' he turned to Kapotas '—wouldn't mind having the aeroplane and its cargo out of the way – earning money, remember – while your big wheel from London comes snooping through? Roy told me about him.'

Kapotas looked thoughtful. I said: 'I hope they know what charter rates are like. '

'I was moderately honest about it,' Ken said. 'They're paying a hundred quid – they're saving the air fares, remember – and it won't be more than three hours there-and-back so you'll see *some* profit. The lad from London will think you're marvellous.'

Kapotas was beginning to like it. I said firmly: 'Dynamite into Hell, yes, but I'm not flying that load into Israel. Of all places—'

Ken waved his non-drinking hand impatiently. 'It's still

transit cargo. They won't care as long as it stays in the Beech.'

There was a long silence except for the shufflings of the waiter in the dining-room end. Kapotas was back to gloom again.

I slapped both hands on the table. 'All right. This time. But Ken – *you* go by airline. Eleanor won't look suspicious and Mitzi should get by with Braunhof on her passport, but the name Cavitt could blow the whole expedition.'

He saw the sense of it. 'Okay, I'll get booking.'

I followed him into the lobby; there was nobody around. 'You got the hundred off the girls in advance?'

He nodded. 'I didn't want to mention it in front of Kapotas.'

'Quite so. But give me fifty now; I've got to refuel.'

'Sure.' He split a wad of Cyprus notes and gave me half.

'Thanks. And I learnt one thing: somebody saying they were the Israeli Embassy rang about Spohr on Friday evening. He talked to Papa, then Papa went out and resigned from there.'

He got the point of Friday evening straight off. 'But an Israeli accent?'

'Kapotas thinks so.'

He considered. 'I doubt Papa knew Israel. He might've been ready to go shares with somebody who did.'

'And who knows us.'

'Say again?'

'One reason why he didn't kill you: if he recognised you he'd guess I'd be somewhere around.'

He scratched his nose with the earpiece of the phone. 'Plenty of people who know us and Israel . . . Only one I can think of here is that Israeli agent – Mihail Ben Iver.'

I nodded. 'I love him, too.'

'Come off it, Roy. The Ha Mosad's pulled some dirty tricks down the line, but . . .'

'Who says he's their secret service, except you?'

After a time he said softly: 'That's right, isn't it?'

23

These unexpected flights really louse up your laundry, and the
Castle hadn't been doing any delousing since the crunch. Now I
had two dirty khaki shirts, one dirty white one and two others
that hadn't quite drip-dried. In the end I put on the dirty white
and my blue uniform trousers, bundled everything else into the
bag and was at the airport by half past one.

Sunday's a quiet day at that season. A couple of parked airliners with nobody working on them, a Piper Navajo – the one
where the props spin in opposite directions – buzzing down the
approach. I watched it on to the runway, smoothly. No turbulence.

Ken's flight wasn't due till a quarter to three and he'd be
bringing the girls out with him. I ordered seventy gallons of
fuel, cash waggled in advance, then studied the met chart and
ate a sticky bun to wipe the beer off my breath. Weather was
no problem, and Airway Blue 17 went straight from here to Tel
Aviv, so I flight-planned myself on it, counting on a three
o'clock takeoff. I still had an hour and more.

I paid for the petrol, got cleared out airside and walked down
to the Queen Air. It was some distance away, on the Number 8
stand they use for visiting private aircraft, just past the customs
bonded store. The Piper Navajo was parked not far away.

I climbed into the Beech and sat staring at those bloody
boxes. By now I was convinced they'd be happiest at the bottom of the sea, and me too, if you see what I mean. Stage an
engine failure and have to lighten the load? It sounded pretty
unconvincing, particularly to an insurance company. But maybe
the cover had lapsed by now.

That didn't solve my immediate problem. Maybe the customs would let me store it in bond, make it real entrepôt cargo,
for a few days. I'd got time to try . . . then I remembered Jehangir's automatic: if the Israelis gave the aeroplane a real frisking
. . . I untangled it from the seat springs and dropped it in among
the maps in my flight briefcase. I could sling it out of the window into the grass at the runway end.

As I climbed down, Jehangir, Janni and a third man came round the tail.

'How very convenient,' Jehangir smiled. Today he was the respectable banker again: dark green silk suit, old school tie and white shirt. Even Janni looked moderately neat in a striped shirt and dark trousers.

Their hands were empty.

I said: 'How's the leg today?'

'Expensive, thank you. I'm having to use an old-style one that I keep as reserve, and I'd forgotten how uncomfortable these belts and shoulder straps are. However, we came to talk about champagne, not legs.'

'If you get rough I'll scream for my mummy.'

He shook his head firmly. 'There is absolutely no need for any violence. All we have to do is go and inform the customs that the champagne you arranged to sell us, and we have come to collect, has – you now tell us – turned out to be small arms. Naturally, we felt it our duty to report this.'

Janni grinned. He probably didn't understand a word: he was just working from my expression.

At least I tried. 'The manifest says it's for Beirut. That implicates you.'

'No, no, no. My name isn't involved. And will Cyprus care, anyway? Their records show you already took one box through customs here.'

'That'll land Kapotas in it, as well.'

'Frankly, old boy, that doesn't concern me in the least.'

It was blackmail, but very good blackmail. I shrugged. 'Okay. What do we do?'

'We simply trans-ship the cargo to our plane. My pilot says this is quite normal procedure.' He nodded at the third man, who was wearing a cotton khaki uniform with knife-edge creases, big sunglasses and a dark moustache. I couldn't see much more.

'That Piper?' and the pilot nodded.

I went on: 'You need two matching manifests, and the customs have to supervise the transfer.'

Jehangir nodded. 'So my pilot says. We have the papers here, ready to make out. Perhaps we might do it sitting in your plane. Will you lead the way?'

*

Half an hour later it was all finished. Jehangir wasn't too bothered that I'd dumped the two open ones – and I think he believed I really had – since any honest customs officer couldn't resist having a snoop into an opened box. As it was, this one only wanted to make sure nine boxes labelled champagne went from aircraft A to aircraft B as per manifest and not eight or ten. Inside could be atom secrets or human meat pies for all he cared.

Then he walked away across the tarmac and I'd lost my chance.

Jehangir half-turned to me with a revolver peeking out from his folded arms. 'Now, of course, you are quite innocent. So we must take precautions to ensure that no anonymous phone call reaches Beirut before our plane does.'

I stared at him, trying to look puzzled. Janni nudged my shoulder and started us walking round the far side of the Queen Air, away from the terminus. The field was very quiet and Sunday afternoon.

I said: 'You forgot about the money angle.'

'Ah, that was when we were talking about a more voluntary exchange.'

'I wasn't thinking of personal profit. Just how I explain to Castle Hotels that I gave away their champagne for free.'

'It is a problem, I agree.' But not for him, apparently.

The Piper's right engine grunted and spun into a crackling roar. Janni kept me walking towards it. Jehangir slowed and fell back a bit.

I raised my voice above the engine noise. 'I've asked for a three o'clock takeoff.'

'Just a slight technical delay,' Jehangir called over my shoulder. There was a faint click-snap and I looked back. His revolver now had a long fat tube on the barrel. A silencer. Janni grabbed my left arm but instinctively I was already looking front again, shocked as if I'd seen Jehangir unzipping his trousers.

They were going to kill me. And my mind didn't want to know.

But they were going to *kill* me.

Well, of course, they were. Even if I couldn't get Beirut to intercept the guns, I still knew who'd got them. It was too much of a risk to let me stay alive.

So they were going to kill me. *Me.*

Like hell they were. My mind was catching up. The briefcase was still in my right hand.

I must have tensed, because Janni's grip on my arm tightened. I tried to relax. 'Never flown one of those Navajos.' What would they do with my body? 'Flew an Aztec for a while.' You don't actually need a body to start a murder hunt, but you certainly start one if you've got one. 'I suppose left- and right-handed engines make sense for private pilots, but not for professionals.' Of course: they'd take me with them. I'd just vanish.

When would it come? It could be any time now, with that engine running; that's why the pilot had started it. A silencer doesn't really work, but on a small-calibre gun close to the racket of a 300-horse engine – it works.

We came up to the left side of the Piper, away from the live engine and out of sight of the terminus. I gently swung my briefcase across and dropped it at Janni's feet.

He checked, loosened his grip on my arm. I stepped in front of him and stabbed my fingers at his eyes.

I never got near nor expected to. His boxer's instinct got his hands up, but it was still a boxer's instinct. He was wide open for the old stamp-kick that rips down your shin and crunches your instep. He screamed and swiped at me, but his foot was just about welded to the concrete.

I snatched the briefcase open. Jehangir took a clumsy side-step to get a clear shot past Janni; I jumped the other way. My hand touched the butt of the hidden Mauser.

Jehangir took another step, hesitated – perhaps because the Piper was right behind me – then fired. I didn't hear a thing, but didn't feel anything, either. The Mauser was coming clear, my thumb crunching down the safety-catch . . .

Janni swayed into the line of fire, then flopped on his knees. I fired over him, cranking the trigger as fast as I could, wanting Jehangir to flinch from the flash . . .

His mouth opened wide and he sat down backwards with a silent thud. The gun tumbled loose.

I'd fired – three times, was it? I counted the echoes in my head. They weren't loud, in that noise. Three it had been. I walked around Janni, picked up the other gun, looked down at Jehangir.

Two had hit him. One high on his left arm, the other somewhere below his heart. His mouth said things I couldn't hear.

Janni got painfully to his feet, hating me. I waved the guns and gestured him to get Jehangir. He hated me a moment longer, then hobbled over to help.

The pilot suddenly stepped down beside me and nearly got the two-gun treatment. His hands jerked high.

'Get them on board!' I shouted. 'And get took off!'

The pilot stared at Jehangir, now on his feet but bent over clutching the bloody patch on his shirt. 'But he may be dying!'

'In his trade he's always been dying. If he does, dump him in the sea. Dump the boxes anyway: Beirut's getting a phone call.'

He went wide-eyed. 'This could lose my licence.'

'*Don't* come that brother-birdman act with me! You knew what was happening.'

Janni had Jehangir in his arms, carrying him like a baby and still with breath enough to yell at the pilot. Who turned back to me: 'He wants to get a doctor now.'

I shrugged. 'Tell him his boss goes now or we all stick around for fifteen years minus good behaviour.'

He must have said something like that; they all got on board. I stuffed both pistols in my briefcase and walked away. I heard the second engine start behind me. By the time I reached the Queen Air, the Piper was moving.

Suddenly I didn't feel like climbing the steps, so I sat on them and began to shiver. But not with regret. And it didn't last.

24

We got airborne just about on time, estimating Ben Gurion airport at four-ten, given a helping wind. Ken's flight would land about half an hour ahead. I'd just reported joining Blue 17 at 9,000 as we reached the coast, set up the engines for cruise power and was fiddling with the mixture levers when Mitzi leaned tentatively in over my shoulder.

I waved her into the right-hand seat. 'Just don't hang your handbag on any knobs.' She smiled, eased cautiously into the seat, and sat looking puzzled at the instrument panel.

'How do you not get muddled with all the clocks like this?'

'You don't look at all of 'em all the time. Like a reference library. You don't need to keep staring at your outside air temperature or fuel state; only when you want to know.'

The loudspeaker crackled: 'Whiskey Zulu, change to Nicosia Control, 126.3.'

'Whiskey Zulu, over to 126.3. Thank you.' I changed both comm sets.

Mitzi asked: 'What is that about?'

'Just changing to a different controller. This one listens in case I report both wings have fallen off over the sea.'

'Then can he do anything?' She looked serious.

'Sure: he lights as many candles as I've got passengers.'

She stared for a moment longer, then smiled.

I checked in with 126.3, then switched in the autopilot. Given luck, now I didn't need to touch anything except the radio and navigation knobs until we reached Israel.

After a while, I asked: 'Did you have much to do with your father's work?'

'Ah yes. I also have a degree in archaeology. Before I married I worked much with my father. And when my marriage ended, I was going back with him – but then he was put in prison.'

I made sympathetic clicking noises.

'It was a very bad time, that year. It was so difficult for me to get money from my father, and there is no work for archaeologists who are not teachers. I washed floors, watching out with children, work like that. Then my father is out of prison and it is going to be all right and . . .' she shook her head slowly.

'His first time, was it? In prison?' Tactful question.

'Pardon?' She frowned and blinked her sharp eyes.

'Well . . . he did have a reputation for not always reporting his finds.'

'Perhaps . . .' She nodded reluctantly. 'But who should own what is lost a thousand years and nobody knows it existed even? King Richard did not give in his will the sword to Israel. Israel was not clever enough to find it. My father was.'

'He was good.' Trying to make amends.

'Oh yes. They do not let him dig if he is just a . . . a bulldozer. He was like Schliemann: he walked on a site and could say: "Here they put the wagons, that was the wine *Keller*, on the corner is the most profit-making shop in the town." I think it is like a man who plans towns except backwards.'

And once she'd said it, I could see the Professor as a medieval merchant prince – with the silk robe, the neat beard, the air of fastidious toughness. Fingering a bale of cloth here, sniffing a handful of spice there, clinking the gold coins in his satchel . . .

If the gold had been there. 'Straight archaeology isn't a sort of high-paid business, then?'

She flicked her hand sharply. 'If you are writing the big picture books that nobody is reading, or making television programmes for people who sleep with open eyes – yes, there is money. But if you wish to do only the real work, to dig, you are only famous.'

'Pure knowledge spreads pretty thin on bread.'

She thought this out. 'Yes, that is right.'

One radio-compass needle was pointing firmly at what it thought was Tel Aviv's beacon, but we were at too much of an angle to the coastline for me to trust it. I tried switching the VOR around to get a bearing on Ben Gurion airport itself, but we were too far and too low for a very-high-frequency gadget.

'What is that?' Mitzi leant across to look.

'A mixed affair. Combined Visual Omni-Range and Instrument Landing System. Reads on to the same dial. The VOR navigates you – points at a radio station – then when you get there the ILS, both needles together, give you height and course to fly so you come down a glidepath on to the runway. Bad weather and night.'

'You can land without seeing?'

'No, you've still got to see the runway at the last moment. But on ILS I'd bring an aeroplane like this down to 300 feet in cloud.'

'And if then you could not see?'

'Then I'd go away and land somewhere else.'

Time buzzed gently by, a calm sea crawled away below. I took out a pre-prepared pipe and added to the collection of matches on the floor.

Finally I said: 'Your father can't have found many million-dollar swords. I mean, when you've found one the pressure must ease up a bit.'

'You must not say "million-dollar sword",' she said impatiently. 'That is museum talk. Do you think my father first thought that when he saw it?'

No, I didn't. Allowing for inflation in the last eighteen months, he probably said: 'There's an $800,000 sword.' But that was wrong, too – or incomplete. It must have meant something else as well – knowledge, truth, beauty – for him to be good at his job at all. Some well-engineered aircraft mean more than money to me. No sword's *intrinsically* more beautiful than the original 049 Connie.

I nodded. 'But what are you going to do when you've got it?'

'I must sell. I would want to give it to a museum in Vienna in the memory of my father, but ... I have to live also. But even in New York I can make sure my father's finding of it is known.'

Professor-Doktor-convict Bruno Spohr's last round-up? But I didn't say that. Soon after, she went back to the main cabin.

My estimated time of arrival turned out just about right, and just before the coast I remembered to open the little quarter-light window at my side and shove out the two guns. Jehangir's silenced job turned out to be an old Smith & Wesson 'Victory' .38, one of the few models actually made with a screw thread for a silencer. Probably quite a valuable antique in its own right by now.

*

At Ben Gurion International they parked us well out, away from the ranks of airliners, and told us to *wait*. After about ten minutes the customs gave the aircraft a quick frisk and we were clear to haul our baggage over five hundred yards to the terminal, watched by strolling guards in sloppy uniforms and an easy sureness about the way they held their sub-machine guns. You can't mistake Israel for a country at peace, and I don't think they shoot off their own feet much, either.

I did the paperwork for the aircraft and then went through the meat-grinder they call customs and immigration. Eleanor and Mitzi were waiting on the other side. They hadn't had any trouble.

'Just for interest,' I said to Eleanor, 'what profession do you have on your passport?'

'You don't say on an American passport, now.'

'That could help.' So then we got Mitzi into a *sherut* – a communal taxi that looks like an American hearse – for Jerusalem. It's only thirty miles, though with Israeli driving it can seem both shorter and longer.

'Give us a ring when you've got a hotel,' I told her. 'Remember we're at the Avia. Ken'll phone us later.'

She was away in a cloud of hot rubber, and we found an ordinary cab for ourselves.

*

The Avia is just around the airport perimeter, in flat dull country that's fine for building an airfield, but not historic or pretty enough to suit tourists. So the hard core of its clientele are airline crews and occasional batches of stranded passengers, which makes it a good place for getting a drink at breakfast or breakfast at teatime.

By six o'clock I'd showered, hung up my two damp shirts to finish dripping, got back into a dirty one and was sitting down behind a Maccabee beer in the first-floor dining-room. Eleanor wandered in soon after.

'No bar?' she asked.

'No, but you can drink what you like here. Airline influence, I suppose.' Despite my personal example, aircrews aren't big boozers.

She ordered a gin and tonic. 'So now we wait?'

'I have to, but you can go down to Tel Aviv for dinner. It's only ten miles.'

'I'll see.' She'd changed into a bright red trouser suit with a ruffled white blouse and a gold whatsit on a chain around her neck. Since she'd sat down there'd been some high-intensity radiation coming off a TWA crew that was breakfasting on turkey sandwiches at the next table, but she let it bounce off.

Her gin arrived, and she said 'cheers' because I was British and drank. 'I thought you said Ken had been deported.'

'Yes, but they changed their minds.' Would she ask why the change? Would I tell her my guess – a trap?

She didn't ask that. 'What was he . . . charged with?'

'Espionage.'

'*What?* And he only got two years?'

'Three with one off for good behaviour. But they call everything espionage over here. We were in the usual business : a load of small arms for Jordan only we landed in Israel instead.'

'That's a habit you can't afford often,' she said dryly. 'Wait – you said *we*?'

'Uh-huh. We were coming out of the Lebanon into Syria, in thick weather. There's a couple of bloody great mountain ranges around there, Mount Hermon and all, and your safety height's about 11,000 feet. So we lost an engine in between them, and we were overloaded so she wouldn't hold more than six thousand feet on one fan. Couldn't go back, couldn't go on – not unless we could see – so the only place to go was south. And that's the Jordan valley. You know it goes on down and becomes the Red Sea and then the Kenya Rift Valley?'

'But you didn't reach Kenya,' she said gently.

'We nearly made Jordan. But when we came out of cloud over Galilee we found we'd got a fighter escort. Ken put her down on a road just south of the lake.'

'And *you* got away?'

'Israel's got a lot of frontier to guard, and they guard it against an army – not just one man.'

So then the TWA crew decided it was takeoff time, but not so urgent they couldn't get a closer look at Eleanor on the way. The captain, a solid man with cropped grey hair, nodded at me and said pleasantly: 'Haven't met here before, have we? You fly?'

He was looking at my shirt, which had the little pen-holders stitched to the outside of the breast pocket.

I nodded back. 'Business and charter.'

'Ah.' His Dow-Jones rating of me slumped several points. 'You do a nice line in stewardesses.'

Eleanor gave him a quick flashgun smile. 'No, I'm his employer.'

The captain sighed. 'And we get Howard Hughes. Come on, boys; it may be the wrong business, but it's the only one we know.'

Eleanor watched them to the door, sipping her drink thoughtfully. 'But Ken got caught?'

'Somebody had to stay and argue, or they'd just have confiscated the whole aeroplane right off. And somebody has to be on the outside paying for defence lawyers. He came close to an acquittal.'

She looked at me curiously. 'How did you decide who stayed? Spin a coin or compare stiff upper lips?'

'No. It was his turn.'

'It was ... ? You mean you've been in jail, too?'

'Nearly three years, in Persia. Same sort of reason. It goes with the job.'

Then the waiter called: 'Mees Travis, telephone for Mees Travis.'

She went to take it. I called for another round, then started scraping out a pipe. I'd just got it packed and lit when she came back. 'Mitzi: she's booked in at a place called the Holy Land, West Jerusalem.'

'Long way out. I suppose things are getting jammed up, there, with Passover and Easter coming on.'

She sipped her new drink. 'How did you get set up as gun-runners?'

'*Please* not that filthy phrase. We weren't illegal. Well – we were sort of arms-running for the RAF in Transport Command and 38 Group, so we learned something, and then when we came out it was the only cargo on offer for small outfits, so we sort of specialised.'

'But not illegally.'

'Straight government-to-government deals; compared to that, the illegal stuff's peanuts. Britain sold £400 million in arms abroad last year, France did better and God knows what America did. A lot of that's fighters and ships and tanks, but a lot's small stuff: rifles, ammunition, radar bits. High value and always in a rush: perfect air freight. But the big airlines won't touch it: not respectable. So . . .'

'And if you didn't, somebody else would.'

I lit my pipe again. 'Actually, I believe in the right of small countries to bear arms.'

She was puzzled. 'Who said "small countries"?'

'I see: you think America should scrap its armed services, too. Or did you just mean small countries that have to buy its arms abroad? Like Jordan. Like Israel.'

After a while, she heaved a sigh, and I mean heaved: a nice bra-busting movement. 'I guess that's so. And it's all legal?'

'That rather depends on which side of the ol' river Jordan you land.'

'I never knew being a merchant of death was so tricky.'

So then it was my turn to take a phone call, down in the lobby.

*

'It's your loving Uncle Moishe,' said Ken's voice. So we were going to try and play it in code. 'How d'you like our beautiful country? Have any problems on the journey?'

'Our old friend from the race-course turned up again.'

'*Did* he? Was he being impetuous?'

'Yes, but I got even more so.'

'Fine . . .' he couldn't expect any more detail, not on the phone. 'Have you heard from your second cousin yet?'

'Who? Oh, yes. At the Holy Land, West Jerusalem. Any contact yet?'

'Yes, but only India Foxtrot.' I suppose 'Instrument Flight' meant not visual contact: he'd only rung Gadulla. 'Looks hopeful. And something else: I checked with shipping offices in Haifa. Old three-stripes was booked on a tourist boat that got in today. No show, of course.'

'No sign of the gent from . . . from the Establishment?'

'No, but he wouldn't book on the same boat, just pretend he had, maybe.'

'He'll be on his way. Watch your back, uncle.'

'And yours, nephew. Love to cousin Ellie. Shalom.'

When I got back to the table, Eleanor was glooming at the menu.

I said: 'Ken, all right. Some progress. D'you want to eat here or go in to Dizengoff?'

'Where?'

'Tel Aviv's Broadway or Boul' Mich'. Or something.'

She put the menu down with a slap. 'So why not live a little?'

25

We ate at a small restaurant just up from Dizengoff Circle. Sunday isn't as lively as Saturday, with the Sabbath just out, but the gentle night air had brought enough of a crowd to give it a bit of a swing.

I made coffee-drinking gestures at the waiter. The food hadn't been anything to write home about, not unless your mother knew those sort of words already, but the Israelis take coffee seriously.

Eleanor said: 'You and Ken – you've been together a long time, now?'

'Twenty years or something. We don't actually give each other flowers on the anniversary of that first day I nearly landed up his chuff on the West Malling runway.'

'You're going to go on?'

'Yes, of course.' Then I stopped to think why 'of course'. 'I suppose ... you've got a man you can work with, you trust, he's good at his job, you can talk to him but you don't have to ... most of life is seven to four against, as somebody said, so why change?'

'But don't you *like* Ken?'

'Of course I like the crummy bastard.'

She looked at me carefully. 'Men.' Then: 'And neither of you ever got married?'

'I did once. Nearly.'

'What happened?'

'Three years in a Persian nick.'

'Oh. And she didn't wait?'

'I felt bad for a time, but ... I'd never promised to give up merchanting death. I suppose a woman wants a man home more than once every three years.'

'Most marriage services imply that,' she said dryly. 'Are you going to give it up now?'

'I dunno ... You've got young outfits coming up, now: kids who can't believe they'll ever land on the wrong side of the river. And past forty, you haven't got the years to spare in jail.'

'I guess I know how you feel . . .'

The waiter brought our coffee. 'Don't tell me your best years were spent in Allentown jail?'

'No. But . . . when a girl gets to thirty . . . in her thirties, she can get the feeling the train's done gone.'

'There must have been plenty of hire cars on the way.'

She looked at me with cool blue eyes but a twitch at the sides of her mouth. Suddenly she grinned outright. 'I guess so – but sometimes you wonder about a ride that lasts a bit longer.'

Sometimes you do. How many café tables had I sat at, listening for the moment when I knew this conversation would last the night? But tomorrow – tomorrow there'd be a cargo for Amman or Ankara or Lagos.

How many café tables had she been at, waiting for a spark, the moment of decision? We shared something already.

I reached and held her hand on the table. She gripped mine.

I said: 'That's what happens when you put the job first, maybe.'

'Maybe. But you don't get to work at the Met because there's no job at Macy's glove counter.'

I waved for the bill. 'D'you want to stroll a bit – first?'

She smiled gently. 'Sure.'

We walked hand in hand up the wide – well, fairly – road lined with trees and bright cafés. But slower than the rest of the crowd. The young Israelis strolled with a sense of purpose, a hungry edge to their gaiety.

Eleanor shivered and clutched my hand tighter. 'They're . . . growing up too fast.'

'That's life as lived on the edge of war. These kids have never known anything else.'

'What can it *do* to them?'

I shrugged. 'Too much teenage rumpus – for a Jewish society – use of arms in crime . . . the way they drive, even. The price of liberty is eternal vigilance. Now we're learning the price of eternal vigilance.'

Though some people must have known before. Myself a bit.

Just enough to know when I'm being followed – not tailed expertly, mind, but followed.

We stopped at a lighted bookshop. A tubby gent twenty yards back put on his brakes, too.

The window showed a book with an old sword on the cover. Eleanor said thoughtfully: 'Did Mitzi ever say just what she plans for the sword – when and if?'

'One-track mind. Let's cross the road. There's a dark alley I want to show you.'

'This is so sudden, sir.' But she gripped my hand and we got through a squadron of hell-diving taxis and private jeeps intact.

So, a moment later, did my tubby non-acquaintance.

I said: 'She's going to sell it, she said. And if the Met can raise the money, you're home and dry.'

'It can find the money. Where's this dark alley?'

'Men were deceivers ever. I just wanted to prove we're being followed.'

'Oh shit.' She looked back. 'You know, that's the bit I'm worried about: getting the Met mixed up in an undercover deal.'

'Don't I remember something about the way they got hold of a vase from Italy a couple of years back?'

'Yes. *They* remember it, too. They don't want those sort of newspaper stories twice. Who's following?'

'No idea. Let's have a beer and find out.'

We sat down at the next café; an open-fronted Parisian place. Before we'd ordered, a face peek-a-booed in from the street. I beckoned it across. It grinned and came.

He was dressed in an inconspicuous – for Dizengoff – shambolic way, with an open-necked shirt, a smudged lightweight jacket weighed down by too much in the pockets, thick grey trousers. It was only his chubbiness that made him noticeable; Israel isn't a fat country.

'Then you must be Captain Case. Thank you.' He sat down. 'I was waiting to see if you noticed me – I'm not very good at following – and I thought, if he notices, he must be him. Most people don't notice even me.'

I said: 'Miss Eleanor Travis. She's *touring*. And you are . . . ?'

'Yes, of course. Inspector Tamir. Attached to the Department of Antiquities at the Ministry of Education and Culture.' He tried to shake hands with us both and show a tattered warrant card at the same time. 'I tried at the airport, then the Avia, then I learned you'd taken a taxi to Dizengoff, so . . .'

'What are you drinking?'

He and I chose beer, Eleanor coffee. She asked: 'What do you inspect, Inspector?'

'Normally, normal police things. Now I'm bothered about . . .' he searched his pockets and found a piece of paper; '. . . Captain Cavitt. And something about Professor Spohr. I know he's dead. And Cavitt is in Israel.'

'I don't know where,' I said.

'Oh, we know: at Akka.'

'Acre?' What in hell was Ken doing there, nearly a hundred miles from Jerusalem?

'Yes. And that was where Professor Spohr was digging.' He routed his pockets again and stuck a wide-bowled briar pipe in his mouth. 'You see . . . the Professor had, there was a story in Beit Oren prison he had, he found something. Valuable. Not reported. Ah—' The waiter put down our drinks.

I carefully didn't look at Eleanor, just sipped my beer. 'And so?' —

'Then we heard he was dead. The Professor, I mean. Shot.'

'Suicide.'

'But can you be quite sure?'

'Ask the Nicosia police. They proved he had terminal cancer.'

He frowned and scratched his scalp, just a sun-blotched dome with a poor crop of long grey strands. And dandruff; a few flakes drifted down into his beer.

'But cancer victims don't . . .' He stopped and sighed. 'In Beit Oren we get people who could make the chicken seem to walk into the soup.'

'I believe that. But—' I took out my own pipe '—but *somebody* fired a gun in that hotel at around nine in the evening. It was an empty wing, so nobody was too likely to hear, but ... And if it wasn't the Prof, somebody got in and out without being noticed. Those two things needed luck; a man who could fake a suicide that well wouldn't rely on luck to get away with it.'

He nodded violently and scattered more dandruff. 'Ah. Yes. You *are* the Captain Case I wanted. Try some of this.' He pushed over a rubber tobacco pouch. 'I mix it myself.'

He mixed it coarse and dark and smelling like old armpits. 'Thanks, but I don't think my flying licence covers that stuff.'

He grinned, not apologetically. Had it been a test? To see if I felt a need to flatter him? Why am I so suspicious of policemen? Why do policemen come and talk to me and never say exactly why?

He lit his pipe, but burning that stuff didn't improve it. 'So perhaps, as it always is on television, it was an inside job? By your colleague Cavitt, maybe?'

'Ken and I have alibis. We were out with a couple of ... you might say ... bar girls.'

'*Were* you?' Eleanor's voice said from somewhere around the last ice age but three.

Tamir smiled sadly. 'Prostitutes make good witnesses. They have little shame and they dare not annoy the police too much. *Lo asson*, it was just an idea; to kill other people is normal – killing yourself, who can understand it?' He gulped the last of his beer. 'Why did the doctors tell him he had cancer? – they do not, usually.'

'Probably because he had.'

'You may be right.' He stood up. 'Are you staying in Israel long?'

'No, but it depends on my company. Castle.'

'Ah yes. Thank you.' He shook hands again. 'I hope you enjoy Israel Miss ... er, yes.'

He shambled off.

'A weird one,' Eleanor commented.

I just grunted; I had an idea that inside that fat man there was a very sharp one quite able to get out. 'What the hell's Ken doing in Acre?'

'Probably digging for bar girls.'

202

'Look, that night, he'd just come out of jail and anyway, in the confusion I never ...' I wasn't improving things; the evening was dead on its feet. 'Ready to go?'

We had to walk back to Dizengoff Circle to find a taxi, and she kept her hands to herself. The crowd had thinned as people settled in cafés or headed home for an early Monday. A few soldiers, some with weapons and all with bundles of food from mother, were beginning to hitch rides back to camp.

After a while, she said: 'Did that Inspector think some other crooks from jail are in on this?'

'There's one Israeli racketeer involved. I think he was trying to locate the Prof with phony letters,' I admitted. 'He wasn't in jail at the right time, but he'd have friends who were.'

'My God. What am I getting the Met into?' After a little longer: 'Could he have killed Spohr?'

'Same objection: he was an outsider.'

'Then somebody else on the inside?'

'Sergeant Papa? Or the cooks or the barman or chambermaid? Kapotas? Where's the motive – who gained anything by his death?'

'The Sergeant got those letters.'

'If he'd wanted them he could have taken them anyway and sworn he'd posted them. He was a carrion bird, not a hunter.'

'He's still the best suspect,' she persisted.

'Wanna bet? The police would take Mitzi any day.'

'Oh no. Her own father? But what's *her* motive.'

'She was related to him. That's motive enough for most murders.'

'That's just cynicism.'

'No, it's statistics.'

'Well ... do you think she *did*?'

'I'm one of the downtrodden minority who believes he actually committed suicide.'

She just shook her head, dissatisfied.

I tried to get cosy on the back seat of the taxi, but might just as well have tried it on a Centurion tank. Some woman can get a bit uptight about where you put it last. Or maybe, as a medievalist, she just preferred older men.

26

It rained in the night – the warm front coming through – but had just about stopped by the time I got up. We'd be due the cold front some time today.

Eleanor wasn't around the dining-room so I read the *Jerusalem Post* and stretched breakfast into coffee and watched the aircrews migrating in and out. Ken rang at about a quarter to eleven.

'How are you doing, favourite nephew?'

'Surviving. What's your news?'

'Victor Foxtrot and established on the glidepath.' I decoded Visual Flight to mean he'd met Gadulla and things were going well; close to an end, maybe. Anyway, he couldn't still be in Acre.

'Fine. So?'

'Listen: I think the Queen should go to the throne of Kings.'

'The – huh?' Then I got it: he wanted me to fly the Queen Air to Jerusalem Airport. Just a single-runway affair they'd taken over from Jordan in 1967, used mostly for tourist sightseeing jaunts. Masada and Eilat and all. But the real point was it was only thirty miles away, and you don't use an aircraft to go thirty miles. Not in Israel.

I said: 'Look, dog's-bollocks – and that's not code – the thing's so pointless it's obvious. It's not a regular customs field, either. We can't go direct abroad from there.'

'Trust your old uncle,' he said soothingly. 'And your own nasty tricky mind, of course. You'll think of a way.'

'But even the weather's due to clamp for an hour or ...' My own nasty tricky mind had already got an idea. 'Oh God. All right. Any mandatory reporting point?'

'Where else?'

That could only be the bar of the King David.

*

I rang the airport Met office and confirmed that there was still a cold front tracking in. Estimated over the airport at 12.30. About. I got a different extension and told them I wanted to be clear to fly by midday; full flight plan when I got there. Then I called Eleanor's room.

'Roy,' I said. She didn't seem vastly enthused. 'Ken says things are good and wants us in Jerusalem. I'm flying up, but I suggest you make your own way.'

That suited her.

I said: 'Bus or *sherut* from the airport, or a train from Lod town, it won't take you an hour. Contact Mitzi at the Holy Land and wait to hear from us. Okay?'

She said it was okay. So I suppose it was.

*

By 11.20 I was leaning on an airport counter filling in my flight plan when Inspector Tamir breathed in my ear. I couldn't forget that tobacco.

'Mr Case, good morning. Meet Sergeant Sharon.'

Aircraft indent., yes, flight rules and status, yes . . . I turned round to meet Sergeant Sharon.

She was small and neat, with black hair drawn back in a severe style and dark unsmiling eyes. Light blue uniform blouse with badges, dark blue miniskirt, black pistol belt. Otherwise, young and pretty, and a cop.

I said: 'Shalom,' but she just jerked her head. Maybe she didn't believe me.

Tamir asked: 'You are leaving?'

I turned back to the flight plan. Aircraft type: BE 65. Comm and nav equipment . . . 'Yes. Just after twelve, I hope.' The front had moved in a little quicker than estimated.

'But you have just come.'

'Pilots are always leaving as soon as they've come. Drives women mad.'

But I don't think they got it. I filled in aerodrome of departure: LLLD for Ben Gurion and 1205 for predicted time. Tamir peered over my shoulder.

'Ah, so you have forms for everything, too.'

'Five copies. One gets telexed ahead to your destination.'

'Where are you going?'

'Nicosia.' Flight Information Region boundary point and time: LCNC at – let's guess – 1223. Meaningless, anyway.

'With passengers?'

'No passengers. Company just wants me back again.' Speed and flight level: 0170 at F080.

Sergeant Sharon said: 'Not even Mr Cavitt?'

'Not even anybody.' Route: B17 to LCNC.

'Where is he?' she asked crisply.

'I dunno.' I didn't *know*, did I? 'What's wrong with Acre?'

'We cannot find him there.'

I glanced at Tamir; he smiled a fat sad smile. 'Quite true.'

'Maybe he doesn't want to be found,' I suggested.

Sharon wound up like a little cyclone. 'Or you are planning to smuggle him out, perhaps!'

I filled in destination and time: LCNC at – a loose guess – 1315. 'Come out and search the aeroplane, then.'

'We were going to.' Tamir said apologetically.

'For *Ken*? What's to stop him leaving the country anyway?'

'Why did he come back?' he countered.

Alternate airfields: there aren't many, for Nicosia. Put in Akrotiri RAF base – that's LCRA – and back here, LLLD again. 'Maybe he got homesick for Beit Oren.'

'You are not being serious!' Sharon snapped.

I put down the operator's name as Castle Hotels, which was about as true as the rest of the plan, then my estimated endurance. 'I'm planning for two hundred miles in bad weather over water. To me *that's* serious.'

Tamir said: 'You mean the weather is going to be worse?'

'Much. Didn't you bring a coat?'

He groaned. 'I left it somewhere last night. With my luck, I could lose my right hand and left glove in the same day.'

I grinned at him, then crossed out most of the emergency/survival equipment list – I only had life-jackets on board – and signed the form.

'So let's emigrate,' I suggested, and picked up my bag and briefcase.

*

The searchers gave me a proper search, despite my escort. I told them Sharon was carrying a gun but nobody smiled. Tamir routed in a pocket and took out a revolver. 'So am I.' I don't think he was talking to the searchers.

How we could get a yard of sword past this sort of check . . .

I suppose Jerusalem did make some sense. As a customs-only-on-request field we should be able to take off without let or hindrance provided we landed at Ben Gurion to clear customs there. By then the sword might be under the floor panels, hopefully not carving through the control wires.

Outside, the sky was as per menu: about five-eighths lowish stratus leaking occasionally like an old dog, patches of blue showing through. Nothing serious yet, though the wind was beginning to gust nervously.

We walked across the wet tarmac, and even there nobody was trusting us; twice snoopy sub-machine gunners stopped us to ask Tamir what was going on.

I unlocked the Queen Air and waved them on up. Tamir put his hand in his pocket and went first. At a generous estimate, it would take one man about ten seconds to decide that nobody was hiding aboard an aeroplane that size: there's just no place. Tamir looked hopefully at the rear bulkhead that seals off the tail cone, but it was obviously permanent. He climbed ponderously down again and stood looking sad, with the wind whipping his thin hair.

'There are no other luggage compartments? I think some planes have them in the nose.'

They do, the Queen Air doesn't, but this was a touch of luck. I led them round to the port side of the nose and, without saying a word, started undoing the twenty-two Dzus screws holding on the electronics access panel. By the time I'd got half of them loose (four of them weren't even holding, which shows the standard of pre-flights I'd been doing) even Sergeant Sharon had lost a little faith. But the panel's nearly two square feet so just conceivably somebody could squeeze through.

I lifted it out and they could see the two solidly-packed racks of electronic black boxes – these mostly grey-greenish – each about the size of a carton of 200 cigarettes.

I called: 'Come on out; we know you're there!'

Sergeant Sharon said: 'Don't be stupid!'

Tamir hushed her, then: 'All right, please close it up.'

I fitted the panel back. 'How did you think anybody could get on to the airfield with security like you've got?' I did up only four of the screws.

'Real security is not trusting your security. Too much has happened at this airport. Is it safe to fly like that?'

'No, but I want to open it again and check one of the inverters for sparking when I've got main circuits on.' I hoped he hadn't studied electronics in night school.

But he bought it. 'That is all for your radio and radars and things?'

'Two comm sets, two ADF's, VOR/ILS, radar, marker – this aeroplane's under-equipped. When I first flew jet fighters, at night, we had just one ten-channel comm set and a transponder thing that never worked. The big changes in aviation haven't been jumbos and supersonics.'

He nodded. 'So – what do you do now?'

'Pre-flight check.'

'Please . . .' So I went back to the door and started again. Normally, a pre-flight isn't something you have to be too sincere about, particularly if you're the one who last flew the aeroplane. Just check the wheels for punctures or cuts, the wingtips and tail in case some hit-and-run pilot taxied into them, take off the pitot head cover and waggle the controls. But you can also do it by the book, and this time I did.

I was conscientiously poking a pipe-cleaner into the static air entry holes by the tail when it began to drizzle again. Tamir hunched his shoulders. 'I think we leave you now. Happy landings.'

'You've been watching too much TV.'

'Where else can one learn how to be a detective?' He shook my hand, Sergeant Sharon didn't, and they hustled away towards the terminal. Now I had to work.

I whipped off the electronics panel again. Up on the bulkhead that separates the compartment from the cockpit is one non-electronic thing: the brake fluid reservoir. Why Beech put it there I don't know, but today I was glad they had. It doesn't look much: just a fat metal-polish can with a screw top and a plastic tube leading into the bottom.

I unclipped the can from the bulkhead, took off the top, and poured out the equivalent of two ounces of tobacco into an empty tin. The human race must have invented nastier liquids than hydraulic fluid, though Greek wine is the only one that springs to mind, and even that doesn't smother your hands in sticky rose-coloured muck that smells like a robot's brothel. But I don't suppose it does as much harm to a VOR/ILS box when you pour it carefully into the joints, either.

That would look too selective, so I sprinkled the last drops around obvious but non-dangerous places where it would show if anybody came looking.

Then I jammed the cap back on against the screw thread, to show how it had slopped out, and clipped the can back in place. Panel back on and *all* screws twisted home. Then wash my hands in petrol from the fuel tank drain and I was on board only a minute behind my schedule.

27

'Ben Gurion ground control, Queen Air Whiskey Zulu. Request start-up, please.'

'Whiskey Zulu, stand by.' They always say that while they sort through the bits of paper to find if they've got one about you. But I'd started up already anyhow; I don't like working the radio off the batteries.

'Whiskey Zulu, clear to start up. Set QNH 981 millibars.'

That put the pressure as far down as I'd seen it in the Mediterranean. The low had tracked closer than predicted. I ran through the rest of the cockpit check, including radar, marker receiver, ADF's and VOR/ILS on. The ILS needles shivered and swung to one side, but the 'off' flags went out; it was still in business. I set the ADF's on the local beacon and Tel Aviv, but without much faith.

'Whiskey Zulu, taxi clearance.'

'Whiskey Zulu, clear to taxi to holding point runway 30.'

'Whiskey Zulu.' I started moving, checked the brakes, rolled on. Nothing else on the field seemed to be moving. The armed guards sheltered, shaking wet feet, under Boeing wings and watched me pass with expressionless eyes.

'Whiskey Zulu, are you ready to copy your clearance?'

'Go ahead.'

'Whiskey Zulu cleared to Nicosia on Blue 17 Bravo flight level 80.'

That didn't need copying. 'Blue 17 flight level 80. Whiskey Zulu, thank you.'

'Change to Ben Gurion Tower, frequency 118.3.'

'Whiskey Zulu, 118.3.'

I switched both sets over. 'Queen Air Whiskey Zulu listening out.'

I stopped at the holding point and did a careful run-up on both engines, checking for mag drops. Nothing much.

'Whiskey Zulu, ready for takeoff.'

'Whiskey Zulu, Met advises line of electrical storms approximately fifteen kilometres west, inbound flights report severe turbulence.' The clipped voice was as carefully unemotional as a laundry list.

With the midday temperatures and coastal effect, the front was winding up tight. Well, if it was rough upstairs it would be bad below stairs; that's what I'd wanted, wasn't it?

'Thank you, Tower. But haven't you heard of heroes?'

'Whiskey Zulu cleared for takeoff on runway 30, wind now reported 270, 25 knots gusting to 40. Climb initially to 3,000 feet, maintaining runway heading until outer marker, then resume normal navigation.'

'Whiskey Zulu, rolling.'

But not for long. The airspeed needle flickered almost before I'd got the throttles open. I stayed on the ground well past 90 knots – a sudden drop in the wind could slam me back with a crunched under-carriage – and when I lifted off we went up like a nervous lift. Half the wet-shiny black runway still stretched ahead when I was wheels up and throttled back into the climb.

The Tower came back: 'Whiskey Zulu, airborne at oh-seven. Change to Ben Gurion Approach, 120.5. Shalom.'

'120.5. Not up here.'

As I reached to switch channels again, something moved on the main panel. When I looked back, the ILS dial was dead. With its dying volts, it had managed to put up both OFF flags, and I hope I go as thoughtfully.

*

The first cloud came at 2,500 feet. Just thin wet stratus without any extra turbulence – in fact things were smoothing out as I got clear of the rippling effect of the ground. After another half minute the grey turned to a gentle golden glow, the rain drained off the windscreen – and I was in a new world.

A hard bright sun blazed over my left shoulder and glared back off the fluffy white cloud below – the top side of that dank stratus I'd just cleared. The total was as bright as a ski-slope; I blinked and squinted before I got my sunglasses on. But ahead . . .

It reached higher than I could see with the cockpit roof in the way, and far out of sight to either side. A bulging, boiling wall of cloud, blinding white in the sun but so dense it threw black shadows on itself below the bulges. As I watched, one of the black patches flashed green-blue with internal light.

For a pilot, this is the wall of the eternal city. Its ramparts higher than Everest and older than Jerusalem, yet so transient that it can build itself and fade inside a day. And you can spend that day in the bar – but there'll come another. A day when there's just you and the wall and a reason to get through.

But not me, not today. All I had to do was get blood on my sword. I'd still have settled for a nice calm sea fog, if Israel went in for that sort of thing.

I had a couple of minutes left; the aeroplane hung steady as a picture on a wall as I switched off the loudspeaker and plugged in the earphones, ready for things to get noisy, and turned up the radar brightness. It was still playing up, not reaching beyond ten miles, but that showed enough: a ragged but solid bar of shimmering light, from about five miles onwards. Rain. Rain thick enough to throw a reflection like a hillside. I turned the contour switch.

The screen blinked and the line hollowed out to an irregular row of dark holes, almost linked. The thunderstorm cells, churning private cauldrons of up-and-down draughts. The strong points of the wall. I weaved the nose to give it a better view south and north, but no obvious weak points.

Did I really want one? Half of me did; even twenty years of built-up flying instinct wanted the safest way. Problem: how to get into trouble safely.

I could try one thing. 'Ben Gurion Approach, Whiskey Zulu. Request clearance to descend on track and try to get below this stuff.'

'Whiskey Zulu, stand by.' I tightened my straps, pushed up the carburettor heat levers.

'Whiskey Zulu – negative on descent. Continue climb to flight level 80.' What I'd hoped for – what half of me had hoped for. The Israelis don't like aeroplanes down low off their coast; they want them up where radar gets a proper view.

The light glowed on the marker receiver: I was just about on the coast.

'Ben Gurion Approach, Whiskey Zulu on outer marker. Turning to intercept Blue 17.'

I hauled around to the right, steering 340 in the hope that it would give me a track of due north. By rights, the VOR should be giving an exact track, but I'd bypassed those rights.

Approach came back at me: 'Whiskey Zulu, change to Tel Aviv Control, frequency 124.3.'

'Whiskey Zulu, roger.' I made the change. Now, briefly, I was flying parallel to the bubbling white wall, but it was moving on me as I headed north and it came east.

'Tel Aviv Control, Queen Air Whiskey Zulu.'

'Whiskey Zulu, go ahead.'

'Whiskey Zulu passing 6,000 feet . . .' I reset one altimeter to the standard atmosphere figure of 1013 millibars; my indicated altitude wound up by almost a thousand feet . . .

'. . . airborne at 12.07, estimating Blue 17 at 12.28 . . .' I spelled out the whole meaningless formula. A glance at the ADF needles, which should have been pointing somewhere behind. Instead, they overlapped, both quivering like bird dogs and sniffing east, at electric power sources a thousand times stronger than man-made beacons.

'Whiskey Zulu, call at flight level 80.'

I wasn't quite going to get there before I had to turn into the wall. Close up, the scale of the thing is always unbelievable. The tiny crafted details you see at twenty miles become vast crude brush-strokes – live ones. Lumps the size of cathedrals bubbled and rolled like breaking waves. It's the hungry surge of a thunderhead that the paintings can never get.

7,000 and I must be about on the line of Blue 17. I turned left, switched up the cockpit lighting full – and just remembered to take off my sunglasses. I had my head down and was settled into the rhythm of instrument flying before the cockpit went dark around me.

*

110 knots, nose above horizon, going through 7,400 feet, climbing about 900 feet a minute, heading 325, start again: 108 knots, push the nose down a fraction, just over 7,400, climb rate dropping, heading steady, start again . . . a constant sweep of the eyes over the panel, tiny corrections passed to the hands, almost bypassing the brain. Never concentrate on one thing. You have five items to watch; stare at one sheep and the other four are

scattered to hell. Speed, horizon, height, climb, heading. Again ...

The wings rocked stiffly and the neat pattern warped; pat it back into place. A faint rattle of rain nibbling through the drone of the engines, but skip the wipers: I don't want to see out anyway.

The windscreen blazed with light, half-dazzling me despite the cockpit lighting and my deliberately bowed head. When I caught up with my reading again, the nose was down, airspeed going up, climb almost nil, heading five degrees off. Less smoothly, I dragged the pattern together.

It began, now. The whole aeroplane lifted and stayed lifting. The climb needle paused as if it was surprised, then shot past 2,000 feet/min. I let us go, just tried to keep the wings level and nose not too high. You don't fight thunderstorms, you just roll with the punch.

The sky fell out from under, jerking me up against the harness; the needle whipped down to a 2,000 feet/min descent. The heading wavered between 320 and 330 degrees.

'Whiskey Zulu, what is your altitude?'

'You tell me.' Whatever the altimeter said was a lie; it just couldn't keep pace. Now it was rushing down through 7,500.

'Whiskey Zulu, maintain climb to flight level 80.' The voice was clear and clean; thunderstorms don't meddle with the highest frequencies.

We hit bottom with a thump, but stayed there for the moment. I shuffled us back into a gentle climb on a heading of 320; already the wind was rougher than I'd expected, so I was probably being blown right off track. Almost ahead, the radar showed a bright line between two storm cells. If I could slide through there ...

The wings rocked and I tried not to fight the heavy ailerons. The nose jolted around in a circle, swaying five degrees either side of my heading. But at least we weren't in a lift-shaft. I snatched a look at my watch and I'd been airborne ten minutes.

Say the front was moving at 25 knots, then it had crept four miles closer to Ben Gurion. And I'd started with it ten miles away, so ... another five minutes. I'd hold out for that.

The radar went out.

Just dead. I reached and twiddled but it stayed blank. Maybe the last jolting had finally parted a loose connection. Hell.

But now, at last, I was about on 8,000. I let the nose sag and the speed come up – but I wasn't trying for my planned 170 knots. You hit this sort of turbulence as slow as you dare. I set 30 inches boost and 2,500 revs.

'Tel Aviv, Whiskey Zulu at flight level 80. My weather radar has gone unserviceable. Over.'

'Whiskey Zulu, do you want clearance to return?'

'Negative. I'll keep trying. It should – Jesus Christ!'

The aeroplane was on its side. Just like that.

'Wrong frequency, Whiskey Zulu. We're all Jews down here.'

I twisted the yoke and pushed the nose down. For seconds, she hung there shuddering, lightning exploded on the windscreen, and at last we fell off in a swerving plunge.

Then up again. The needle hit the stop at just over 4,000 feet / min and the altimeter blurred as it spun. My heading – the hell with the heading, what about the speed? It was down to a sick 95 and if we tipped again we'd stall. I rammed the nose down, throttles up.

The engine noise suddenly vanished in a roar like a waterfall – and it was. The windscreen flooded; water sputtered explosively in at the tight-shut side windows and over my lap.

The lift-shaft reversed and we fell. I was jerked off my seat, my sunglasses lifted out of my pocket, bounced off my cheek and on to the roof. The wind computer rose out of my open briefcase, hung weirdly in the air, then smashed down again as we bottomed out with a slam that set the whole instrument panel shaking in its mount.

That did it. 'Tel Aviv, Whiskey Zulu request return clearance.' My voice sounded clenched.

'Whiskey Zu . . . to turn . . . up omni rad . . . 7,000 feet . . .'

Oh no. 'Tel Aviv please say again.' But my own voice was jumping in and out of an echo chamber. The radio was packing up.

I tried to hold the aeroplane with one hand while I reached to change to the second set. And be damned to a clearance anyway. I was turning around.

I pushed into a gentle left turn. Into a storm cell or away from one?

The second VHF set came in clear: '... do you read? Over.'

'Tel Aviv: Whiskey Zulu. I have one comm failure. Please say again my clearance.'

'Whiskey Zulu, are you declaring an emergency?'

Am I saying I'm beaten, I quit? In public?

'Tel Aviv – any traffic?'

'Negative, Whiskey Zulu.' So at least no mid-air collision.

'Then just clear me.'

Formally: 'Whiskey Zulu cleared to turn left pick up 336 omni radial descend to 7,000 feet.'

It was time to make my confession complete. 'Tel Aviv, my VOR and ILS have also gone unserviceable.'

And then I knew what it was all about. I reached my toes beyond the rudder pedals and touched the brakes. No resistance at all. The first bump of the storm had shaken off my carefully jammed-on reservoir cap; now a whole tide of the foul stuff was sloshing around every box of electronics in the nose.

'Whiskey Zulu, still no emergency?' He sounded faintly incredulous.

'*All* right, then. Whiskey Zulu, Pan, Pan, Pan. Now are you happy?' But I'd still compromised by making it only an 'urgency' call. 'I have located my trouble, anyhow. Brake fluid leaking into the avionics. So I could lose this comm set and my ADF's at any time. Also no brakes. Request radar assistance.'

'Whiskey Zulu, stand by.'

By now I was heading roughly 145 and for the moment the vertical currents weren't too bad. It was like being dragged downstairs on your bottom, but no worse than that. And I was going out a lot faster than I'd come in; now I'd got a major component of the wind behind me, and my ground speed must have gone up a good eighty knots.

Tel Aviv came back. 'Whiskey Zulu, are you getting a useful reading on your ADF?'

'Negative.'

'Whiskey Zulu, steer 148 degrees, maintain 7,000 feet until overhead Bravo Golf November beacon. Change to Ben Gurion Approach, 120.5.'

'Whiskey Zulu.' They'd bring me over the airport, turn me around so I could let down in the holding pattern on the coastline, then back in a sweeping plunge for the runway.

'Ben Gurion Approach, Whiskey Zulu. What is your latest actual?'

'Whiskey Zulu, stand by.' Was it as bad beneath as I wanted it?

'Whiskey Zulu: wind 280 gusting 50 knots, visibility 300 metres in heavy rain, two octas six hundred feet, eight octas eight hundred feet. Understand you may suffer total electrical failure any time.'

'Something like that.'

'Understand you have no brakes. Is your marker receiver okay?'

'Don't know. Haven't been over any markers recently.'

'Whiskey Zulu, stand by.'

I knew what was worrying them. Me, too. The weather on the deck was as bad as I'd hoped for: just possible for an ILS approach but still dicey. I could come below cloud safely on a timed descent from the outer marker, but I'd still be going exactly the wrong way. Then I'd have to do a procedure turn at 500 feet in 300 metres visibility and an erratic strong wind to find the runway again. I was prepared to try.

They weren't. Not with my last radio likely to blow at any moment.

'Whiskey Zulu, unless you declare a full emergency do not repeat not attempt to land at Ben Gurion International. Divert to Jerusalem; weather there is still in visual limits.'

The aircraft heaved like a sick stomach and hit a patch of hail that clammered on the roof like road drills. A ball almost ping-pong size broke on the screen, jammed in the wiper and dissolved slowly.

'I suppose so.' I said, trying to sound reluctant. 'Will you notify Nicosia?'

'Wilco, Whiskey Zulu. Maintain 148 and we'll turn you on the beacon for Jerusalem. Go and crack up on *their* runway.'

'Repeat, please?'

'Shalom.'

Four minutes later I swam into vivid calm sunshine just fifteen miles from the eternal city. And the best thing was, I hadn't even suggested the idea myself.

28

I reached the King David at two o'clock, which happened also to be the middle of a thunderstorm, possibly one I'd already met personally. I walked straight through the big lobby and up the corridor to the bar and just stood there, dripping on to the polished floor. Ken stood up from the gloom, looking pleasantly dry on the outside.

'Where's the aeroplane?'

I jerked my head and sprayed water over an approaching waiter. 'Where you wanted it. Whisky sour, please.'

I took off my jacket and hung it over the back of the chair. The bar had an air-conditioned chill and my shirt was wet as well. The hell with it. I put the jacket back on and sat down.

'Could be worse,' Ken said. 'You could be flying in this stuff.'

'I was. Where d'you think this front was, an hour and a half ago?'

'How did you swing it?'

'Sabotaged the ILS and took off for Nicosia. Decided I couldn't penetrate and by then Ben Gurion was clamped for anything but an instrument approach ... so they diverted me here.'

'Neat. Could you have penetrated?'

'I'm not sure I could.'

His eyebrows lifted a fraction. I'd wanted to tell him, somebody who'd understand, more of what it had been like. But no need. He'd know.

'It must have been slightly intrepid.' He knew, all right.

'Just moderately slightly.'

The waiter put down my whisky sour and I took a gulp and the flight was just an entry in my log-book.

But – 'One thing, Ken. I may have screwed up the whole idea. I managed to louse up most of the avionics; they probably won't even let us take off until we've got a lot of it replaced.' I'd ordered some replacements, but I could hear Kapotas's blood-pressure bubbling at 200 miles.

He didn't seem worried. 'No rush. Once we've got the sword,

we can pick our own time to get it out. A grounded aeroplane that's opened up a bit, you visiting it twice a day – that's a nice cover for getting something on board. Did you have any trouble at the airport?'

Apart from landing on a downhill runway without brakes? 'No, it just took an hour to get a customs man up to clear me out.'

'You weren't followed?'

'No. But it's no secret that I'm here. A bit of hurry—'

'Sure. What happened to Jehangir yesterday?'

'I may have killed him.'

'Christ . . . Well, it couldn't happen to a nastier guy. But what about a comeback from Cyprus?'

'It all happened airside and he had a private aeroplane so I pushed him in and . . .' Should I say he'd taken the champagne boxes as well? I wasn't too proud of letting them go. And Ken would start rhubarbing about 'capital' again. He might even be right. So I said: 'What were you doing in Acre last night?'

He stiffened. 'Who said that?'

'We got picked up by a cop in Tel Aviv last night. He works for the Antiquities Department. Ken, it *was* a trap.'

'Of course it was. They were behind me from the start – that's why I went to Acre, where Bruno was digging. Always give the client what he suspects, anyway. They're probably ripping that town apart looking for buried treasure.'

'And you. How did you get away?'

'Got up early and caught a train. Have you any idea what time the trains get up in this country?'

'Well . . . they'll soon know I'm in Jerusalem and they could guess about you. Anyway, if I was looking for Cavitt and Case I'd put a man in the bar of the King David and forget the rest of the country.'

He looked around quickly. Only a dim yellow light came in through the Olde Englyshe windows behind him, and they hadn't turned on the main lights. But nobody seemed to be bending an ear at us. The rest of the crop seemed to be normal tubby tourists.

Ken relaxed and grinned. 'They don't know us *that* well. Anyway, Israeli cops can't afford to drink here.'

'Neither can we. After this one, let's get operational. Have you really got a deal?'

'I spent an hour with Gadulla before I rang you today. We've got a deal.'

'Let's get started on it, then.'

'Look, nothing much can happen before night.'

'We can get spotted, *that's* what can happen. It's a small country, Ken. The cops know each other. The word gets around fast.'

Thunder ripped the invisible sky and didn't even shake the drink in my glass. Just sound and fury; harmless.

Ken nodded at the ceiling. 'In this clag?'

'That's all right. I'm wet already.'

*

No taxis, of course, and the half mile to the Jaffa Gate had stretched in the rain to a good mile-and-a-half. But behind us, beyond the weird great sultan's palace of the YMCA, the sky was clearing to a copper-sulphate blue. The front was almost through.

We moved at an Olympic walk, the rain bouncing up around our ankles.

'Great idea,' Ken said in a sodden voice. 'Now we can plead not guilty by reason of pneumonia.'

'It's all in the mind. Did Gadulla mention anything about a letter from the Prof?'

'He was expecting one, all right. So it existed.'

'You didn't say what had happened to it?'

'Why complicate things? He probably hasn't heard of Papa getting dead and wouldn't connect it up anyway. If he likes to think the letter never got written ...' He took his hands out of his pockets to shrug more expressively, then hastily stuffed them back.

Then there was the City ahead of us, the squat grey-gold walls and ramparts reflected and exaggerated in the shapes of the thunderheads above. At least the rain had flattened the dust that usually blows in your eyes at that corner.

We went in by the Jaffa Gate – really just a gap torn in the wall by some Turkish slob in the nineteenth century – and about that time, the rain cut off. Just like that.

Ken said: 'Just ten minutes and we could have got here without total baptism.'

Around us, the sun was hatching out taxis, tourists – and a handful of khaki-uniformed coppers. Ken jerked his head. 'Come on.'

The Old City's been around a long time, but once you're inside, it doesn't feel particularly old. Not like those tall quiet back streets in Florence or Venice. This is all too quick and busy, and the Holy Sepulchre itself, over Christ's tomb, just beats Southend funfair but only just. King Richard didn't miss much.

But our part of town was the narrow jostling souks and alleys, sometimes covered with vaulted roofs and ventilation holes half blocked with weed so the sunlight comes down in pale green shafts into the blue smoke drifting from the metal-workers' shops. Each shop a tall narrow cave stretching back into what could be primeval rock but is probably the brickwork of Suleiman the Magnificent or even Herod. So maybe the place does feel a bit old, when you stop and think. We weren't stopping.

We weaved through the crowd, banging our heads on baskets and dresses hung overhead, brushing off Arab boys shouting: 'Hey, my friend, I am your guide . . .' until I was properly lost. As far as you can get lost in a place only half a mile square. Just Ken's way of shaking off any tail.

I found myself getting a close-up of a goatskin jacket hanging over a clothing shop while Ken scouted our back trail. Until then, the air had smelled of spices and coffee and that vegetable smell that rain brings out anywhere. Now the late goat had it all his own way.

'Any bogeymen?' I asked.

'No, I don't think so.'

'So we can move on? – this jacket's getting friendly.'

'Tell it you're engaged.' He led the way around one more corner into a souk that was mostly metal and jewellery shops, with crumbling old boys sitting behind counters brazing brass pots with blow-lamps. Ken stopped at a cave lined with spearheads, pots, swords, helmets – most of them so obviously reproduction that the few aged pieces looked pretty good by contrast.

A chirpy Arab boy in jeans and a V-neck sweater came forward to start his sales talk.

Ken said: 'Gadulla's expecting us. Cavitt – and my friend.'

The kid gave a smile of recognition and scuttled back into the shop.

We eased in a couple of steps off the street and waited. Opposite was a barber's with a glassed-in front. The Old City supports more barbers than an Army training camp, but everybody still seems covered in hair. Just another economic factor I'll never grasp.

A quiet gritty voice said: 'Ahlan, ahlan ...' and we turned round.

Why had I expected an old man? – because the Prof had been? – because of the antiques angle? This one was tall, lean and several years younger than us. Dressed in a slim, coarse gallabiya, jacket and red-and-white check head-dress tied with black silk. A thin triangular face you might have called hawk-like if the hawk hadn't flown into high ground some time and bent its beak, the bend exaggerated by the symmetrical little moustache beneath. But the eyes were dark and calm.

He touched Ken on both shoulders in a ceremonial embrace, bowed to me. 'It is a pleasure, Mr Case. Please come through.' He held back an old smoke-stained curtain and we went down the cave and around a rack of modern shelving holding rows of 'antiques' and into a back chamber the size of a cell. I looked quickly at Ken, but perhaps even his dreams had forgotten by now.

'Coffee, perhaps?' Gadulla offered. 'Please sit down.'

Ken took off his jacket and shook it, then shivered. I knew how he felt.

Gadulla said: 'Of course ...' and yanked a one-bar electric fire from under the low round table that held a telephone and small spirit stove.

29

A few minutes later we were sitting half-naked on chairs shaped like camel saddles and our clothes were turning the little room into a steam bath. There were no windows – just a couple of doors – and a single lamp in a beaded shade, and when you'd been there a while, the time of day stopped mattering. The room had been built without sun or stars; a place for quiet secrets.

'Is there a back door?' Ken asked.

'Perhaps fifty.' Gadulla gestured at the two doors. 'If you have the keys – and the friends. The whole street is so much connected, above and below.'

'Fine. Is the sword here?'

'It will be. Did you bring the plane with no trouble?'

I nodded. 'No trouble.'

'How good.' He walked to the front of the shop and called something to the boy. I got up and turned my half-toasted trousers around.

From the rough-plastered walls, and Gadulla himself, you couldn't guess whether the man was waiting for the soup kitchen to call or the armed guards to haul out the day's takings. His robe was plain wool cloth, his jacket a grey pin-stripe – old but well-cut – the head-dress clean.

He came back. 'The lad is bringing coffee. But I forgot—' he reached below the table and put up a bottle of Johnny Walker Black Label. 'Perhaps you would like some of this?'

Ken glanced at me. 'Maybe a spot – just to balance the wet on the outside.'

Gadulla poured two careful shots into decorated glasses. 'I hope it is good. I was rather strictly raised; I am one of your Coca-Cola Muslims.'

We sipped, and Ken had been right: it just matched that electric fire sizzling my shins.

After the second sip, Ken said: 'It wasn't till I got talking to some Arabs in Beit Oren that I knew strict Muslims don't really disapprove of alcohol – they just won't touch it in this life. In

Paradise they're going to sit around all day smashed out of their knickers. Have I got that right?'

Gadulla said inscrutably: 'It is not quite that simple.' He looked at me. 'I believe you first saw Professor Spohr dead?'

'More or less.'

'Did he leave any note? – any letters?'

'Not that I saw. But he rang you, didn't he? – what did he say then?'

He thought about it. While he did, the boy came in with a tray of coffee from the local café. Gadulla handed round the tiny cups. 'Later I will make my own, but now, this is quicker.' The boy grinned and went away.

'Bruno – the Professor – said he would send instructions, but I could expect to sell the sword half and half with somebody from elsewhere.' He looked calmly at Ken.

'Beirut?' I suggested.

'He said no names on the telephone.'

Ken asked: 'Did he sound as if he was going to kill himself?'

'A terrible question. Now ... now I think yes. That he was saying goodbye.'

There was a long silence. Then Ken got up and eased himself back into his trousers. 'Oooh, lovely. Like wading in hot cheese. I'll tell you one thing Bruno *didn't* do: make it easy for his loving daughter to inherit that sword.'

The afternoon crawled by. The boy came with more coffee; Gadulla talked to a few customers beyond the curtain. But mostly we just sat and looked at the wall and listened to my stomach. Somewhere down the line, I'd forgotten to have lunch.

'The kid could buy you a snack,' Ken suggested.

'Like a couple of sheep's-eyes? I prefer my own judgment.'

'Once it gets dark we'll go out and find a café.'

We waited on.

*

About five, Gadulla pulled down a metal blind over the front of the shop and padlocked it to steel hoops set in the floor. 'Now would you care to see from the roof?'

It made a change. He unlocked one of the doors, led the way up steep, winding stone steps. At one landing there was a short

224

dark corridor with two other doors and no sign of life but a yellow plastic bucket. We went on up. At the top, Gadulla unlocked another door and we walked out on to a small, flat, walled roof garden.

Over behind the YMCA the sun was sliding down among a few scattered clouds trailing after the front. And away east, you could just see the distant ramparts of the storm, calm and white and incredibly detailed. Somewhere well over into Jordan.

Gadulla clucked sympathetically at his rain-beaten potted plants, then waved a hand over the edge of the wall. 'You see? This is just one more way out.'

A maze of other flat roofs, all at different levels, rambled away on both sides. A little bit of athleticism and you could be a dozen houses away in a couple of minutes.

'D'you live here?' Ken asked.

'Not usually. I have a house—' he waved northwards '—with my workshops.'

'Made any good antiques lately?' I asked politely.

He grinned his lopsided grin. 'Is it fair that only one person should own something that is unique? I just help the spread of knowledge. But before I knew about the plane, I had an idea for taking the sword from the country. I would make a mould from it, then cast perhaps another forty – in metal with the same weight – and put a glass for the jewel and something for the crest and sell them to tourists. Very cheap, so I sold them quickly and they all left Israel in one or two weeks and the airport searchers got used to them. But the forty-first ...' He grinned again. He'd obviously have liked to do it just for the hell of it.

Ken smiled back, but not so widely. As we walked back down the stairs, he muttered: 'I think we'd better have Eleanor and Mitzi over for an expert opinion. I'm not sure I'd recognise a moulding.'

I'd been thinking the same thing.

*

By six it was dark enough. Gadulla led us out through one of his back doors: up one flight of steps, unlock a door, down a stone corridor, around a couple of corners, another door and we were at the head of some outside steps leading down into a narrow cul-de-sac of an alley.

He showed us a bell-push beside the door. 'An hour, perhaps? I will be here then.'

By night, most of the Old City seems empty but not dead, only lurking. A few cafés are open, near the gates, and you get an occasional glint of light from a shuttered window, a whisper of music from TV or radio, the echo of somebody else's footsteps around a corner. You find yourself walking quietly and listening hard.

After a few turns we came out on to David Steps and up towards the brighter lights near the Jaffa Gate. We went into the first restaurant we saw, not too close to the gate.

I ordered while Ken borrowed the phone. The place was a simple tourist joint making a 60-watt attempt to look like a nightclub. The cheery Arab mine host was the only staff on view, and at that time no more was needed. Just a family group at another table and a couple of soldiers drinking pop at the bar, Uzi sub-machine guns on the counter between them. I think there's some regulation about you *must* go armed in Jerusalem.

Ken came back. 'I got Mitzi. Eleanor's got there but she's out at the moment. What did you order?'

'Lamb and chips.' The menu was basically tourist, with a few simple Arab dishes for those who wanted to boast they'd tasted real atmosphere.

'Steak tomorrow.' He sat down. 'Mitzi should be able to tell if it's real antique and it matches the description. That's all we need: he hasn't had time to cobble up a fake from genuine old parts.'

'He's had over a year.'

'Until a few days ago he thought he was dealing with Bruno. He wouldn't bother to try that on him.'

It figured.

'Mitzi knows the address?'

'Yes, but she's meeting us near here. Ten to seven.' He glanced at his watch, but there was half an hour to go.

Then our lamb arrived. Not at all bad, though lamb's one of the safest things to order in Israel. And a bottle of Negev wine. I sipped and chomped for a while.

Ken suddenly put his knife and fork down. 'Mint sauce. I knew there was something missing. It'll be worth getting back to England just for that.'

'And they say travel broadens the mind. Mint sauce kept us out of the Common Market for ten years.'

'Worth every minute.'

After another while, I asked: 'What's Gadulla getting out of this deal?'

'Mitzi agreed to twenty per cent.'

I chewed. 'Nice of him to accept, seeing the Prof told him he could expect half.'

'You think the letter said that?'

I tried to write the missing letter in my head. *Dear Mohamed* – it would be in English – *Dear Mohamed, I'm sending documentation on the sword to a man in Beirut, Pierre Aziz. Get in touch with him and split the profit.* But what had stopped Gadulla selling the sword already? It was worth something, even without the description. The letter must have said something else: *Dear Mohamed* . . .

I woke up. 'Just Dear Mohamed. A handwritten letter wouldn't say "Gadulla" or his address. That's what Ben Iver was torturing Papa for: Gadulla's full name!'

Ken took a bit of meat from his mouth and looked at it curiously, put it down. 'What about the envelope?'

'Papa wouldn't keep it. With uncancelled stamps, it's proof he was robbing the mail train.'

He nodded thoughtfully. 'It works . . . How would Ben Iver expect to find who "Mohamed" is, then?'

'Find one of us and follow.'

He looked quickly sideways, but the place was as empty as before. The family had gone, another couple had arrived. The two soldiers still at the bar.

The proprietor stood up and grinned helpfully, but I shook my head.

Ken said softly: 'No way he can be behind us two. But when Mitzi gets here, I'll lead her around the houses, you tail us to make sure nobody else is.'

'Wilco.' I chewed on. Maybe mint sauce, now I was thinking of it, *would* have helped. 'How's anybody going to pay Gadulla anyhow? The Met won't fork out for weeks at least.'

Ken looked at his watch again, then waved to the proprietor. 'Getting near time. Gadulla's prepared to trust us, that's all.'

'The word of a white man, huh? Balls. He's got some scheme of his own running.'

Ken shrugged. The bill arrived and he paid it. 'Maybe he's just honest.'

'Ken, nobody in this is honest, starting from you and me.'

'Two minutes.' He stared at the table. 'Well, all right – we're finally getting rid of that champagne.'

The room went cold and quiet. 'To Gadulla? You want him to have *that* stuff?'

'Why not?' he whispered fiercely. 'I knew it would come in useful. Capital always does – and that's all it is, just like all the other boxes we've carried. Only this time we got lucky and we own it. And now we can cash it in for a share of that sword.'

'New lamps for old, hey? Ken – Gadulla was probably born a Palestinian. You know what he'll do with nine boxes of guns in Jerusalem. He'll give—'

'Not him. He'll sell them.'

'To the same people. I see why you wanted the aeroplane up here. You couldn't have unloaded at Ben Gurion. This airfield's not so well guarded. I suppose his boys were going in at midnight and—'

He stood up. 'Time. They *are* going in around midnight.'

They weren't, but he didn't know why. I followed him to the door, and the proprietor rushed to open it, wish us a good night and come back soon.

'Ken—' but Mitzi was already strolling – as much as her rather nervous walk could become a stroll – past. Ken closed up and took her arm.

I gave them seven seconds start, then strolled after, though the whole thing was pointless by now. When Gadulla the Bold found there weren't any nine boxes of untraceable small arms in the deal, then his interest in twenty per cent of a vague promise was going to reach nil. I still did the covering well enough, stopping to listen behind me, skittering ahead cat-footed to keep Ken and Mitzi in sight.

Going back, the City was even quieter and emptier than it

had been. Once we'd turned off David Street, the alleys were just dark echoing links between sparks of light from little lamps on occasional walls.

After ten minutes, when we'd passed the front of Gadulla's shop twice and were just reaching the back steps, I caught them up. 'Nobody's behind. Ken, before we see Gadulla—'

But he went on up the steps and pressed the bell. Mitzi followed, then halfway up she stumbled and dropped her handbag. It hit the stone below with a sharp glassy pop.

'*Scheisse!*'

I picked it up. 'What the hell have you got in there?'

'It was just a little pot I had bought. I thought to ask Herr Gadulla if it was real.'

'I hope it wasn't.' I took it up the steps. The door creaked open and dim light filtered out. A pot goes *pop*? I opened the handbag and shook out the ruins of a light bulb.

Or signal gun.

A soldier ran into the alley behind us, pointing an Uzi.

'Please do not move,' said the voice of Mihail Ben Iver.

30

Of course, he *was* a soldier; any Israeli his age would still be on the reserve. And if you happen to want to take your sub-machine gun to a party, you'd attract comment in civilian dress and no second glance in uniform.

He arranged us competently: Ken, Gadulla and me in chairs jammed into a corner, with nothing we could reach or kick within range. But not until Mitzi had searched us. Gadulla didn't like that. Not one bit he didn't.

Mitzi stood back, mousey eyes glinting and smiling watch-fully.

Ken asked: 'I suppose young fuzzy-chops found out where you were staying and came a-calling?'

Ben Iver said: 'Miss Spohr decided to change her agent. She thought I might get her a better deal.'

Well, maybe. He could cut out Ken and me and Gadulla – if Gadulla agreed to turn up the sword at all – but he'd also be cutting himself a big slice of the action.

'Is that the gun that killed Papadimitriou?' Ken asked.

Ben Iver grinned. 'Hardly.'

It had been a ridiculous question. But the answer had solved Papa's death, all right.

'Any more questions?' Ben Iver asked cheerfully, his glasses twinkling in the lamplight. 'Or shall we move on to item three, like where is the sword?'

Nobody said anything, Gadulla in particular. Mitzi looked hopefully at Ben Iver. He held the gun one-handed – you can do that easily with a small, compact gun like the Uzi – and took out a smallish colour photograph.

'You know this, of course?' He waggled it at Gadulla. 'It was the original redemption ticket you gave Professor Spohr in return for the sword.'

'He stole it from me,' Gadulla said bleakly.

Mitzi looked a bit sharp, but Ben Iver nodded. 'That sounds more likely.'

I asked: 'Are we too young to see this picture?'

'No, but I would prefer to describe it. It shows Mr Gadulla in happy conversation with a certain Palestinian terrorist leader who lives in Beirut – or is it Damascus? Anyway, the likenesses are very good. I really don't know why people allow such pictures to be taken.'

Nor do I, yet you see books about the French Resistance with wartime group photos, everybody clutching a Sten gun and grinning like a toothpaste ad, and what the Gestapo would have done if they'd found one of those pictures ...

'It isn't evidence,' Ken said.

'Evidence, schmevidence. We know it would at least put Mr Gadulla across the border into Jordan, stateless, homeless, all his property here confiscated. Ha Mosad – which you kindly thought I belonged to – doesn't need legal evidence.'

He held up the photo. 'So I have here one pawn ticket for one sword.'

'It was in the letter Spohr wrote to Gadulla?' I asked, just to get things straight. 'Did Papa know what it was?'

Ben Iver shook his head without looking at me. 'Not exactly. But he had the sort of mind that understands blackmail. Now, please – the sword.'

Gadulla went on looking like a bent hawk for a moment longer, then nodded. 'If I may stand up?'

'Carefully.'

Gadulla went to a thin, colourful rug hanging on the wall, unhooked it and lifted the sword down from the pegs behind.

'Has it been there all the time?' Ken asked, staring.

'Only a few hours,' He laid it carefully on the table under the lamp and sat down. Mitzi moved quickly across to look.

I'd never really expected to meet it and so hadn't any high hopes about it, but even so I wasn't much impressed. It was just a big, very sword-like sword. A long straight, slightly tapered blade two inches wide at the top, and with occasional little nicks of rust. But painted with some brownish-red stuff – probably a rust inhibitor the Prof had slapped on.

The hilt looked oddly thin: just a bar of rough metal leading up from a straight crosspiece and loosely wrapped with a tangle of grimy gold wire. There'd probably been a grip of wood, long rotted, with the wire binding it in place. And at the top, fat as a small plum, the pommel, with the crest on one side, a wine-coloured jewel on the other.

Mitzi had her sharp eyes right down on it, almost as if she was trying to pick up a scent. 'Ufert ... the name is right ... and three leopards, passant guardant ...' she rubbed the crest carefully with her thumb; '... that is right ... and the jewel. Yes!'

'*Is* that a ruby?' Ken asked.

'Ruby?' Ben Iver leant forward.

Mitzi shrugged. 'Miss Travis told you: they did not put yet real gems in German swords.' She had a ring on her finger with a tiny diamond; she scratched at the 'ruby'. 'No, it is what you call "balas".'

'Spinel,' Ben Iver said sadly. I think he'd have been more at home with a genuine gem and a doubtful sword, but you can't have everything.

Mitzi lifted the sword reverently. It must have weighed like a bad conscience and I'd hate to have been on the consumer's end, but it still looked just a rather crude old sword.

Not to her. 'It was mine and now I *have* it!'

Ken said gently: 'Bruno didn't plan on you getting it.'

She swung round on him. 'He had no right. *I* am his daughter. When he is dead his money is mine, not to some criminals in here and Beirut!'

I said: 'But he wasn't going to die ...' then remembered he was, anyway. Then I knew why he'd died. '*You* told him he'd got cancer. The doctors had told you secretly, the way they do, and you got into a row that night – it would be about money, wouldn't it? – and you said "Screw you, dear daddy, you'll be dead in two months and it'll all be mine anyway." The jolt of that, and knowing he'd got just two months of pain to come, he rings Gadulla then posts the two letters ... It figures.'

Mitzi was looking at me with a little mousey Mona Lisa smile.

Ken swallowed. 'If he's determined to do her down, why not leave a note saying what happened?'

'Let's put in one more scene. For neatness. She doesn't go out. She hears a shot. She goes in next door: one dead father, one suicide note. She confiscates that, maybe she goes through his papers. But nobody's come running. So she can walk out, to prove her uninvolvement – *and* get rid of the note. She daren't dispose of that around the hotel.'

Ben Iver said: 'Please do not go on. These family dramas make us Jews feel very sentimental.'

Mitzi turned and glared at him. 'I did not know he would kill himself!'

I nodded. 'It caused you a lot of trouble when he did. You just wanted him to appreciate his last two months to the full.'

Beside me, Ken gave a little shiver.

Gadulla said calmly: 'If I may have the photograph?'

Ben Iver seemed surprised to find it in his hand, then crunched it and tossed it across. Gadulla picked it off the floor – Arabs aren't ball players – uncrumpled it, looked at it unemotionally. Then stood up again slowly. 'May I?'

He went to the table and lit the spirit stove. 'Of course, you may have copied this.'

Ben Iver shrugged. 'So may the Professor. But you have what you always expected. And we are both in business . . . there may be a time when we can work together.'

Gadulla nodded briefly, held the photo to the stove. There's something about flame that makes you watch it. Ben Iver said: 'I think that is the best—'

Mitzi hit him with the sword.

It was a simple back-hand swing, and if she couldn't put much weight behind it, the sword had plenty of its own. Ben Iver got his arms up and the sword chopped into them, swept them back past his head and sliced into the bridge of his nose, exploding his glasses. And stuck there. He slammed back against the wall – and then I got my eyes shut.

I heard the Uzi clatter free, then the thud and clang as Ben Iver's face hit the floor. Reluctantly, I looked again.

Mitzi was grabbing for the gun, Gadulla pushing the stove off the table and it bursting in a whuff of flame around the gun. Ken took two long strides, kicked the Uzi clear.

I got on my feet to watch Gadulla. He went quietly back to the corner and sat down again.

Ken snick-snacked the Uzi's bolt and a cartridge clunked on

the floor. Loaded, all right. 'First, you'll be wondering why I called you here ... somebody put that fire out.'

I pulled the rug off the wall.

Mitzi screamed: 'Give me the gun! I want it! That is why I did it!'

'Going for a hundred per cent, huh?' Ken said. I threw the rug on the flames and tramped it down, then bent over Ben Iver.

I think he moved as I touched him, but never again. The blood was oozing where it should have been pouring.

Mitzi was still screaming. Ken pointed the gun at her. 'Stand aside and shut up. You don't get a third chance.'

She took a pace back and stood there, looking a little mad.

I said: 'Ken, forget about Ben Iver.'

'Fine. I didn't fancy explaining him at a hospital.'

Gadulla said, calm as ever: 'I do not want him found in that uniform in this place.'

Ken said: 'Amen and join the club.'

The phone rang.

Ken and I looked at each other. He said: 'Ben Iver must have friends.'

I turned to Gadulla. 'His or yours?' He made a tiny shrug.

'Answer it – in English.'

All he had to say was 'Hello', then listen a moment. Then hold it out to me. 'He wants Mr Case or Mr Cavitt.'

*

It seemed a long time before I got to saying: 'Roy Case.'

'Inspector Tamir.'

I mouthed *police* at Ken. His face hardened.

Tamir said: 'I am sorry to trouble you but I want you to know the shop is surrounded and all gates to the City watched. So it would be simplest if you came out quietly, and with the sword.'

I absorbed some of this, then asked: 'What's your number?'

He gave it. Probably the police barracks just inside the Jaffa Gate.

I rang off. 'He says we're surrounded and come out quietly.'

Gadulla shook his head. 'You cannot surround a street like

this, with all the back doors ... And they will not use much force in the City. They are afraid of riots.'

Ken looked at him steadily. 'But somebody sold us out. Again.'

He spread his hands. 'For what? What would the police offer me?'

I picked up the phone, dialled the number. It was a police station, all right. 'Do you speak English? – good. I want to speak to Miss Eleanor Travis. The American lady. I think she came with Inspector Tamir.'

'Yes. I will find her.'

I put the phone down, feeling suddenly tired. 'Little Eleanor, all right. She met the cop in Tel Aviv. She discovers the sword for the government, they give her the inside track for the first bid.'

Mitzi said: 'But I promised her first refusal.'

'But this way,' I said, 'it's legal and above-board and the Met's reputation isn't hurt. Fame and promotion for our Eleanor.'

Ken leant against the wall. 'We're in real Judas country, aren't we?'

Mitzi suddenly panicked. 'But when the police come in, what will they think about *him*?' She flustered a hand at Ben Iver.

'They won't believe he committed suicide,' I said. 'What you mean is you murdered somebody and you'd rather it didn't become public knowledge. You should think of these things in advance. Can we manage to lose him?' I asked Gadulla.

'We will have to,' he said calmly.

Ken nodded. 'Right. And then out the back door.'

I said: 'Ken – they're watching the gates, and at night they don't need many men for that. There's only seven ways out of the City.'

'There's always another way.'

Gadulla shook his head dubiously. 'The City was always a fort. It still is.'

'All *right*, we'll hide out somewhere here until we've grown beards like rabbis! They'll get tired after a month or two.'

'I can just see Mitzi with a beard.'

And that was it. Unless we kept her nailed down, she'd be off like the good news from Ghent to Aix doing a new deal that swapped us for whatever the police had on offer that week. Ken sighed and nodded.

I said: 'We can walk out now – without the sword. No sword, no body – no crime. Eleanor can't prove the thing existed. So they'll screw us around for a day and let us go.'

Gadulla liked it. Ken didn't. 'No-o. I've come a long way to find the damn thing and I'm not letting go.'

Of course, if the sword stayed with Gadulla so did the profit. I picked it off the floor and wiped it clean on the charred rug. The gold wire was crumpled around the hilt now, but otherwise it wasn't harmed from tasting blood for the first time in nearly eight hundred years.

I swung it gently. Heavy, all right, but balanced. A simple killing weapon, worth maybe a million dollars. Logic, please.

I shook my head to clear it. 'Ken, we've never been much good on swords. Just forget it.'

'No! That's *it*! Our years in jail and losing the aeroplane and all.'

'And growing old?'

He took a slow breath. 'Like running out of time. Dying a loser.'

The phone rang again. I took it out of Gadulla's hand. 'Yes?'

'Shalom. Mr Case? You have ten minutes. That's what they usually say on TV, so it must be right.'

'Shalom.' I put the phone down. 'Well, they may not have the place surrounded but they know which front door to kick in. Ten minutes.'

'Move that body, then, if you want to.'

I looked at Gadulla. After a moment, he stood up. I passed the sword to Ken.

We wrapped the rug around the arms and face, then carried it down the basement steps, winding full circle or more so at the bottom I didn't know what direction we were facing. Gadulla turned on a torch and wedged it under his armpit, aiming down a narrow arched tunnel that smelt of rats'-piss and was lined with flaky patches of dry lichen. We took a couple of turns, past heavy old wooden doors with modern padlocks and up a short flight of worn stone steps.

At the landing, there was a metal grille, its bars rusted thin with time, set in the wall. We put Ben Iver down and Gadulla lifted the grille clear. Beyond was a sort of chimney, leading up and down, and I could hear the bustle of flowing water at the bottom.

'It only fills after a storm,' Gadulla said. 'At other times it is dry. Perhaps Suleiman planned that – who can know?'

'Where does he come out?'

'Never. When it is dry you can hear the rats.'

I paused a moment, then picked up my end. He made a shallow splash that echoed like a bell. Gadulla muttered something and lifted back the grille. The stone blocks at the lip were rounded with centuries of wear, so maybe Ben Iver wouldn't be lonely.

'What did you say then?' I asked. I mean whispered.

'*Allah-hu ahkbar*. God is great.' And I suppose that about covered it. 'What will your friend Cavitt do now?'

'You mean what will we do, him and me. Lead the way and we'll find out.'

*

As we came back into the shop Mitzi had just finished wiping the floor clean. Ken was on the phone; he seemed a little surprised to see us, but just dropped his voice and went on talking. '... nearly a hundred, I'd guess ... Just a clear passage out of the country *with* the sword ... Yes, nine boxes and *not* here so don't waste your time looking ... Okay.' He put the phone down.

Nearly a hundred what? In nine boxes? I sat down because my knees suddenly felt like it.

'You were quick,' he said. 'I got to thinking we could maybe arrange something—'

'Not you, Ken. Not you as well.'

He looked blank, but he'd always been able to. 'What d'you mean?'

'I mean ...' I mean twenty years and a million flying miles and the girls and the booze and the failed engines and times like in Isfahan ... Why can you only think of the pieces of something after it's busted? '... I mean not you.'

'Look, just—'

'I mean nine boxes marked champagne! You swap a terrorist plot for a clean getaway. *Who stays behind this time?*'

The Uzi waggled vaguely in my direction. 'Ah, well ...'

'Of course, it's my turn, isn't it?'

'Just a couple of years—'

'Ten, for terrorism.'

'Roy, it's at least half a million dollars! I'll be waiting.'

'So you do the ten and I'll do the waiting.'

His face hardened. 'I'm never going back.'

I nodded. The room was thick with over-breathed air and the smell of that spirit stove. Gadulla and Mitzi didn't seem to feel like contributing.

'Ken – you – you're a fuckup even as Judas. There's no boxes. Jehangir got them before I could reach him.'

'Ahhh.' The sub-machine gun wilted towards the floor. 'I wish I'd known ... I never was much good at the business side. And you don't look much like Jesus, either.'

I stood up. 'Fine. Dump the gun and we'll walk out of here.'

'No.' And oddly, his face seemed suddenly younger. Untroubled. He flicked the gun at Gadulla. 'I want the keys to the roof!' He got them. 'Coming, Roy?'

'Not this time.'

'See you then.' He picked up the sword and went through the door to the roof stairs.

*

I snapped at Gadulla: 'Open your front door. Maybe we can distract them.'

He shrugged fatalistically, but led the way to the front of the shop. As he got the padlock clear, he turned. 'What will happen to me?'

'If they catch Ken, you could have a problem explaining the sword.'

'But I looked after the sword, when I could have sold it—'

'You looked after it because you were being blackmailed and you were being blackmailed because you're a Goddamn terrorist and frankly I don't much care what happens to terrorists. Open it *up*.'

He pushed up the metal curtain and I stepped cautiously out into the patchily-lit alley. Figures moved at either end, stepping back into doorways.

Somebody called: 'Put up your hands!'

I put them up and waited. A couple of police, one with an Uzi, the other a pistol, scuttled up and frisked me, then Gadulla. Sergeant Sharon appeared out of the shadows, muttering into a small walkie-talkie.

Then she said: 'You can put your hands down. Who are these?'

I introduced Mitzi and Gadulla.

'Where is Mr Cavitt?'

I jerked my head at the shop; instinctively, both the other cops levelled their guns at it. Sharon lifted the radio.

Machine guns went *brrrap* in another street. Two bursts. Then a third. Then silence.

*

He was huddled along the bottom of a house wall, the sub-machine gun in one hand, the sword glinting dully in the middle of the dark alley.

'Don't touch him,' Sharon warned.

I didn't need to. A burst had caught him across the chest. I asked: 'Did he kill anybody?'

'No, but he hit one of our men in the legs.' Her voice was cold, almost contemptuous. 'What did he hope to do? There are only seven gates to the City. No other way out.'

'No?'

She stared at me. 'But why did he try to fight?'

I shrugged. 'I don't know. He was growing old. You die of that, too.'

Tamir materialised at my shoulder. He looked down at Ken. 'Ah.' Then, sounding a little breathless: 'Have you been told you are under arrest?'

'I guessed.'

'The charges – we can work those out later. But you will probably go to jail for a small time anyway.'

I nodded. 'There's nobody waiting.'